OPERATION ANGUS

Also by Terry Fallis

The Best Laid Plans

The High Road

Up and Down

No Relation

Poles Apart

One Brother Shy

Albatross

OPERATION ANGUS

A NOVEL

BY TERRY FALLIS

McClelland & Stewart

First edition published 2021

McClelland & Stewart and colophon are registered trademarks
of Penguin Random House Canada Limited.

This is a work of fiction. Names, characters, places, and incidents in this novel are
either the product of the author's imagination or are used fictitiously. Any resemblance
to actual persons, living or dead, events, or locales is entirely coincidental.

Library and Archives Canada Cataloguing in Publication
data is available upon request.

ISBN: 978-0-7710-9472-9
ebook ISBN: 978-0-7710-9473-6

Book design: Matthew Flute
Cover art: (Silhouette) siraanamwong / Getty;
(Parliament Buildings) JDawnInk / Getty
Interior art: (Footsteps) alashi / Getty
Typeset in Electra LH Regular OsF by M&S, Toronto
Printed in Canada

McClelland & Stewart,
a division of Penguin Random House Canada Limited,
a Penguin Random House Company
www.penguinrandomhouse.ca

1   2   3   4   5   25   24   23   22   21

For Nancy, Calder, and Ben, again.

PART

NO.1

CHAPTER 1

"An MI6 agent just asked me to meet her in an hour at a pub around the corner," I blurted out. "And, well . . ."

"And what, man?" Angus asked. "You're seeking advice on what to wear or who should pay?"

He stood in the doorway decked out in pajama bottoms and a white T-shirt that proclaimed *Hovercraft lovers do it on air.* By the look of him, he'd been sound asleep when I knocked. Mind you, whether in the House of Commons or his boathouse workshop, day or night, his long hair and beard almost always looked as if he'd just driven through a hurricane in a convertible.

"Well, um, I don't really know. I guess I just wanted to tell somebody that I'm meeting a secret agent in a London pub late at night for a clandestine meeting," I replied.

"Well, Daniel lad, by my reckoning, if you're saying that out loud in a hotel corridor, you haven't quite grasped the fundamentals of the spy game," Angus deadpanned. "Did she actually use the words 'clandestine meeting'?"

"Well, no, I guess I'm just projecting, given the circumstances and all."

"Well, you'd better come in. I'm bleedin' awake now anyway," he said. "And this hallway is not the venue for a conversation about MI6."

"Sorry, Angus. It's still early. I figured you wouldn't quite be asleep yet."

"After the day we had, I'm knackered," he said as he waved me in and closed the door behind me. "Nothing is quite so enervating as an interminable and mind-numbing meeting where people talk too much but say too little."

We were almost at the end of April and had been in London for two days, with one more to go before flying back to Ottawa. It was our last stop on a whirlwind tour of European capitals—Rome, Paris, Berlin, and London—for meetings. In case you don't follow Canadian politics, Angus McLintock had won re-election a few months before—a crazy tale all on its own—and was appointed Minister of State for International Relations. To be clear, he was not the Minister of Foreign Affairs, one of the true plum postings in Cabinet. No, think of him more as the junior minister supporting the Minister of Foreign Affairs. And Angus and I were just fine with that for his first time at the grown-ups' table. We handled lower-profile—read: *lower-priority and less important*—policy areas and assignments, like international aid and those choreographed and often substance-free visits by foreign leaders to Canada.

On this trip, Angus and I were part of a Canadian delegation in London for discussions with our G8 counterparts about the upcoming summit in Washington. Of course, Angus was not responsible for Canada's involvement in the G8. After all, the G8 summit is a big deal, so naturally the Minister of Foreign Affairs has the lead. What Angus and I were on the hook for was planning a very brief stopover meeting in Ottawa between our Prime Minister and the Russian President, Vladimir Pudovkin, as the feared former head of the KGB travelled back home to Moscow.

While Angus and I had a bilateral meeting lined up with the Russian delegation the next day to discuss security for the President's brief visit to Ottawa, the real reason for the London trip was a formal briefing on the G8 summit preparations. As hosts of the upcoming summit, the Americans led the formal briefing, which covered all facets of the annual G8 shindig.

Our Minister of Foreign Affairs was there with her considerable entourage, as were delegations from the other G8 countries. Angus and I were also there—well, sort of. To be

honest—a practice I fully support, particularly in politics—
Angus and I were just bit players at this major London meeting. Proximity to the action is one clear measure of just how
important you are perceived to be. So, when I say Angus and
I were bit players, I mean we were in the room for the big
U.S. briefing, but we were seated on the extreme periphery
of the proceedings, nearly in a different postal code from
the boardroom table. But we were *really* only there to hear
about flight departure protocols and timing for President
Pudovkin's short hop from Washington to Ottawa. In the
four-hour briefing, the specific information that we cared
about consumed about four minutes. Yep, four scintillating
minutes that kept me on the edge of my sleep. Even hours
later, back in my hotel room, I was still feeling the effects of
the stultifying briefing. But the mystery text I'd just received
shook me from my stupor.

> I was in the briefing with you today (the no longer young
> woman seated at the far side of the room from you and
> saying nothing). I'm MI6. Please meet me at 22:00 at the
> Copper Cup pub, back corner table. Dark-blue dress.
> It's important, strictly confidential, and very unofficial.
> While frightfully cliché, tell no one, and do come alone.

I read her text through several times, and my heart rate moved
up the dial from *lethargy* right past *well, this is exciting,* and
held steady midway between *red alert* and *battle stations.*

4

The fourth time I read it, I decided her words were unlikely to change, so I lowered my phone and instead paced up and down my room until I left a discernible trail on the carpet. That only took about five minutes. I don't think it was quality broadloom.

I'd always thought the idea of one's hair standing up on the back of one's neck was a myth carefully cultivated by thriller writers and horror films. Turned out I was wrong. I pushed mine back down, then sat on my bed and thought long and hard about what to do. How to respond. There were so many options: Go to the meeting at the pub. Go to the head of the Canadian delegation. Go to our British government contact. Go to a movie. Go to sleep. And then, in the midst of this maelstrom of possible responses, the answer materialized before me with crystal clarity. Of course. Go to Angus.

"All right then, lad, from the top," Angus said as he collapsed back on his bed.

"Ten minutes ago, which would have been at 20:50," I began in my most authoritative voice, but stopped when Angus lifted one eyebrow so high it threatened to break free from his forehead. "What?" I asked.

"20:50? Have you joined the military?"

"I'm just trying to bring some clarity to the story's details and avoid any confusion."

"It just sounds a tad pretentious, and I fear it would soon be annoying."

"Annoying? Well, I don't know why, I've only been doing it since . . . 21:00," I said, checking my watch. "Besides, I'm really just trying to get into the spirit of the evening. They always use the twenty-four-hour clock in spy novels. James Bond never arrives twelve hours late for a secret rendezvous, because MI6 uses the twenty-four-hour clock."

"Oh, sorry, lad, did you say something? I must have drifted back to sleep there," Angus needled. "Now, can you move the sheep into the shearing pen with a wee bit more alacrity?"

"Of course, but I don't know why we have to bring sheep into this," I huffed. "Anyway, the text came in to my personal cellphone, not my government-issued mobile. So the message was clean, off the grid and off the books."

"Who are you spouting now, Tom Clancy or that Ludlum lad?" Angus shook his head. "Sufferin', Daniel, get to the point."

"Okay, okay, so here's her text," I said, handing him my phone.

His eyes moved across the screen. Given the ensuing pause, I suspect he, too, read the text more than once. Eventually, he looked back to me.

"Well, I dinnae know how we're going to find you a dark-blue dress to wear in the next hour," Angus said.

"Um, I think that's what she's going to be wearing."

"Ye gods, Daniel, can you not tell when I'm having you on?"

"Right. Sorry," I said. "I'm a little nervous, and maybe a little excited."

"So where is this Copper Cup? I've not heard of it."

"I Googled it," I explained. "It's just around the corner from here. She must know where we're staying."

"Daniel, she's MI6. She probably knows what you had for breakfast and the brand of underwear you favour," Angus said. "And one thing's certain, you'll not be goin' on your own, a lamb to the slaughter. I'll be your . . ." Angus snapped his fingers in search of the right word.

"Watson?"

"No, not him."

"Robin to my Batman?"

"Certainly not."

"Sancho Panza?"

"Och, no. There'll be no tilting at windmills tonight."

"Wingman?" I suggested. "And that's my final offer."

"That's it!" Angus said, raising his hands in triumph. "Aye, wingman. I'll be your wingman."

I wasn't sure a wingman was a good idea. On the other hand, two heads are better than one when venturing into uncharted waters. A paddle wouldn't hurt, either.

"But her instructions were not to speak to anyone and to come alone," I pointed out. "She might bolt if we both show up."

"No, I dinnae think so. Not if I arrive after you've already sat down. Besides, a few fingers of single malt would aid a smooth return to the horizontal when we get back here."

I replied to her text, agreeing to meet her. Then Angus and I cooked up a plan—or, at least, the pale imitation of something that approached the impression of a hazy semblance of a plan.

At 21:45 I texted her again to announce I was on my way, but my message bounced back with a notice that the number was not in service. I went anyway. Perhaps she'd been using a burner phone. Spies are always using burner phones in espionage novels.

It was raining when I emerged from our hotel. (Knowing that it was London in the spring, though, you probably didn't need me to mention the rain.) The pub was only a couple of blocks away, so I just lowered my head and trotted through the drizzle. The Copper Cup was at the end of a dark alley a little ways from a major thoroughfare. It seemed like a sensible location for a clandestine meeting with an intelligence operative, but I still felt a little jumpy.

The establishment appeared to be an above-board operation, but it was not above ground. I had to descend an outside staircase before entering the basement pub. It was dim inside, but since I'd been walking in the dark my eyes had already adjusted. I'd decided I needed to turn up my observational powers for the meeting, so I casually scanned the room, trying not to give the impression that I was scanning the room. Turning 360 degrees on the spot probably wasn't the right approach. There were booths lining three walls of the room, free-standing tables and chairs occupying the interior space, and a long, dark wooden bar along the remaining wall. Sconces gave off a yellow-orange glow that seemed warm and welcoming without illuminating very much.

I saw her just where she said she'd be. She sat in a booth at the rear of the pub, in a blue dress, with her back to the corner, giving her a full view of the pub's interior. Standard procedure in spy novels. I recognized her immediately from our meeting: shortish hair, with grey and sandy duking it out; the grey was winning. I pegged her as late fifties or early sixties, though I'm not gifted at estimating women's ages and have the scars to prove it. When our eyes met, she nodded almost imperceptibly. I kept my cool and waved enthusiastically, causing patrons at four neighbouring tables to wave back tentatively with *Do I know you?* plastered on their faces. She rolled her eyes. Embarrassed and halfway to humiliated, I crammed my hand in my pocket, made my way over to her, and sat down.

"Did you wish me to alert the media that you have arrived?" she asked, seeming annoyed.

"Sorry, I'm new to the whole late-night MI6 meeting thing." She winced when I said MI6. "Right, sorry, again. Um, I'm Daniel Addison."

"Yes, you are," she agreed.

I waited for her to continue. When she didn't, I prompted, "And you are?"

"Taking a big risk meeting you and violating umpteen provisions of the Official Secrets Act." She looked up to the ceiling, perhaps for patience, and sighed before lowering her eyes back to me. They were softer now. "You can call me Fleming."

I nodded.

"A bit of context to start," she began. "I'm a career MI6 officer. I've committed more than thirty-five years of service to Her Majesty's government. I spent much of that in the field in various international postings, often attached to our High Commission, but not always. For the last ten years I've been languishing at a desk job, and I'm about to retire in less than a month."

"Can I ask how you got my personal cellphone number?"

She smiled. "Daniel, you're an official delegate from Canada and I work at MI6. We actually have your contact information. It was circulated to dozens of civil servants, including me. And even if I didn't already have it, I could find your mobile number without difficulty. I could also remotely scan your contacts, review your call log, and track your location. It's what all intelligence agencies do."

I suspected as much but was still a little surprised to have it confirmed in casual conversation. Welcome to the real world, Daniel.

"Right. Good to know," I conceded. "But why reach out to me? I'm not exactly at the apex of power in Canada, and I'm certainly not part of the intelligence establishment."

"You just answered your own question." Her eyes looked past me and widened as Angus hove into view beside us. He'd tamed his hair and beard to the best of his ability, which meant that it merely looked messy and unkempt rather than chaotic and frightening. He was dressed neatly enough, but it took observers a while to work their way down from his memorable head to his unremarkable clothes. I made room for him on my side of the booth and he slid in.

"Hello. I'm Angus McLintock. Good to see you again."

Despite the addition of Angus to the cramped quarters, the temperature in the booth dropped precipitously. This suddenly felt like a very big mistake.

"Angus, um, this is Fleming," I said.

But she just stared at me. Sometimes it's hard to discern the feelings behind a look, but in this case, there was no confusion at all. None. Fleming looked at me with unmistakable anger and what I would charitably describe as visceral contempt. I expected tendrils of smoke to issue from her ears and nostrils at any second. Did I mention that it now felt like a very bad idea to have Angus drop in?

"I'm sorry." I shifted in my seat. "I didn't really know what to do."

"But you did something anyway," she whisper-snapped. "You told somebody else."

"I know he was supposed to *come alone*," Angus said. "But that's just such an old and shopworn espionage trope, right up there with the trench coat, a gadget-heavy Aston Martin, and the dead drop."

"The dead drop remains a simple and very effective way to exchange information secretly, but that's neither here nor there," Fleming hissed. "I'm nettled because doubling your number at this meeting means doubling the odds I'll spend my declining years in prison."

She was agitated, her eyes darting around the room in search of additional surprises.

"Please, the lad was nervous," Angus said. "And we're a team. We tend to do things together, in lockstep, joined at the hip, including a clandestine rendezvous in an obscure London pub."

"Sorry, I should have just come alone, I know," I jumped in. "I'm sorry. But we can be trusted."

"You don't even know what this is about yet," Fleming said. "Look, I didn't want to draw an elected MP and minister of the Crown into this directly. It could complicate matters and put you in a difficult position." Her eyes were on Angus.

"But you see, I'm afraid it's the way it is," Angus said, almost in a whisper. "Besides, he was going to tell me anyway, now wasn't he? That's the trust we have with one another."

Fleming then nodded, stood up, and walked out of the pub without another word. We turned in our seats and watched as she climbed the stairs to the street and disappeared.

"Blast and damnation!" Angus said. "I fear we miscalculated."

"We?" I glowered at him. "I should have just followed instructions and come on my own."

"Damnation again. I'm sorry, lad, if I've ruined the moment."

"I sensed it was just about to get very interesting," I said.

"Aye, and I did find it bracing when she used the word 'nettled.'"

We brooded in silence for a few moments as I tried to decide if I was nettled by Angus.

Suddenly, Fleming was standing before us again. She resumed her place in the booth with her back in the corner and her eyes alternately on us and scanning the pub.

"Very well," she said. "I'm not partial to surprises, or to having my instructions ignored. Please don't do that again." I nodded with whiplash vigour. Then she looked at Angus. "You *are* needed for this, but I'd hoped to work through Daniel here, at least at the outset. But you're here now, and as my young colleagues are so fond of saying these days, 'it is what it is.'"

The barkeep approached and we ordered—tea for Fleming, Coke for me despite the hour, and a single malt, Dalwhinnie, for Angus. We said nothing until the drinks arrived. It was awkward, but neither Angus nor I wanted to risk saying anything that might trigger Fleming's next and perhaps final exit.

She sipped her tea, took a deep breath, and again let her eyes circle the pub. It wasn't very crowded, but there was enough background chatter to make eavesdropping on our conversation unlikely. Finally, she leaned forward, and so did we.

"Before I get to the crux of the matter, let me lay out the reality of this little encounter. It never happened. I have never spoken to you. You don't know me, and I don't know you. You will never, ever point a finger anywhere near my direction. This is strictly confidential and off the books."

I gave Angus a smug look at hearing her last statement, but he ignored me. When I turned back to Fleming, she looked puzzled.

"Sorry, inside joke," I said quickly. "We understand. Absolutely confidential and off the books. So, can I ask, is Fleming your real name?"

"What do you think?" she replied. "I haven't had a real name for more than two decades."

"Cool!" I said. It was surreal to be seated across from a bona fide spy. This wasn't a movie. This was real! She glared at me. "Sorry, that just slipped out."

"I am about to provide important intelligence, strictly unofficially. It is not supposed to find its way into your hands. But here we are," Fleming said. "My government, through the misguided decisions of my lunatic boss, has specifically directed that this information not be shared with Canada or any other ally. In all good conscience, I cannot simultaneously honour that directive and the pledge I made so many years ago to serve my country." She took a deep breath. "That is why we're here. After I convey this information, I will be extremely vulnerable, and open to prosecution under various pieces of legislation should you ever reveal your source. I am torn between the primacy of my convictions and the laws I've sworn to uphold.

I'm counting on you to act on this information to prevent a significant geopolitical incident, protect innocent and perhaps not-so-innocent lives, and uphold international security agreements, all whilst not exposing me. This is not a trifling thing I ask. Do we understand each other, gentlemen?" Even though I was the one she'd arranged to meet, she was staring down Angus.

"You have my promise as an honourable man that we will never betray you," a solemn and serious Angus said. "I can assure you, my word, my honour, my integrity, my guiding principles mean a great deal to me, and I hope to others. And I can speak for Daniel on this front, as well."

"Absolutely," I added. I fear I say "absolutely" too often. It's a word I seem to lean on, particularly in the far too many meaningless meetings I attend. But in this case, I thought it perfectly, even absolutely, suited the moment.

"Your reputations precede you both. You come with endorsements from a trusted friend, so it was no coincidence that I reached out to you over others," Fleming said. "I'm staking my comfortable, and I hope tranquil, retirement on your promise."

"I'm curious," Angus said. "May I be so bold as to inquire who has supported the lad and me as upstanding, stalwart, and trustworthy?"

"You may certainly inquire, but I will not answer," she replied, her response softened by a nascent smile. "So, with the ground rules established, let's get to it, shall we?"

She glanced past us again to scan the room, a habit she exercised every minute or so. A final deep breath, and she started.

"The desires of the Chechen people to govern their own country, and Russia's brutal suppression of that dream, is our point of departure. Gentlemen, I have reason to believe that while President Pudovkin is in Ottawa, in exactly eleven days, there will be an attempt made on his life. I'm here in this pub late at night because apparently, no one else at MI6 wants to thwart it."

Angus and I looked at one another, horrified. Angus turned to face Fleming again.

"You have certainly snared our attention. I will stifle the myriad questions darting through my wee brain and let you get on with your briefing. We are in your hands."

She nodded.

"And soon, gentlemen, I will be in yours."

The woman we knew as Fleming proceeded to give us a crash course in Russian–Chechen history, including the two costly wars that left Chechnya not just under Moscow's thumb, but under Pudovkin's iron fist. The anger in Chechnya towards the Russian President was fierce and growing. Chechen separatists were believed to be the architects of more than one assassination plot against Pudovkin. Both Angus and I knew something of the conflict, as it made its way into our news coverage occasionally, usually when the violence and loss of life were significant enough to warrant the Western media's attention.

"The problem is, Chechen separatists bent on assassinating Pudovkin simply cannot get close enough to him to do the deed in Moscow, or anywhere in Russia," Fleming explained. "The security around the President is much too tight. So the Chechens have broadened their horizons and brought new creativity to their mission. In the last five years, several Chechen sleeper cells have been deployed to carefully chosen cities around the globe. Most arrive as couples, usually through existing refugee and immigration channels. They have always entered their new host countries legally, to make it easier for them to blend in and operate out in the open. The theory goes that these sleeper cells will be activated should the hated Russian President ever visit any of these cities. The logic is that he will be more exposed and more easily eliminated outside of Russia, where security around him is unlikely to be quite so extreme."

Holy shit. Chechen sleeper cells? Assassination plots? In sleepy Ottawa? I could feel my heart racing. I started to raise my hand to interrupt with the first of about a thousand questions I had, but Angus gently pushed my arm back down to my lap.

"Pray, continue," Angus said to Fleming.

The barkeep appeared at that moment for last call, but Fleming waved him off. She surveyed the room again before continuing.

"Look, there'll be time for questions," she said. "But let me get through the scenario first. The information is arranged to give you the insight you need efficiently and effectively."

Angus and I nodded.

"Right, then. Through my analysis of intelligence from MI6 operatives in the field, I am convinced that there is a sleeper cell in Canada, almost certainly in Ottawa, as it has always been the most likely city to be visited by the Russian President. Even if it turned out Pudovkin was to go to Toronto or Montreal, Ottawa is perfectly positioned to accommodate these two other locations. And if my intelligence is sound — and I believe it is, or I'd not be risking my career and freedom in this pub — the sleeper cell has been in Canada for two years. By my reckoning, Pudovkin's upcoming visit to Ottawa, and his meeting with your Prime Minister, represents the perfect opportunity to activate the sleeper cell."

"And to try to take him out on Canadian soil," I added.

She nodded.

"Saints preserve us," Angus said under his breath.

"So why wasn't any of this mentioned in our formal briefing today?" I asked. "Or, put another way, why are we learning about it late at night in the back corner of a down-market pub while personifying the dictionary definition of 'furtive'?"

Fleming shook her head. "This has made me angrier than anything else in my thirty-five-year career in British intelligence, and believe me, there is plenty of competition for that distinction. It's just not right. This intelligence should be shared with you. It must be. In fact, we're obligated under the terms of the UKUSA agreement to share this with you, but we're not going to, at least not officially."

"You lost me, madam," Angus interrupted. "UKUSA? What's that?"

"Right. Sorry, an insider's acronym. UKUSA's more colloquial name is 'Five Eyes.'"

"Right. I've read about Five Eyes," said Angus.

"It started out as a bilateral intelligence-sharing agreement between the U.K. and the U.S.A. in the post–World War II era as the Cold War took hold, but it was eventually broadened to include New Zealand, Canada, and Australia. Five nations, five eyes," Fleming explained.

"Right. Then why the wee discrepancy? Why are you abrogating Five Eyes by not officially sharing this information?"

"Two reasons," she replied. "First of all, my crackers zealot of a boss, Kendal Acton, an Eton-Oxford prat, and son of another Eton-Oxford prat, Sir Richard Acton, and grandson of a third world-class Eton-Oxford prat, Sir Wisdom Acton, doesn't consider this to be fully baked intelligence. He says it's just a crazy theory of mine, and therefore not solid enough to share. But that's just an excuse." Her eyes yet again flitted about the room before returning to us. "I believe the real reason, given the U.K.'s troubles with Russia and Pudovkin's brazen operations on our soil—"

"Like poisoning his former citizens?" Angus cut in.

"Precisely," said Fleming. "The real reason is that my boss doesn't want to do anything that might hamper the Chechen separatists' efforts to take out Pudovkin. He'd like nothing more than to help them finish their mission, even if it puts the citizens or leaders of our allies at risk. It's unconscionable." She was really steamed. "It's a violation of Five Eyes at best, and illegal at worst. And our silence puts *your* Prime Minister and Canadian citizens at risk."

"That is outrageous," Angus seethed.

Ideas, questions, and feelings were ricocheting around my brain, leaving me without a coherent thought, let alone a contribution. I understood what Fleming was telling us; I just found it hard to fathom that it might actually be happening within our own borders.

"I'm convinced my analysis and the theory it yielded are well supported and easily pass the threshold of reasonable credibility to require sharing the theory with Five Eyes partners. It's valid and true, but no one above me believes it. So a decision was made not to share this with Canada, even though I'm more convinced than ever that this assassination attempt will happen. Canada is the perfect location for such an operation."

"Why?" I asked.

"Simply put, you are a very civilized, progressive, and enlightened nation, one not yet plagued with violence and terrorism," Fleming said. "There is not a pervasive security culture or presence. You don't have police squads packing machine guns patrolling your airports and downtown areas, as are commonplace in Europe. It's safer. What better place to plan an assassination?"

Angus and I looked at each other and nodded, acknowledging her compliment and logic.

"But in the end," she continued, "I can't point to water-tight proof. I think the evidence is powerful and convincing, but technically, it's only circumstantial."

"If you would, can you take us through the evidence?" Angus asked. "I want to judge what your superiors have rejected, if we're to take this on."

"An entirely reasonable request," she said. "All right, then. Through MI6 operations in other countries, I have independently tracked nine Chechen couples who arrived in their new host countries, usually together. Some claimed refugee status as opponents of the Russian government, while others in more welcoming countries simply applied through the normal immigration channels. It has taken several years to make it all happen, but they're in no rush. Pudovkin isn't going anywhere, so it's worth taking the time to ensure the mission's success."

She paused to sip her tea.

"The cities where they have ended up are revealing. Washington, Berlin, London, Canberra, Paris, Strasbourg, Madrid, Rome, and Ottawa. Given our current relationship with Russia after the poisonings here, there's no way Pudovkin will be visiting London anytime soon. In general, the Russian President only makes foreign visits outside of the old Eastern Bloc nations for summits, which are often held in capital cities. Security is always extremely tight at summits, but less so for bilateral meetings before and after summits. For instance, the Russian President did meet with the Spanish President following the recent Rome summit. And this is where it gets interesting. The day before the Rome summit ended and Pudovkin was to travel to Madrid, a small apartment building exploded and collapsed in the Spanish capital. It was reported in the media as a leak from a faulty gas main, but that was just the cover story."

"I remember that story," I said. "So it wasn't a gas leak?"

Fleming shook her head. "Intelligence from our assets on the ground reported traces of C-4."

"Aye. Plastic explosives," Angus said, and I nodded.

"Six people died in the blast, including both our Chechen nationals, who had moved into the building two years earlier. The blast was likely caused by mishandling the explosives while assembling the bomb."

"But I thought C-4 was very stable and unlikely to explode by accident," Angus said.

"That's true, but the detonation mechanism, usually a mobile phone, is tricky to set up correctly. So, the C-4 was just as stable as it always is, but they probably detonated it by accident while setting up the mobile fuse. The meeting between the two leaders went on as planned, with no incident. This suggests that the FSB bought the whole gas main disinformation and had no concerns for their President's safety."

"FSB?" I asked.

"Sorry, the Russian successor to the old Soviet KGB."

"Ah," I said. "Right. I remember now from my thriller novels."

"The most likely assassination scenario was to plant an explosive device in the sewer in front of the Spanish President's private residence. Sewer lids are welded closed as a standard security measure, but we had an asset enter the sewers half a mile away and she made it unobstructed to the President's residence. Clearly, they did nothing more than weld down the lids. There, our operative found fresh, shiny, and newly installed metal brackets fixed onto the vertical shaft of the sewer just below where the Russian President's car would stop to let him out. The brackets would have supported a sizable bomb, like the one that brought down the apartment house the day before."

She paused. Angus and I just stared at each other, and I could actually feel my fingers trembling. While I believe we've already established that I'm no intelligence expert, clearly Fleming's evidence was convincing and downright terrifying. I could tell from the pained expression Angus wore that he, too, was persuaded. How could MI6 not take this seriously, I wondered.

"Is some kind of explosive device the likely approach for the Ottawa attempt?" Angus asked.

"I would think so," she replied. "I've reviewed the itinerary. There are no public appearances scheduled, so no close and easy access to the President. And I think it's a lot to expect that one of the Chechens might be a skilled long-range shooter, so a sniper play seems unlikely. Plus, I'm told the paint is not yet dry and the carpets barely laid in that strange new building you're using for the meeting. So heaps of people are still going in and out on a daily basis, making it easier for deep-cover operatives to plant explosives secretly."

"Yes, the Champlain Centre is nearly finished, and yes, it is a strange design," I said. "The Pudovkin meeting will be its inaugural event."

Angus cut in. "Please, dinnae get me started on the architectural embarrassment that is the Champlain Centre. Let us remain focused on the more pressing matter. The theory you've developed out of the Spanish incident seems all too compelling."

"And Madrid sets the bomb precedent, too," I said. "But I still can't understand why no one would accept your theory. It certainly seems solid."

Fleming shrugged. "I suppose all of this evidence is still technically circumstantial and definitely not a priority for my boss. In fact, given the Russian poisonings on our territory, none of my colleagues would shed a tear if Pudovkin were killed. So, Kendal Acton shut me up, shut me out, and shut me down."

"So, is that the whole story thus far?" Angus asked.

"Almost," she said. "In my mind, Pudovkin's brief stopover in Ottawa after the May G8 is the next best opportunity. As far as I know, there remain two Chechen nationals living in Canada, likely in Ottawa. We have no IDs for any of the couples, but I believe we have their operational code names."

"Where did you get their code names?" I asked.

"An MI6 asset in Chechnya, in Grozny, found the list of names and cities on an encrypted thumb drive she obtained, but there was no context for the information until I started snooping around and putting it all together."

"Can you share the names?" I asked hopefully.

"Their operational names seem to be couples from Russian literature," Fleming said. "The Madrid team was known as Anna and Alexei."

"*Anna Karenina,*" I said.

Fleming, unimpressed with my grasp of Russian literature, continued. "The Ottawa couple are code-named Tatyana and Eugene. I forget what Russian novel they're from."

"*Eugene Onegin,*" said Angus.

"Pushkin," I added. "Nicely done, Angus. If this were a *Jeopardy!* category, we'd be killing it."

"So now you know what I know, and it's over to you," Fleming said. "But I implore you to act on this information in a way that protects me, or I will deny everything, and stopping the attempt on Pudovkin's life will be that much harder."

"We will not betray you," Angus promised. "We couldn't, and we won't."

"Well, without descending into melodrama, I truly believe you now have the life of President Pudovkin and my future freedom in your hands. Please do not give me reason to regret my decision."

"We won't," I said. "But how can we reach you? The number from which you texted me is no longer in service."

"Yes, that was a single-use number."

I nodded. "Right, a burner phone."

"Yes, that's what they call them in the movies," she said. "I'll be in touch with you."

"Just before you go," Angus said. "Why us? Why not reach out to, say, our ambassador here at Canada House?"

"Three reasons, really. Firstly, this is completely unofficial and under the table. I'm on my own and far out on a limb on this. So I needed to find the right entry contact. The ambassador is too official to approach quietly." She smiled. "Secondly, as I noted earlier, I have it on very good authority that you, Mr. McLintock, are a man of principle who can be trusted, and who has earned a reputation for making the right call even if it's not the popular call. That goes for Mr. Addison, too."

"I really wish I knew who's been spreading these rumours about us," I joked.

Fleming just shook her head and almost smiled at my quip, but not quite. "I've already shared quite a few big secrets tonight, but I'm not going to share that one."

I hadn't expected her to. Besides, I had quite enough to process from everything else we'd just learned. I was exhausted, excited, and scared all at the same time.

"Finally, and I'm not one for signs, but back at the office, when theories gain a certain momentum, we're required to give them a code name starting with whatever letter we happen to be up to in the alphabetical cycle. When it was time for me to name this pet Chechen-sleeper-cell theory of mine, we happened to be back at the start of the alphabet. Believe it or not, long before I ever knew of your existence, Mr. McLintock, let alone your public service track record, I somehow chose the name Operation Angus." Then Fleming stood and left the booth and pub for the second time that night.

Angus and I didn't talk much on our walk back to the hotel. I was too nervous to say anything out loud about our surprising encounter with Fleming, so I waited until we were safely back in Angus's hotel room.

"So?" I said, looking at him.

"So what?" He sat on the edge of his bed rubbing his hands on his forehead, his eyes closed and face clenched.

"So, do you believe her?" I asked. "Do you think the Chechen-sleeper-cell theory and the plot to kill Pudovkin are real?"

Angus paused before answering. "It's beyond our ken right now, but her theory certainly sounded legitimate and well supported as she laid it before us," he said carefully.

"That's what I thought, too. I don't understand why Fleming is not being taken seriously by her boss. He sounds like a complete and utter tool."

"Daniel, if my dear Marin were here right now, she'd wonder why you're so surprised that the fruits of a smart woman's intellect are not accepted by the man to whom she reports. It happens every day in workplaces around the world."

"I know. I get that," I said. "But Madrid? The traces of C-4, the code names from Russian literary couples, the sleeper cells conveniently located in national capitals, the Chechen hatred of Pudovkin—she's put it all together. It all lines up. Isn't that enough to go on? To act on?"

"One would think, unless her superior, this highborn Kendal Acton, supports the goal of the plot. Remember, Russia has killed and injured some of their critics, their own former citizens, on British soil. Bold and outrageous acts indeed. I'm not surprised that some Brits would like to see a regime change in Moscow, and if it's at the hands of Chechen separatists far away in Canada, all the better. MI6's hands would be clean."

Angus walked over to his suitcase, which was resting open on the circular table by the window, and began pulling off his shirt.

"But their hands would not be clean, because they possess convincing intelligence that would enable them to stop the plot," I said. "MI6 would be guilty for not acting on what they know."

Angus was now kicking off his shoes and reaching for his belt. "Aye, but only if that intelligence is credible, accurate, and unimpeachable. And apparently Fleming's theory has not crossed that threshold, at least in Kendal Acton's judgement, which may well be biased at best and reckless at worst."

"Um, Angus, you're not about to take your pants off, are you?" I interrupted. "Because if you are, I'd just as soon avoid that spectacle."

"Well, you can grant your own wish simply by turning the other way."

I spun away just in time to avoid the most revealing part of his act.

"But what are we supposed to do with this?" I asked, now staring at the door. "How can we stop this, assuming it's real at all?"

"I'm not yet certain. We need to think upon it a wee bit. But at some point, it seems clear we'll need to talk to the good folks at CSIS and maybe the RCMP, given that both have a role in security for the Pudovkin meeting."

"Well, that's just great." I sighed.

"What's the matter, lad?"

"Angus, I don't think talking to CSIS and the RCMP is going to work, especially if we can't divulge our source. Remember who's now in charge of both agencies."

"Don't be silly, lad," Angus replied. "Surely all that swirling, choppy water is well under the bridge, around the bend, and long forgotten by now."

"Oh, Angus, your childlike innocence is one of your more endearing traits," I said. "I hate to be the bearer of bad news, but allow me to offer a reality check. That troubled water will be churning for years before it flows anywhere near your bridge. Scorned politicians have very long memories."

"Blast this world of politics," Angus grumbled. "I cannae abide it much of the time."

"I know. And to add to it all, we're going to have to bring the Prime Minister's Office into the circle on this—without betraying Fleming, of course. Is it safe to face you?" I asked.

"I'm decent—dressed or not, but I have donned my night-clothes now, if that's the answer you were seeking."

I turned, and Angus was back in his pajama bottoms and T-shirt.

"Lad, this is a serious and dangerous business, and we must treat it as such."

I nodded as I reached for the doorknob.

"No reminder needed, but it will be heeded," I said solemnly. "By the way, your shirt is inside-out."

DIARY
Tuesday, April 29
My love,
You willnae believe it, Marin, but I'm in London, though I figure you already know. Aye, that big, grey city a wee bit south of Scotland. Sadly, there's no time this trip to visit my homeland. But whilst here, we've been handed what just may be a ticking time bomb. Young Daniel and I will have to take care with it when we return to Ottawa. But that's not why the pen is in my hand.

You see, love, I'm better now. I reckon the passage of time, my unexpected foray into public service, and now a seat at the bleeding Cabinet table, if you can fathom it (for I cannae), have all helped me. Aye, they have. I'm better. I miss you no less than I did the day you left the living—the day you left me—but I seem to have assimilated the longing. The grief is still there and always will be, but its edges are softer, and they fit a wee bit more easily into my life, though "easily" will never be the right word.

In the beginning, your absence weighed so heavily on me, I could barely move and seldom did. Now, in time, I seem to have created space for your love and loss, and I can carry it around with me. It's still a damnable burden, some days more than others, but it no longer lays me so low. These pages have been a blessing for me but I dinnae need them now the way I did then. You can see I'm better, love.

AM

CHAPTER 2

The next morning, Angus and I were back at the Foreign Office for a meeting with three Russian officials, led by Russia's ambassador to Canada, Mikhail Koskov. Built like a pit bull and shaped not unlike a spark plug (if you can simultaneously conjure both of those mental images), the ambassador did all of the talking, not even introducing his colleagues. He was smart. Most Russian ambassadors were.

Much of the discussion revolved around the benign and inconsequential joint announcements that our Prime Minister and the Russian President would make following their tightly scripted encounter in Ottawa. We agreed on increased academic exchanges as well as joint research on the impact of global warming on the Arctic—a region in which, to put it mildly, we enjoyed shared interests.

When the announcements are made after these bilateral meetings, it might appear to the casual observer that the two leaders just rolled up their sleeves and hammered out these deals in the preceding two hours. But everything is negotiated and choreographed long beforehand, including the leaders' wardrobes and words, the agreements announced, the news releases issued, and the canapés passed at the reception. It's not unlike professional wrestling in that it's all new and fresh to the audience, but making it look spontaneous takes plenty of people and planning. It must be said, though, that there is slightly less potential for drama, histrionics, and hubris in wrestling.

In addition to cooking up the joint announcements for our respective bosses, we also spent far too much time deciding how to frame and disseminate the news stories that we hoped the meeting between our Prime Minister and the Russian President would drive. Never before in the course of human history has so much time, thought, and effort been committed by so many to the announcement of so little. But the talks were to establish a framework for the future negotiation of trade deals and other economic partnerships, so I had to stay focused on the fact that Angus and I were responsible for organizing this little bilateral tête-à-tête, and that neither side wanted to leave anything to chance.

Towards the end of our session with the Russians, the conversation turned to the state of the new Samuel de Champlain Centre, the nearly finished conference facility being constructed just east of Parliament Hill. One benefit of negotiating with Koskov in English was that we always knew · where we stood with the ambassador. His grasp of English simply did not permit nuance. His words tended to be blunt instruments with which he occasionally bludgeoned us. But it certainly saved time.

"We liked first version of building," said Koskov. "Maple leaf was so Canadian. But now is no longer maple leaf. Now is giant ugly spider on cliff. What happened?"

Viewed from above, the original design had featured a large maple leaf–shaped building cantilevered out from the side of the cliff, with a sheer drop straight into the Ottawa River.

"Mr. Ambassador, I can certainly understand your confusion and your verdict on the, shall we say, aesthetic shortcomings of the redesign," Angus began. "I think you know the story, as the *Ottawa Citizen* has devoted an unconscionable aggregation of stories to the matter. But in summary, the original design, which I agree is quite striking, depends on the cantilever effect that comes from embedding the steel beams that form the veins of the maple leaf deep into the rock of the cliff. Those embedded beams allow for that free-floating look of the building. The geological studies and core samples all showed that the cliff's rock formations could easily support the design. Unfortunately, when testing the extremes of architecture and engineering, one cannot always ascertain the geological stability of a cliff through studies and core samples alone. The true test is in the actual construction."

"So you start to build, and boom, beams start slipping in the rock?" Koskov asked.

"Well, that's as good a description as any," Angus conceded. "The deflection of the beams is constantly monitored, and the numbers revealed that the rock face simply is not stable enough to support the original design. We thought it would be. We were wrong. So, to ensure that our Prime Minister and your President don't die when the building falls into the river, we've had to take remedial measures."

"Remedial measures," Koskov repeated, nodding and chuckling. "So remedial measures are big black spider legs."

"Aye. The government, in all of its wisdom, thought it was best to salvage the original design with these reinforcing braces above and below the structure, rather than start over and create an entirely new building."

"That is one thing about democracy I don't like. People with no brains or taste can vote, too," Koskov said.

"In this case, it was a Cabinet decision, and it would be unseemly for me to assess the allocation of brains and taste across our numbers," Angus said in a voice that suggested he was just getting warmed up. Uh-oh. I had a bad feeling about this.

"But, regrettably, let me report that when the debate was done, cooler heads most assuredly did not prevail!"

"Angus?"

"Oh no, we needed a few more cooler heads before there'd be any prevailing," Angus continued, at a higher volume than was really necessary in the room.

"Um, Angus, I'm sure Ambassador Koskov . . ." My cut-in was cut off as Angus barrelled right past the very obvious DANGER, PROCEED WITH CAUTION sign I was waving.

"That's right, despite every reason not to, somehow the blessed group of us decided to go with the spider legs and turn a breathtaking design into an arachnoid abomination!" Angus declared with, shall we say, enthusiastic finality.

The ambassador was now smiling, while his entourage looked a little nervous. I tended more towards anxiety.

"Whoa, okay, Angus, okay. Thanks for that colourful intervention," I leapt in. "Um, the key point to remember here is that the Cabinet came together and voted to add the reinforcing, um, legs, to the building to make it safe and oh-so-distinctive. And that's the way it's going to be. It is on track to be fully finished in time for our meeting. Maybe it's not quite as attractive, but it will be safe."

Angus, who had not yet fully mastered the concept of Cabinet solidarity, looked puzzled at my explanation, but Ambassador Koskov saved me by jumping back into the fray, a wry smile on his face.

"And you have now protestors against ugly spider maple-leaf building. In Russia, we don't have protestors. It is easier without protestors. Trust me."

"Yes, well, be that as it may," I said, eager to move on, "I wonder if we could turn our discussion towards security at the meeting."

"Of course," Koskov said. "Security experts from our staff in Ottawa and President Pudovkin's personal team in Moscow have toured in and around ugly spider centre. Spider hangs off cliff with only one driveway in and out. Good for security. We are satisfied with ability to defend and protect our President."

"Well, to be clear, our RCMP and CSIS will be securing the airport, the motorcade routes to the Russian embassy and then to the meeting, and of course the ugly spider centre, too," Angus said, looking directly at me.

I slipped into my best poker face. I'm very good at hiding my annoyance in mixed company.

"Canada is safe nation," Koskov said. "We will protect President Pudovkin if you secure travel arteries and ugly spider centre."

"Mr. Ambassador," Angus began, then paused. "May I ask if there are any security concerns that might originate outside of Canada?"

"I'm not understanding what you mean," he replied.

"President Pudovkin is a strong and powerful leader," Angus said. "Sometimes that means not everybody is very happy with him. Are there groups among the old Eastern Bloc countries that might want to, hmmm, well, harm the President, and might try to act while he's in Canada? It would be helpful to know as we finalize our security protocols for the meeting."

I noticed a slight frosting of the air in the room.

"Mr. McLintock, President Pudovkin is most popular Russian leader we have since revolution," Koskov said confidently. "He keeps getting re-elected. The people love him. So, you worry only about inside Canada. We will worry about outside, and there is no problem. No threat."

"Nothing at all?" Angus asked.

"Is like I already said," Ambassador Koskov said, staring Angus down. "Is not for you to think about. Is for only me to think about."

"Yes, but Mr. Ambassador, if you think something could happen in Ottawa, then we have to think about it, too. The safety of President Pudovkin when he is in Canada is at least partly the responsibility of the host country."

"I have great faith in Canadian people," said Koskov. "Who would try to harm the President? Let us stop talk of violence. We are very good protecting him. Your RCMP will clear roads for motorcade, and then it is done, how you say, sound and safe."

Angus glanced at me. I nodded and he turned back to the ambassador.

"Well then, I think we've accomplished as much as we can this afternoon," Angus concluded. "I do believe the sun is over the yardarm, and you know what that means, don't you, Ambassador?"

"This phrase is unfamiliar for me," he replied.

"It just means, perhaps a wee tipple of single malt for me and a vodka for you would be the appropriate way to close our very successful meeting."

"*Da*. Yes. Vodka is familiar for me. On behalf of my government, I agree. Drink now would be very nice. But I will try your single malt. Vodka is very familiar for me."

We were in the departure lounge at Heathrow that afternoon before our flight back to Montreal and then Ottawa. Naturally, we were flying commercial—economy class, too. Angus had insisted. I, too, was concerned about the prudent expenditure of taxpayer dollars. But on the way over, about halfway into the seven-hour flight, with my knees pressed into the seatback in front of me, my commitment to fiscal responsibility wavered. Not so for Angus, who was shorter than I. And the flight home, against the prevailing west wind, is about an hour longer. Excellent.

We'd not yet been called to board, so I was stretched out, making the most of the ample legroom in the departure lounge for as long as I could.

"So, Angus, about the meeting with the ambassador," I started.

"I thought it went quite well," Angus replied. "He was a tad curt when we ventured into the security realm, but that's to be expected. When I asked him about unnamed forces that might oppose Pudovkin and visit misfortune upon him, I figured his hackles might rise. And they surely did. I was just testing his limits."

"I was thinking back to even earlier in the meeting when you made it abundantly clear that you opposed the government's decision on the Champlain Centre's redesign," I said. "I just wanted to remind you that when Cabinet makes a call, we all line up behind it. It's part of the privilege of sitting at that table."

"I don't recall expressing any views that suggested I might hold a contrary opinion." Angus looked genuinely puzzled.

"Hmm, that's very interesting. So you don't remember rather vehemently uttering the phrase 'arachnoid abomination' and punctuating it with what sounded to me like at least three exclamation marks? It's an alliterative gem that is not easily forgotten."

Angus sighed.

"Aye, I know you're right. We must put up a common front, show a united team. Aye, I know. I know. I'll try a wee bit harder to bear it in mind."

"That's all I ask."

Angus turned to stare at me.

"Okay, okay," I said, raising my hands in surrender. "You're right, I'll probably ask for more, but not right now. Sitting here, in this moment, it's all I ask."

We sat in silence as the business-class travellers were called to board. I looked longingly at the passengers who would soon be sprawled out in spacious, feather-soft seats that could easily hold two of me. "Oh, and just to close the circle on next steps, we will need to brief Bradley Stanton when we get back, ideally tomorrow morning if the jet lag doesn't leave us both comatose. We're obligated to tell the Prime Minister's Office. This is too big to freelance on our own but we'll keep Fleming out of it."

"Must we?" Angus asked. "Mr. Stanton is a bampot of the first order and I find it preferable to avoid all contact with him."

"I haven't yet added 'bampot' to my own growing lexicon of Scottish epithets, but I assume it bears negative connotations."

"You always were a bright lad," Angus replied. "Aye, 'bampot' is an obscure but most useful and appropriate word when dealing with the likes of Mr. Stanton. In simple terms, which I always try to employ when jabbering with him, 'bampot' means idiot."

"Then I can understand why you chose it," I said. "Nevertheless, meeting him together is better if we're going to protect Fleming. You know, support each other, put up a common front, show a united team, you might say."

"I know, I know. All right, all right. I'll do the blasted meeting, but let's not draw out the infernal encounter any longer than need be."

Our seats were at the very rear of the plane. I squeezed into the window seat, my knees—and the person sitting directly in front of me—already protesting. Even though it was early afternoon, Angus was asleep before we'd levelled off at cruising altitude. His beard sprawled and splayed across his chest in a vision of perfect chaos. It looked like an oversized grey bib and served a similar function, in that both captured errant bits of food. He slept almost the whole way home, while I spent the entire flight in a futile quest for a sitting position that was merely uncomfortable rather than painful.

Much to my surprise, I was awake at my regular time Thursday morning. Lindsay was still asleep beside me, so I carefully and quietly slipped out of bed. My left foot with all of my weight behind it came down on my iPhone charger, which was inexplicably on the floor. It hurt. A lot. Let's just say it was the non-parent equivalent of standing on a Lego brick, and just as painful. I released an inadequately muffled profanity, but Lindsay barely stirred. I'm convinced I could rev up a snowblower in our bedroom and she'd not be roused.

I loved our apartment. It was the second floor of Angus's boathouse on the shores of the Ottawa River, just outside of the lovely town of Cumberland, and as I scarfed down a bowl of cereal by the kitchen window, the river filled my field of view. I pulled on some work clothes, left Linds a note on the kitchen table, and slid behind the wheel of my less-than-sporty Mazda CX-5 for the half-hour drive to Ottawa. The only sporty aspect of the CX-5 was its colour, bright red. Angus was driving in later, in our ministerial car.

As I approached the downtown core, I decided to head a little out of my way to check on the progress of the Champlain Centre. I hung a left onto St. Patrick Street and drove along past where it merged with Murray Street to the dead end that was once the Alexandra Bridge. It had collapsed three months earlier, courtesy of infrastructure decay, on the very night Angus was re-elected. In fact, when the bridge fell into the Ottawa River, it set off a chain of events that would land Angus his seat at the Cabinet table. But that's another story.*

The road was completely blocked off where scores of construction and salvage workers laboured to clean up the twisted wreckage that angled from the street into the river below. But I wasn't there to monitor progress on the bridge cleanup. Just to the east and above was Nepean Point, where a statue of Samuel de Champlain towered over the scene. The site, which overlooked the river and Parliament Hill, had once provided tourists with one of the best views in Ottawa. Just next to the figure of Champlain, the Astrolabe Theatre had featured outdoor plays, concerts, and other events.

---

* *The High Road*, McClelland & Stewart, 2010

But over the last two years, Nepean Point had become a construction site. The theatre seats were gone, and just past the statue, the nearly completed concrete-and-glass Samuel de Champlain Centre sprouted out of the cliff. Even before the recent redesign fiasco, many citizens had been upset at the loss of the outdoor theatre. It had dominated Ottawa City Council debates, prompted thousands of letters to the National Capital Commission, and even been raised in the House of Commons.

I stared at the building as best I could while keeping the CX-5 on the road. Man, the artless black braces were the very picture of ugly. It really did look like a big spider clinging to the cliff.

And even though it was still only mid-morning, about fifty protestors had already gathered at the gates of the building site with placards, bullhorns, and boundless anger. As with many protest rallies, creativity was in short supply.

The nearly never-ending chant "Hey hey, ho ho, spider legs have got to go!" was so loud, I suspect you could hear it all the way to Parliament Hill. I rolled down my window as I pulled an illegal U-turn and slowly cruised by the roiling assembly. A woman wearing a tie-dyed T-shirt and jeans was speaking through a megaphone. If she'd donned a headband, she would have been straight out of Woodstock central casting.

Her rhetoric, delivered at full rage and volume, was only briefly a welcome change from the chant.

"... these grotesque spider legs now marring the clean and beautiful lines of the original building have turned an architectural wonder into a visual atrocity! We call on the government to tear down this bastardized and brutalized eyesore. Sweep this tarantula from the cliff and start again!" she shouted.

Then she started a new chant that was immediately embraced by her followers.

"Kill the spider. Kill the spider. Kill the spider. Kill the spi . . ."

I closed my window and the noise of the protest faded. I scanned the crowd as I drove past, just to make sure Angus wasn't chanting along with the rest of them. I didn't see him, but he was there in spirit. Frankly, so was I. What a mess.

I headed for our Centre Block office. I may not have mentioned this, but the Prime Minister had also asked Angus to serve as House Leader, given his proven knowledge of the esoterica of parliamentary proceedings. So in addition to our Minister of State for International Relations office in the Lester B. Pearson Building over on Sussex, we also required a Centre Block office to manage Angus's House Leader responsibilities. The House was in session, so we needed to balance our efforts between the two roles, and not drop any balls in the process.

Shortly before noon, Angus and I were sitting in the reception area of the Prime Minister's Centre Block office.

Neither of us was looking forward to what was to follow, but we couldn't sit any longer on the information Fleming had shared with us.

"Danny boy, welcome home," Bradley Stanton said after we were finally summoned to his office. "And good to see you, as always, Minister."

Angus nodded, barely managing to disguise his distaste for Bradley and everything he stood for. As the Prime Minister's Chief of Staff, Bradley Stanton embodied everything in politics that Angus and I detested. In Bradley's world, it was always about politics and power and never about principles, policy, or people. I know. That's a lot of p words, but I think they work. I guess Bradley had a few redeeming qualities, and even though over the years I haven't yet been able to find them, we'd reached a kind of détente. I had grudgingly accepted that politics would always attract power people like Bradley, and he knew that policy people like me would always be there as a counterweight. It's kind of a universal law in politics.

Angus and I sat down in the two guest chairs.

"Thanks for seeing us, Bradley," I opened. "This won't take long, but we wanted to brief you on something that happened while we were overseas."

"You're not about to hand me a problem, are you, Danny boy? You know how I feel about problems, and you've dumped more at my feet than anyone in the party."

"Mr. Stanton, please, will you just hear him out and we'll be out of your way," Angus said.

"Of course, Minister." Bradley leaned back in his chair. "The floor is yours, Daniel."

"All of our formal discussions related to the G8 and Pudovkin's visit to Ottawa were constructive and productive," I said. "We seem to be working well enough with Ambassador Koskov. But we feel compelled to report on something else we heard, from a confidential but very credible source, while we were across the pond on our little tour."

Then, as concisely and clearly as I could, I relayed a sanitized version of the story Fleming had passed along to us, without once indicating where we'd picked it up. I was careful not to use pronouns that would reveal Fleming's gender or to give any hint as to where she might work. Instead, I emphasized how the pieces all fit together and pointed quite clearly to an attempt on Pudovkin's life by an Ottawa-based Chechen sleeper cell during the Russian President's upcoming visit.

"And that's it," I concluded. "That's all we know right now."

"So, where did this information come from? A stunning maid at your hotel in Berlin? A sketchy waiter at a restaurant in Paris? A Russian exile disappointed by Pudovkin's abuse of power? Where?" Bradley was starting to wave his hands in the air to punctuate his questions. I could tell by his face that he wasn't pleased with what I'd reported. I'm sure it sounded to him like I was in fact just dumping a big steaming pile of problem on his desk.

"Bradley, I said right from the top that we cannot divulge where, how, and from whom we received this information," I replied. "We just cannot. We've given commitments and they helped secure this intelligence."

"Intelligence? Last time I checked, we're all on the same team here," Bradley snapped. "How do you expect me to help on this if you're going to keep me in the dark? I don't have time for this. The PM would laugh me out of his office."

"Mr. Stanton, can you not understand plain English, man?" Angus cut in. "We cannae tell you where this information comes from, and we're not gonnae. We'll not betray the confidence that has been shown us. It should be enough for you that we vouch for the credibility of this intelligence. We are not strangers to you. We are honourable colleagues who have proven ourselves to be trustworthy. We have earned the right to expect that you would accept our word as legitimate and credible. What's more important here is that we act on it, and quickly."

"Why are you telling me about this, anyway? You know who you need to tell."

"Yes, I know, Bradley, but I don't think the Honourable Emile Coulombe really wants to hear from us now, or maybe ever," I replied.

"Spare me your petty feud with Coulombe," Bradley sneered. "That's not my problem. He's the Minister of Public Safety. He's responsible for CSIS and the RCMP, and security around any visits by foreign leaders. So don't dump unsubstantiated musings about an assassination attempt on me, go and dump them on Coulombe. It's his jurisdiction."

"We planned to talk to Emile but thought you should know, too," Angus said.

"Well, thank you, Minister, you can tick that box. I now know about it."

"Will you brief the PM so he's in the loop?" I asked Bradley.

"Brief the PM? Addison, have you been drinking? The PM has enough on his plate getting ready for the G8, without inflicting fantasies straight out of a paperback thriller. Go and deal with Coulombe." Bradley waved a piece of paper at us. "I have other issues to manage."

"What's that?" Angus asked.

"It arrived a few weeks ago. It's a threat of legal action from a group of nutbars called the Society for Public Architecture, pushing us to stop building the redesigned Champlain Centre. They're trying to get some kind of an injunction."

"But it's nearly finished. Pudovkin comes in less than two weeks," I said. "That ship has sailed."

"Regrettably," chimed in Angus.

"And then ten minutes ago, an email arrived for the PM, the Minister of Infrastructure, the Finance Minister, and a long list of other Cabinet members—let's see now, ah yes, including you, too, Minister—from some underground group called the Public Architecture Militia, threatening to blow up the Champlain Centre."

"Geez, Canadians are usually so placid and meek, but build an ugly public building and they turn into the Baader–Meinhof gang," I replied.

Angus checked his cellphone.

"Aye, it's here." He read it and then passed it to me. It wasn't a straight email, but rather a PDF image of letters cut out from magazines and pasted into prose. It said STOP BUILDING THE CHAMPLAIN CENTRE NOW OR WATCH THE LEAF FLUTTER DOWN INTO THE RIVER! It was signed PAM.

"Who's Pam?" I asked. "And how is she involved?"

Angus leaned over towards me. "Daniel, lad, I believe PAM is an acronym for Public Architecture Militia, to which Mr. Stanton previously referred."

Bradley rolled his eyes. "Welcome to the discussion, Addison. I'll try to speak slower."

"Surely they're bluffing," I said, ignoring him. "We have far more serious issues in the country that should be spurring Canadians to action rather than a building that looks like a spider. Where's the outrage over global warming, or our relations with our Indigenous peoples, or the growing gap between the rich and the poor? But some group threatens to bring down a building because it isn't attractive? That's insane."

"Have you seen the building, Addison? It's a helluva lot more than unattractive. I dismissed the threat until I saw the redesigned Champlain Centre for myself. Now I think we need to take this seriously."

"But you won't take the intelligence we just provided seriously?" Angus asked.

"Minister, I'm sorry, it's unsubstantiated information that will continue to be unsubstantiated until you can prove it's from a credible source and can be backed up with hard evidence," Bradley said. "And it falls dead centre in the middle of Coulombe's world. I'm not even going to think about it right now, because it's his problem and your problem, not mine." He stood up. "And now, gentlemen, I have to brief the PM on lots of things that don't include this assassination fantasy. Thanks for popping by. It's been fun."

Emile Coulombe, Minister of Public Safety, did not like me. But he liked Angus even less. To cut a long story short, Angus had inadvertently triggered Coulombe's departure from Cabinet as Finance Minister a couple of months before. You see, when the Alexandra Bridge collapsed in January, the PM asked Angus to investigate the cause and make recommendations. Angus and I consulted with a lot of experts, but as a mechanical engineering professor, Angus already knew his way around a failed steel structure. And I knew where all the bodies were buried on Parliament Hill. In the report we wrote together, the reason the bridge fell into the Ottawa River was clear, incontrovertible, beyond dispute, and certainly much better supported than the bridge itself.

Decades of cutbacks in the name of deficit reduction had left our crumbling infrastructure sadly neglected, and the

Alexandra Bridge was just the tip of the iceberg. Our report set up a shootout at the O.K. Corral, pitting the Finance Minister and his annual budget against Angus and his report. We forced the Prime Minister to weigh a massive but critical investment in our bridges, roads, and ports against Coulombe's significant tax cut. We won. The PM sided with us and the Cabinet followed. Coulombe resigned, nourishing a hatred for Angus that I fear might never be quelled. Luckily for Coulombe, it became clear that the PM needed another Quebec voice around the Cabinet table, and there really wasn't anyone else to consider. Regional sensitivities are always a delicate balancing act. So, after spending a month out in the cold, Emile Coulombe was welcomed back into Cabinet as the Minister of Public Safety, though it was a significant demotion from the heights of the Finance portfolio.

"Jocelyn Massé," said the voice at the other end of the line.

Jocelyn was Emile Coulombe's Chief of Staff. I had called from my cellphone, so there was no caller ID. That's the only reason she answered. It wasn't my first rodeo.

"Hi, Jocelyn, it's Daniel Addison."

Dead silence.

"Hello, Jocelyn, are you there? Hello?" I knew she was there.

"What do you want?" she finally responded.

"Oh, hi. You *are* there," I said. "Good. Um, Angus and I have just come from the Prime Minister's office, where they strongly suggested we meet with your minister urgently, now or at least sometime today. We have information to share from our overseas tour that bears directly on the security of the Russian President's imminent visit."

"No, I don't think so," she said. "Not today."

"I understand that to meet with us would violate your minister's directive of not ever meeting with us, but as I said, it concerns secret intelligence that puts the lives of Vladimir Pudovkin and our Prime Minister, and likely many RCMP and CSIS officers as well, at serious risk."

"I thought all intelligence was secret," she replied. "That's the point of intelligence. It's secret."

"Ahhh, yes, I suppose you're right on that tiny, nearly irrelevant point," I said. "Apologies for the inadvertent redundancy. But we do need to share this intelligence with you and your minister, and preferably senior RCMP and CSIS officials, too, on an urgent basis, either now or this afternoon at the very latest."

"No, I don't think so," she repeated.

"Jocelyn!" I snapped, but instantly realized I had to rein myself in. "Do you really want to be the one responsible for allowing what would be the most significant foreign policy disaster in Canadian history to unfold steps from Parliament Hill and escalate tensions around the world? Oh, and don't forget the part about needlessly imperilling the Prime Minister's life?"

She hung up, but I patiently waited. And five minutes later, she called me back, just as I knew she would.

"You've got fifteen minutes at four thirty today," she said. "Does Angus have to be there?"

"I'm afraid so. He is in charge of the Pudovkin visit," I replied. "And I don't think fifteen minutes will be enough."

"You've got fifteen minutes, so you'd better keep a tight leash on Anguish if you want the meeting to run its full quarter of an hour. Clear?"

"Clear. And thank you. You won't regret it."

"I already regret it." She sighed and hung up.

Nice talking to you, too.

CHAPTER 3

"I wouldn't be surprised if they made us wait a bit," I said as we approached the minister's office at the Department of Public Safety on Laurier Avenue. We were precisely one minute early. "It would be just like Coulombe to grant us a paltry fifteen minutes and then make us twiddle our thumbs for no reason other than spite."

"Aye, spite. And don't forget contempt and a dash of vindictiveness for good measure," Angus replied. "Still, I keep hoping against hope that Emile might grow up and not conduct himself like a toddler on the playground."

"Hello, Suzanne," I said to the receptionist.

"Hi, Daniel," she whispered. "Good to see you, and the minister, too." She nodded to Angus.

"Have you lost your voice?" I asked.

She looked around furtively.

"Ahhh, no. It's just that I am personally happy to see you, Daniel, but it won't do my career any good if I'm seen to be overtly pleasant or helpful to you," she said, still whispering. "Sorry."

"You make it sound as if disliking Angus and me is an official policy of the minister's office," I said with a chuckle.

She laughed, too, but nodded vigorously in the affirmative.

"Gentlemen," she said, in a more conventional receptionist-type voice. "Please take a seat, and Jocelyn will be with you in just a . . . well, she'll be with you, um, eventually."

She mouthed a silent "sorry" to me as we sat down.

At precisely 4:55, Jocelyn appeared and escorted us to the minister's boardroom for our four thirty meeting.

Emile Coulombe sat at the head of the large board table. Seated to his left were two officials who had security and law enforcement written all over them. They had the look. Jocelyn assumed her usual seat at the minister's right hand. All but two of the remaining boardroom chairs had been carefully pushed back against the wall. Even without yellow crime-scene tape, I knew they were off limits. The two empty chairs left for us were way down at the other end of the table. We were on Coulombe's turf, so I figured we'd sit where they wanted us to and hope our voices would carry to the other end of the room.

Emile Coulombe looked unhappy, as he almost always did. His brown hair was stuck flat to his head, and he wore gold-rimmed granny glasses from a bygone era that made him look as if he were from, um, that same bygone era, despite only being in his forties. His English had the faintest French accent.

"What do you want?" he opened when we'd settled in our far-flung chairs.

"Good to see you, Emile," Angus said. "And thanks for fitting us in on such short notice. I'm joined by my Chief of Staff—a highfalutin title if I ever heard one—Daniel Addison."

"Minister McLintock, we have very little time," Coulombe said, tapping his pen on the table in what I assumed was Morse code for *Get out of my boardroom.*

"Just before we start, and I assure you we'll be spritely, could you introduce your colleagues?"

Coulombe waved his hand towards the two people on his left. "Janice Sorenson, CSIS liaison to the minister's office, and Claude Rosseau, RCMP liaison to the minister's office."

"Excellent," replied Angus. "Then let me begin, given what little time we have. Emile, while at our overseas meetings, we have come into credible information—credible intelligence, really—of a plot, perpetrated by a Chechen separatist sleeper cell here in Ottawa, to assassinate Vladimir

Pudovkin while he is here a week this Saturday to meet with the Prime Minister."

Emile Coulombe looked at his CSIS and RCMP liaison staff. They both shook their heads. Claude Rosseau made a valiant attempt, but in the end failed, to stifle a smile.

"Who gave you this information?" Coulombe demanded. "Let us judge if the word 'intelligence' is appropriate."

"Therein lies the rub, Emile," Angus replied. "We cannae tell you the source of this intelligence. But I assure you, we are convinced of its authenticity and of the grave threat it represents. Now, let me offer more details before you pass judgement." Then, in typically succinct sentences, he presented a powerful summary of Fleming's analysis, including the situation in Chechnya, the failed Madrid attempt, the sleeper-cell theory, and the rationale for attempting the assassination in Ottawa rather than Moscow.

"Again," Coulombe said, "I ask, who gave you this supposedly reliable information?"

"Again, I say, we cannae and willnae betray our source. And that is not negotiable."

"Where were you when you received the information?" Jocelyn said.

"Our trip took us to Washington, Rome, Paris, Berlin, and London. That is a matter of public record," responded Angus.

Coulombe leaned over to whisper to Janice and Claude for a few minutes. Given our distance from them, there was no chance of overhearing. Finally, Janice, from CSIS, spoke.

"Thank you for this information, but it really doesn't ring true," she began. "We are in daily contact with our counterparts in the European Union on multiple fronts in our continuing efforts to thwart terrorist groups and other illegal activity, from drug trafficking to human trafficking. And we're well aware of the Madrid situation and the gas explosion that brought down that building and killed those six people. It's our job to know."

"Just to clarify," Angus interjected, "it wisnae a gas explosion as reported. As I stated, traces of C-4 were found at the scene, though that is not widely known. And if you check the names of the perished, you'll find two Chechen nationals among them."

Jocelyn shook her head.

"An unfortunate coincidence that has no bearing on international security matters. It has been thoroughly examined by our counterparts in Madrid. The consensus among CIA, MI6, ASIS, and other intelligence agencies is that while the Chechens are very angry with Pudovkin—who wouldn't be?—they lack the sophistication, the training, and the money to support a network of sleeper cells. It's just too far-fetched. I'm sorry," she said matter-of-factly.

I was growing impatient, and eventually I couldn't restrain myself. "But what if everyone is wrong and the sleeper cells do exist?" I asked.

"I think you may have been reading too many spy novels," Jocelyn said.

I just barely held my tongue. Scorched earth would not help us.

"You have had your say and you will now leave it to the experts," Coulombe said. "You can now get back to managing the catering for the big meeting."

"Emile, please dinnae let a petty grudge you still hold against me stop you from thoroughly investigating this threat," Angus pleaded.

Emile stood. "Do not tell me how to manage our nation's security, and I'll not tell you what colour napkins to use at the Pudovkin meeting," he snapped, pointing at Angus. "You come to us with completely crazy and unsubstantiated claims, with not a shred of evidence, and expect us to jump to attention and pull resources away from other important matters, like the threatening letters about blowing up the Champlain Centre. We don't have time for a wild goose chase in search of a red herring! The answer is no!" He then left the room, his three staff following and leaving Angus and me alone.

"I dinnae think that went as well as we'd hoped," Angus said.

"Looks like we're on our own," I replied, just as Jocelyn returned to the boardroom to escort us out.

"Thanks, Jocelyn." I forced myself to say at the door. "We'll keep you posted if we learn anything more."

"Don't bother."

I closed my eyes briefly and reminded myself to breathe.

"Okaaay, but would you mind keeping us informed . . ."

I stopped in mid-sentence, as she'd already disappeared back into the office without saying another word.

Suzanne looked a little sheepish as she waved us goodbye.

"I think you're right, lad. We are on our own," said Angus as we waited for the elevator.

"What a bunch of bampots." I was annoyed.

Angus frowned. "Daniel, I must tell you, the term doesnae sound quite right rolling off your tongue," he said. "Perhaps stick with 'idiots.'"

At around six that evening, I was at the wheel of our ministerial car with Angus next to me for the drive back to Cumberland. Yes, if we'd wanted, Angus and I could have been seated in the back with a driver doing the dirty work up front. Every Cabinet minister has access to a car and driver. But Angus insisted it was over the top to have a chauffeur, so I drove us both home in our ministerial chariot, a Buick — assembled in Oshawa, Ontario, of course. My car was still parked at our ministerial office on Sussex, but we were leaving from Centre Block, so it made sense to take the Buick. I'd pick up my Mazda the next day.

"By the way," I said. "You added Washington to our itinerary when you briefed Coulombe. We hadn't been to Washington that trip."

"Aye, but they'll not check that. Besides, we did visit Washington a few weeks ago, so I wasn't completely dishonest."

"Just a little misleading."

"Aye, I suppose. But I was trying to make it a little harder for them to figure out who gave us the intelligence."

"Good idea," I said. "When you hear the scope and details of the story Fleming told us, it does seem that the likely source was an intelligence agent."

"Exactly, lad. So let's give them five agencies to consider, rather than just MI6."

"You know, this is a much nicer car than my Mazda."

"Aye, and even nicer again than my little Camry."

I pulled the Buick into the Riverfront Seniors' Residence in Cumberland. We were due for a visit with the one and only Muriel Parkinson, the octogenarian who was the lifeblood and spiritual leader of the Cumberland–Prescott Liberal Association. Before Angus's miraculous and completely unexpected victory less than a year earlier against the man who was at the time the most popular Finance Minister in Canadian history—that, too, is another story** —Muriel had stood as the sacrificial Liberal candidate for the preceding five elections. She had been a legendary Liberal Party stalwart for most of her life. She bled red. I know what you're thinking, but she bled more than blood red—she bled Liberal red. The disease that plagued her (and was also her

_____

** *The Best Laid Plans*, McClelland & Stewart, 2008

surname) was starting to assert a tighter grip on her mobility, but her mind and memory were as sharp as one of those Ginsu knives hawked on TV that can cut through a running shoe in one swipe. Suffice it to say, while she now had tremors and difficulty walking on her own, she was one smart political operative who still worked a day or two each week in our Cumberland constituency office. It was also Muriel who had introduced me to Lindsay, her granddaughter.

We found her seated in her favourite chair in the lounge, the most popular room in the place because of the outstanding view of the Ottawa River. She was talking and laughing with a woman I didn't recognize who was sitting in one of those motorized scooters. She looked younger than Muriel, with closely cropped brown hair. Glasses hung on a string around her neck. She was the only Black woman—or Black person, for that matter—I'd ever seen in the Riverfront Seniors' Residence.

"Oh, Daniel and Angus!" Muriel said with clasped hands when she saw us approaching. "How wonderful to see you both. I'd forgotten about our visit. Come and sit down. I want to hear all about your travels."

"Hello, Muriel, my dear." Angus leaned down to plant one on her cheek. "It's good to see you."

I went in for an embrace, then sat down next to Angus on the couch facing Muriel and her friend.

"Where are my manners? Let me introduce a newbie resident and old friend, Vivian Kent," Muriel said, placing her hand on her friend's wrist. "She's only just moved in a week ago. It's so nice having her here."

Vivian smiled and nodded at us. "Nice to meet you," she said. "I've heard all about you both from your biggest fan here."

"Vivian and I met when my public service career was in its denouement and hers was in its ascendancy," Muriel explained. "I've followed her fascinating path for years now. We've been doing a lot of catching up."

"Where did you work?" I asked.

"Oh, you know, in Ottawa, the federal government, here and there, doing this and that."

"She's being modest or secretive, or both," Muriel said. Then she leaned forward and lowered her voice. "Vivian worked for the RCMP in the late 1960s, in counterintelligence, of all things, and was among the first senior bureaucrats to lead CSIS when it was established in 1984."

Angus and I exchanged a meaningful glance. Hmm. Having a retired CSIS official close at hand might come in handy, particularly if we had to go it alone.

"Muriel, I'm sure they're not interested in my long and boring civil service career," Vivian protested.

"Nonsense, Viv! Besides, it may have been long, but I suspect it was far from boring. Not that you ever spilled any exciting stories about your exploits." Muriel shifted her eyes back to us. "She even spent a few years cloaking and daggering at Canada House in London before finishing her career back here, what, six or seven years ago?"

Vivian rolled her eyes but confirmed it with a nod. "As a lifelong politico, Muriel is still spinning and embellishing stories rather than just telling them," she said. "My career was certainly fascinating and fulfilling for me, but I doubt it would hold much interest for anyone else. I just wish it hadn't been prematurely truncated. I figure I had at least a few good years left."

"What happened?" I asked. "If I'm not prying, or it doesn't involve disclosing state secrets."

"You aren't, and it doesn't. The reason is quite pedestrian," she replied. "At the time, my damn arthritis was galloping, so I certainly was not. In fact, getting around was increasingly difficult. I had a desk job for the last little while but eventually had to retire." She looked wistful. "Sad day for me."

"Of course it was. I cannae say I'm looking forward to retirement either," Angus said. "But how are you feeling now?"

"The disease's progression seems to have slowed, but I still had to give up my little house on the river. Another sad day, but there was no other way. I'd be lost without this little beauty."

"Gentlemen, though I can understand your confusion," Muriel said, "Vivian is referring to her scooter and not to her old friend."

Angus and I dutifully chuckled. I turned back to Vivian. "Do you miss your work with CSIS and the glamorous world of international intrigue and espionage?" I asked. I wanted to learn more about her. She had expertise and experience navigating the very same dangerous waters in which Angus and I were now floundering.

"It is a great misconception that work in the security services ever even approaches glamorous. That is the exclusive domain of Hollywood and the less-than-realistic novels that feed that insatiable beast," she replied. "The bulk of the important work of intelligence agencies is done behind desks and computer screens—so many computer screens. But to answer your question, I loved my work and I miss it every day."

"And how have you found it so far here at ye olde Riverfront Manor?" Angus asked.

"Well, you got the 'olde' part right. But really, it's been lovely reconnecting with the legendary Muriel Parkinson," Vivian said with a smile. "And I am getting used to the food, to the extent that any member of the human species can."

"It helps to eat without gazing too long upon your plate," Muriel added.

"Yes, I keep my eyes on the river. That view makes up for a lot."

I looked out at the river, and in the window's reflection I could see Lindsay striding our way behind us. I'm not gifted when it comes to women's fashion, but I think she was wearing what is commonly known as a black dress. She looked great, even reflected in glass. I turned just in time to watch her hug Muriel.

"Hi, Grandma," said Lindsay. "Sorry I'm a bit late."

"Nonsense, dear," Muriel replied. "You're here and I'm not going anywhere, so I have all the time in the world for you."

Then Lindsay moved to me with a smile on her face, the one that often leaves my heart a little fluttery.

"You look amazing," I said, standing up to greet her.

"Thanks," she said, then gave me a hug and kiss. "You left when I was still asleep this morning."

"I tried to wake you up. Really, I did. I banged two crash cymbals together, sounded an airhorn, and then broke six plates on the bedroom floor while shouting 'Opa!' and you stirred not a muscle."

She laughed and reached for my hand to hold.

"Sorry about that. But I sleep the deep slumber of the happy and unperturbed." She squeezed my hand. "Do you know who said that?"

"Hmmm, no, but it sounds a little like Virginia Woolf," I guessed.

"Nope. I just made it up on the spot. But thanks for the compliment."

She said hello to Angus and gave him a hug before joining me on the couch and resting a hand on my thigh, warming it. It was the most natural, almost unconscious, act. I loved when she did things like that—holding my hand, draping an arm across my shoulders, even walking beside me with a finger hooked through one of my belt loops, physically linking us. Quiet little acts that mean so much.

"Hi, Vivian," Lindsay said, turning to her. "I see you've met the dynamic duo."

"Good to see you, Lindsay, and yes, I have, and I'm still recovering."

We chatted for a few more minutes about nothing in particular before Lindsay stood up and grabbed my hand. "Well, hate to chat and run, but Daniel and I are out to dinner tonight to celebrate his recent return from globe-trotting."

I handed Angus the car keys. "You're actually going to have to drive your own ministerial car back home. I'm not sure that's ever happened in Canadian political history, so maybe snag a selfie when you're at the wheel and we can post it on social media."

"Laddie, I've never taken a selfie, nor ever had the urge to, and I'm surely not going to snap my first tonight. You can rest assured of that," Angus said with mock indignation.

Lute was a new restaurant that had just opened on Cumberland's main drag and was earning rave reviews from the locals. We were led to a quiet table in a back corner of the restaurant, and my mind immediately cycled back to our meeting with Fleming in a back corner of the Copper Cup just a few days earlier. It seemed like a long time ago.

"So, any news from any of them?" I asked Lindsay once we were seated.

"Nothing yet." She sighed. "But I should hear soon."

Lindsay was a week or so away from finishing her master's degree in political science and had applied for doctoral programs at a few schools, including her alma mater, Carleton.

"It would be so great if you got into Oxford or Harvard," I said.

"I don't know." She shook her head. "They're both amazing schools, but I'm not sure it makes much sense for me to go to England or the States to earn a doctorate in political science when my work is on Canadian democratic institutions."

"But Linds, we're talking Oxford and Harvard. They're magical places."

"I know, I know. But objectively, Carleton is the perfect school for me to research a dissertation on the Canadian Senate. I think if I were at Oxford or Harvard, I'd be coming back home on research trips every month or so. That seems crazy. Besides, *you're* here. And a doctorate takes so long."

"Whoa, whoa," I said quickly. "Do not for one second factor me into your decision-making. If I knew you had turned down Oxford so we wouldn't have to be apart, I'd never get over the guilt. Don't do that to yourself, or to me." I grabbed her hand across the table. "And anyway, don't assume we'd be apart. What makes you think I wouldn't drop everything to follow you to London or Boston? I have yet to put my own Ph.D. to use. Maybe I could land a junior teaching gig there. Surely there aren't that many CanLit faculty at either school. Or maybe I could get a start on that book I've been threatening to write. Look, you can move to far worse places for love than Oxford or Harvard."

She said nothing but kept looking at me with enchanting eyes.

"I'm serious, Lindsay, even in the rare circumstance that I somehow couldn't follow you, we can make a temporary long-distance relationship work. And we would. We are fine. We are strong. We have a good thing going here, and that won't change wherever you are in September. This has to be first and foremost about you, not us."

Deep down, I truly believed the words I was saying, but I was still terrified at the thought of being apart from Lindsay for so long.

She smiled and squeezed my hand. "I knew you'd react that way, but that doesn't mean it'll be easy if I end up some-where else."

"Are you kidding? Being apart would tear me up. But we would make it work, for all the right reasons. And I didn't say it wouldn't be hard. I said choosing to stay here just so we could be together wouldn't be fair to you. What would Marin Lee advise?"

"Oh sure, bring out the big guns," she said. "Marin Lee would have advised exactly what you just did."

"No further questions, Your Honour. The defence rests."

Marin Lee and Angus McLintock had been married for nearly forty years. They'd met when they were handcuffed together in the back of a police van after being arrested at a pro-choice rally on Parliament Hill, not long after Angus arrived from Scotland. Many assumed Angus was a staunch feminist because of Marin, an accomplished and respected feminist academic and writer, but in reality he had found his cause before he met her, and their shared beliefs and values literally bound them together in the back of a paddy wagon. It was a solid foundation for a love affair I wish I could have witnessed. Her passing from cancer only a year or so before had left Angus with a gaping void in his heart and his life.

During dinner I recounted all that had happened since Angus's and my fateful encounter at the Copper Cup pub in London.

"So, Emile Coulombe and his major-domo Jocelyn are putting their hatred for Angus ahead of national security and perhaps even the life of our Prime Minister?" Lindsay asked in disbelief.

"Well, that's a possibility, but they also don't accept that Angus and I are in possession of legitimate and well-supported intelligence. They don't believe us, and neither do the RCMP or CSIS. And that kind of makes sense— neither CSIS nor the RCMP has picked up any intelligence that even remotely resembles what we gave them. And none of their allied intelligence agencies have passed along anything like it, either. In a way, I can hardly blame them for being skeptical or dismissive."

"Would they believe it if you betrayed Fleming and explained that your source was a veteran MI6 agent?"

"I don't think so," I replied. "Play it out. Coulombe and his people would check with MI6, and probably speak with Fleming's boss, this Kendal Acton jackass, and he'd assure the minister that Fleming has gone rogue and that the intelligence is bogus. We'd be no further ahead, and Fleming would probably put a liquidation contract out on Angus and me."

"What about the PMO?" Lindsay asked. "Bradley could get Coulombe to move on this."

"The only person who dislikes me more than Emile Coulombe is Bradley Stanton. Unless we can show Bradley clear and incontrovertible evidence of this plot, he won't be raising a finger to help us. He doesn't want the PM anywhere near this."

"What about going to the Ottawa Police?"

"Angus and I talked about that, but law enforcement is a very tight community," I said. "If the RCMP and CSIS reject us, the Ottawa Police will, too."

"So, you and Angus are on your own."

"That's exactly what we keep saying to one another. We're swinging way out there on a limb far too slender to support us."

"Well, I'm with you now, too. I can help. I don't know how, but I'll be ready."

"Thanks, Linds. I wish I knew what we were in for," I said. "And don't think I won't call on you. In the meantime, you may want to watch some *MacGyver* reruns to, you know, get into the right frame of mind."

On the drive home, I remembered some other news.

"Have you ever seen the *Nutcracker* ballet?" I asked.

"Oh, it is fantastic!" Lindsay replied, her eyes alight. "I've seen it several times at the National Arts Centre and once in Toronto. It is a spectacle to behold."

"I didn't know you were a ballet fan."

"Daniel, I took ballet classes until I was thirteen, when it became clear I was not bound for the National Ballet School. I was about nine years old and with my ballet class when I first saw *The Nutcracker* and fell under its spell."

"What do you know about the cannon dolls?"

"They're one of the best parts of the ballet," she gushed. "The two cannon dolls are the comic relief. Their antics onstage mark the start of a big battle. They're hilarious. Why?"

"Well, strange as this might sound, Angus, and I have been invited to play the cannon dolls at the NAC for *The Nutcracker* in December. I was invited by association, of course."

"I don't understand," she said, looking perplexed. "I've seen you dance."

"No, no, you don't understand. In the Toronto production, for years now they've invited local celebrities to play the roles of the cannon dolls. They get about fifteen minutes of rehearsal, then they're dressed up in crazy-coloured jester costumes and do their thing onstage. It apparently adds some local interest to the production, and the audience loves it," I explained. "Anyway, they want to try it here in Ottawa."

"That's the most exciting news I've heard in a very long time!" she said.

"Wait. I just told you there could be an assassination attempt on the life of Vladimir Pudovkin on Canadian soil, and you think the most exciting news is that Angus and I might be in a ballet?"

"Strange, I know. Have you told Angus yet?"

"Ah, no, and I don't plan to for a while. We have plenty of time. It's probably a moot point anyway. I'm pretty sure he'll cut me off and say no before I've finished briefing him on it. I don't think he has much ballet experience."

"Oh, Daniel, it's such a fun thing to do. And it would make him seem more like a real person in his constituents' eyes. Canadians would love him even more if they could see him flouncing around the stage as a cannon doll. He really should do it. He'd have a blast," she said. "Oh, and think about the positive media coverage. There'd be loads! It's good optics and good politics, both nationally and here in the riding."

"You always know just what to say."

"Ah, the Sicilian defence," Angus said as I responded to his opening move.

After dinner, I'd driven us back to the boathouse. While Lindsay headed to bed to read, I picked my way up the hill in the dark to Angus's house, stumbling a few times but never actually going down—first time in a while. I'd promised to check in with him before calling it a night. We often played chess as a way to clear our minds, even though Angus is a stronger player than I. I usually win one out of every five battles, but I do love the game. Fifteen minutes into our match that night, my queen stood captured and helpless just off the board, alongside a few of the other pieces Angus had already snared.

"I told Lindsay at dinner," I said, after moving my one remaining knight to a safer square.

"Well, with the game afoot, we may need her help if she's up for it," he said.

"Oh, she's ready to serve. But I just don't know how we advance this. It feels like we're stuck."

"I think you should poke around a bit and try to learn what you can about the Chechen community in Ottawa," Angus suggested. "I also think we could ask a friendly expert for advice on how to proceed."

"Well, that would be nice if we knew such a per— " I looked at Angus. He was smiling. "Hmm. You mean Vivian. Vivian Kent."

"Well, I dinnae think Hercule Poirot is available," Angus replied. "I took it as another sign that we happened to meet a retired career intelligence officer at the very moment we needed to."

"I thought you were a man of science who always rejected signs," I said.

"For the most part, that's true enough, lad, at least until the signs are so compelling it becomes folly to ignore them."

"I wouldn't admit that to the Society of Professional Engineers," I said. "Do you think Vivian would help? And can we trust her?"

"You heard her. She misses her work every day. And she's a long-time friend of Muriel's. On the strength of that connection alone, I trust her already," Angus said. "Oh, and incidentally, checkmate in three."

"Shite. Shite." Hanging out with Angus so much had given me a whole new inventory of expletives. I looked at the board and eventually saw his stratagem. I worked it through on the squares, over and over.

"Laddie, no matter how long you stare at it, there's nothing for you," Angus said.

Of course, he was right. There was no escaping the noose he'd placed around my neck. Why drag it out for a few more moves? I toppled my king in surrender. "And thrice, shite."

I picked my way back down to the boathouse feeling a bit discouraged at the state of my game. I should have seen what Angus had been cooking up on the board. In hindsight, all the clues and cues were there. I just missed them. Preoccupied? Distracted? Blind? Or all three?

Lindsay was asleep, so I crawled into bed with as much stealth as I could muster and turned off my lamp. I soon discovered she'd not been asleep at all.

PART

NO.2

CHAPTER 4

We started the next morning at our ministerial office on Sussex. Angus and I had driven in together and talked the whole way about next steps. When I made it to my office, I took the first small step in our plan, while Angus sat through a long-planned briefing on our international development programs.

"Hey, Fitz, it's Daniel," I said into the phone.

"Unfortunately, I really can't talk now. Sorry." He hung up.

That was weird. But then he texted me, almost before I'd had a chance to hang up my phone.

Sorry. Call me back on my cell. Give me two minutes.

Roy Fitzsimmons and I had worked together a few years back in the Leader's office, where I was the lead speechwriter and he worked in communications. After the election, Roy didn't follow us over to the PMO. Instead, he left the world of politics and took a civil service job in CSIS as senior manager of communications.

I waited the requisite two minutes and dialled his cellphone.

"Hey, Fitz."

"Addisonian!" he replied. "Nice to hear your voice." We hadn't spoken much in the last few months.

"Are you standing in the middle of Laurier?" I asked. "All I hear is traffic."

"Well, I'm not in the middle of Laurier, but I am on the sidewalk."

"Everything okay?"

"Yeah, yeah, it's all good. I'm just never certain if I can speak freely on my office phone. So I often duck outside for personal calls."

"You mean you think your line is bugged?"

"I just don't know. I doubt it. I'm a small fish in a very big bowl. But it is CSIS, so I don't want to take any chances, especially when I'm talking to you."

"What does that mean?"

"It means that you and Angus are not exactly in our minister's good books."

"Well, I wouldn't call that a breaking news bulletin, Fitz."

"Yeah, well, it runs deeper than just not liking you very much. It's not in writing and it never will be, but he's given a clear directive through the RCMP and CSIS chain of command that no one is to respond to any communications from your office or lift a finger to help you in any way."

"You're kidding me!" I was seething. It was outrageous behaviour by a minister of the Crown.

"I wish I were, but I am not." He sighed. "Danny, Coulombe still has a very big hate-on for your great bearded friend. He doesn't like you much, either."

"Well, I'm not surprised he doesn't like us much after what Angus pulled off in that budget, but this just sounds so petty and personal."

"You mean it sounds like politics?" he asked. "Why do you think I got out when I did?"

"Point taken. Hey, let me change topics for a sec. Does MI6 ever provide information or briefings to CSIS about issues or incidents outside of Canada?"

"Of course. There's a monthly videoconference briefing when we share stuff we've learned from our intelligence operations, and they reciprocate. We do it with other allies, too. When there's a lot happening in the world, we have them more than monthly."

"Are you in those MI6 videoconferences?"

"I wish. That's well above my paygrade. But I do set up the room. I get London's PowerPoint early so I can load it in the secure boardroom and make sure it's all working. Then they kick me out and lower the cone of silence."

"Do you happen to remember if any of the recent briefings touched on Pudovkin's visit to Madrid to meet the Spanish prez?"

"I think so, yes. In the last briefing I seem to recall a few slides about the Madrid bilateral."

"I'm interested in any intelligence around that Madrid meeting, particularly as it relates to security. Do you remember anything?"

"I remember thinking MI6 uses an awfully small font for effective PowerPoint presentations, but that's about it."

"Shite."

"But I think I still have the full PowerPoint on my secure hard drive," Fitz said. "I can't send it to you, of course, but what are you looking for specifically?"

"Yes! You're a legend, Fitz. And this will stay just between us. You may remember that there was an explosion in a Madrid apartment building the day before the confab between the two leaders. All I really need to know is if it was mentioned at all in the MI6 briefing."

"This could cost me my job, you know," he replied.

"Trust me, man, this is important, and it relates to Pudovkin's upcoming visit with the PM. I just need to know what MI6 said about the Madrid apartment explosion. That's all."

"I'll text you at lunch if I learn anything I think I can share without finding myself out of a job or up on charges."

"Fitz, no one will ever know, and I will owe you big time if you come through for me on this one," I said. "Your country thanks you."

"You know, I've always wanted a ride in that legendary hovercraft your boss built."

"Done!" I said. "Hell, you can drive it up and down the river for as long as you want."

I hung up and checked my cellphone, where I'd created a to-do list of things I needed, well . . . to do. *Call Fitz* was number one, and I'd already crossed it off. Busy, busy. Good for me. Number two on my list was *Find Chechen sleeper cell*. That might take me a little longer.

I spent the next hour on the phone with a contact I had deep within the Department of Immigration. I asked her in a meandering and roundabout way about the influx of refugees and immigrants from former Soviet states. While Canada had been a popular destination for citizens of many eastern European countries looking for a fresh start, she said, it was hard to secure solid information about them after they'd completed the immigration or refugee process. There was also the minor matter of Canadians' sacred right to privacy, she told me. Oh yeah, that. Anyway, my hope of being emailed a list of names and addresses for recent Chechen arrivals in the Ottawa area was a nonstarter, if such a list existed at all. My contact was as helpful as she could be, but, well, let's just say it was an hour I'll never get back.

So, I did what I always did when stumped doing research for a speech or policy paper. I turned to that heralded font of all wisdom, Google. I tried various search terms, including *Chechens in Ottawa, Chechen separatists in Canada, Chechen terrorists in Ottawa, Why Chechens hate Pudovkin, Chechen community in Ottawa,* and finally, in an act of desperation when I could find nothing of any relevance, *Chechen sleeper cell in Ottawa.* Nothing. Zero. Oh sure, I found a few oblique references, but they proved to be dead ends in about two clicks. Of course, there is a Russian community in Ottawa, and there may even be a few Chechens as part of it, but given the national tensions and antipathies between the two peoples, Chechens may not have been warmly welcomed into the broader Russian community, or may not have had any interest in joining in the first place.

I was stuck. As I researched more, I found myself, as did Angus, strongly supporting the aspirations of the Chechen people for self-determination and independence. We agreed their desire to throw off Russia's yoke and become a full-fledged sovereign nation was right and just—but we didn't want their battle for independence to find its way to our shores, or, more accurately, the shores of the Ottawa River. Perhaps we could more strongly press Russia through diplomatic channels to make our position clear. Perhaps the Prime Minister might even raise the issue at his meeting with Pudovkin. Our PM didn't have a strong track record as a boat rocker, but it was worth a shot.

There was no real way of moving forward unless we started looking at names and home addresses, on tax returns or through other federal programs. And for very good reason, that information was not available to me. In short, I was searching for the Holy Grail. I would have loved to stumble upon a website with helpful photos, names, bios, and addresses of Ottawa Chechens. You know, something like:

Ludmilla Yamadayev, 28, joined the Chechen Sleeper Cell, Ottawa branch, in 2007 after nine years with the Chechen Liberation Front and another two with the Chechen Freedom Platoon. She has proven expertise in explosives, remote detonators, surface-to-air missiles, firearms, hand-to-hand combat, surveillance, and the broader clandestine arts. She has her G2 driver's licence and graduated with distinction from her high-performance-car-chase course at Mosport International Raceway. In her spare time, she likes cats, playing *Pokémon Go*, and watching *The Voice*.

But my search always came up empty. I even attempted to cross-reference common Chechen surnames I found in Wikipedia with names on Facebook, Twitter, and Instagram. Nothing. Maybe I was casting my net too widely and I needed some way to narrow my search field, to make our haystack smaller before we started probing for the needle. I just didn't know how.

In the early afternoon, my cellphone buzzed.

"Addisonian, it's Fitz."

"Hey, Roy," I replied. "Did you come up with anything?"

"Just a minute, I'm finding a quiet spot on a side street so I don't have to shout," he said. "Okay, this works. Now, I don't have much. Just a few bullet points from one slide. They mentioned what they refer to as the collapse of an apartment building the day before the meeting. They confirmed the cause as a faulty natural-gas intake fitting that triggered the explosion. Six people died. Then there's a 'Security Implications' heading with the word 'none' below it."

"Really?" All this was doing was proving Fleming's theory. It left me feeling empty and depressed.

"That's what it says," Fitz confirmed. "MI6 says it was a gas leak explosion with no connection to Pudovkin's visit."

"Did they even mention who died in the blast?"

"They just said six tenants in the building died."

"Fitz, thanks for this. It means a lot. Now, forget we ever had this conversation."

"What conversation?" he replied. "But let's not forget the hovercraft joyride."

"Don't worry, we'll make it happen. I promise. Thanks again."

—

Fifteen minutes later, Angus and I were driving to the Champlain Centre for our final walk-through before the Russian President's visit a week later.

"There's really only one plausible explanation for the erroneous MI6 Madrid briefing with CSIS," I said.

"Aye. MI6 is deliberately covering up evidence Fleming assembled," Angus said. "Nothing about the C-4 traces, nothing about the Chechen nationals in the building, and nothing about the fresh steel frame in the sewer to hold the device. Nothing."

"They're knowingly providing misleading intelligence to an ally who will soon be welcoming Vladimir Pudovkin," I said. "That is just not right."

"Is there no way we can reach out to Fleming?"

"Not that I can come up with. We just have to wait until she contacts us."

"Aye. Well, let it be soon, then."

The protestors milling around the entrance to the Champlain Centre were still chanting and marching, but their energy seemed to have dissipated, which was not surprising given that this same group had been chanting and marching twelve hours a day for the last two weeks. I was amazed they were still conscious and upright. Even today, they were fixated on the spider image. It had become a symbol of the fight, and central to the protestors' messaging. It was really quite brilliant. Chanting *Kill the spider!* over and over was so much more compelling and memorable than opting for *Hey hey, ho ho, rescind the ugly redesign option and develop an attractive new one!*

Patient police officers, who recognized Angus and me and our official site passes, gently parted the crowd and let us pass through. I followed the driveway down and around until we drove underneath the huge cantilevered concrete canopy that extended over the Centre's main entrance. Lots of workers were hard at it outside, with shovels, large potting urns, garden hoses, and racks of shrubs and flowers yet to be planted. Angus and I entered through the glass doors into the soon-to-be-inaugurated Samuel de Champlain Centre.

"They've done a lot since we were last here," I said. "It looks completely ready."

We entered the main assembly space, which overlooked the river. Even the grey-toned carpeting, complete with a subtle maple leaf pattern, was nearly fully installed.

"Aye, she's nearly done, except for the Skyjack sitting over there."

It did look anomalous: a bright-orange, four-wheeled Skyjack—a motorized elevating platform for changing light bulbs, washing the upper reaches of the windows, or giving Yao Ming a stand-up haircut—parked in the middle of the room. I guessed it was still there for last-minute inspections and final fixes.

We both stared high above us at the ceiling. Steel beams fanned out from the south wall of the building, forming the veins of the enormous maple leaf. The beams extended just beyond the windows to jut into the air high above the river. The view really was spectacular.

With the blueprints for the building in hand, Angus and I walked slowly through the Champlain Centre from stem to stern. We examined every square inch of the place, now that we knew the most likely way to bring down the building—along with Pudovkin and perhaps our Prime Minister, too—was some kind of explosive device. But where and how would it be planted? The Centre perfectly reflected the blueprints, with not even an extra bulkhead that might have housed a bomb. Everything was as it should be.

We had a master key from the site supervisor, and we scrupulously checked every utility room, bathroom, cloakroom, closet, kitchen, office, meeting room, balcony, foyer, and storage space on the premises. Every last one. We walked into every walk-in fridge in the kitchen. We scoured the cupboards, pantries, stoves, and drawers. We searched the physical plant and HVAC systems to the extent we could. We pored over the forced-air furnaces and air-conditioning units, and even opened panels and explored the ventilator shafts. We found nothing that deviated from the blueprints. We headed back outside and clambered around the roof of the Centre where the steel ceiling beams disappeared into the cliff face. Then we slipped underneath the building where the steel floor beams followed suit.

As a mechanical engineering professor, Angus took the lead, so I, as usual, followed, opening doors, knocking on walls, and giving the appearance that I knew what I was doing, an important skill I've gained over my years in Ottawa. We were very thorough.

An hour after we'd arrived, when I figured it was time to head back to Cumberland, Angus had another idea. "I want to take another look at the main assembly room," he said, walking back down the hall. "That's where the two leaders will be face-to-face for the longest period."

As we re-entered the room, Angus went straight to the Skyjack and climbed aboard.

"Um, Angus, what are you doing?"

He ignored my perfectly reasonable question and looked directly above him to the ceiling. "Close, but not quite right." With that, he pushed the green Start button and the Skyjack grumbled to life. He stood at the controls and fingered the little joystick that looked like it was better suited for a PlayStation. The Skyjack lurched backward, accompanied by the now-familiar *beep-beep* sound effects, which were just loud enough to be heard by a pedestrian walking the streets of Hull across the river. I kept waiting for the site supervisor to come rushing in and have some kind of a seizure, or at least attempt a citizen's arrest. But he didn't. Angus looked up as he manoeuvred the Skyjack just where he wanted it. Then he hit another button and the scissor lift raised him up, up, up. He deftly stopped his ascent just as the Skyjack was about to crash through the high ceiling. Angus was so close to the ceiling, he had to crouch down to stop from bumping his head.

This was classic Angus, taking charge of the situation, threats to his safety be damned.

"Angus, I'm not sure you should be doing that," I shouted. "Do you have a licence to drive that thing?"

He looked down and shook his head while pointing to his ears.

"Be careful! You almost pushed your head up through the ceiling tiles," I shouted even louder.

"I cannae hear you, lad," Angus shouted down. "Dinnae worry yourself, I'm just going to push my head up through the ceiling tiles."

I thought he was messing with me, but then he stood up and slowly lifted the ceiling tiles up with his head until he stood fully upright on the Skyjack. He looked like a headless man pressed into the ceiling—but I could still see his one-of-a-kind beard. I'd be terrified up there, but Angus looked quite calm, even at home, perched high atop the Skyjack. It was pointless to tell him to come down until he was ready. While I waited, I was quite happy to be on solid ground, even if it was in a building cantilevered out over the Ottawa River.

Angus reached down to a small tray attached to the controls and grabbed what looked like a flashlight. For about five minutes, he used the flashlight to peer into the ceiling, rotating first to the left and then to the right. Eventually, his face came back into view as he crouched down and slid the displaced ceiling tile back into position. He proceeded to lower the Skyjack about two feet so he could stand fully upright with his head just brushing the ceiling.

Angus turned off the engine. "I cannae see anything above the ceiling that shouldn't be there," he said. "I just cannae figure it out."

He stood there deep in thought and rested his hand on the long steel beam that ran the length of the building above him. "Blast and damnation!" he snapped. "Could it be our friend across the pond was wrong about all of this?" Then, in frustration, he banged the beam with the soft underside of his fist.

"Shite. It seemed so convincing and real," I said.

"Aye, it did. Our source was certainly believable. But we've kicked over every stone and there's nothing here. We're missing something. It's dangling just out of our reach, but I sense it."

"Maybe the bomb isn't here yet," I suggested.

"Aye, but starting in the next day or so, there'll be so much security crawling around these precincts, outside and in, that it would make no sense to try to bring in and hide a device then."

"We should get moving if we're going to make our stop before they have dinner," I said.

Angus looked at his watch and nodded. "Stand clear, I'm coming down."

It was nearly five o'clock when we made it back to Riverfront. As arranged, Muriel, Vivian, and Lindsay were waiting for us in a remote corner of the lounge so that there was no danger of us being overheard. If you looked over to us, closely clustered, you might think Angus and I were about to provide a top-secret briefing on an impending incident with global repercussions. So maybe it wasn't the most secure of locations, but give us a break. It was our first top-secret briefing on an impending incident with global repercussions.

As the only other person beyond Angus and me who understood what we were dealing with, Lindsay leaned forward with a very serious look on her face, waiting for us to speak.

"Thanks for attending this wee gathering," Angus started.

"As you can surely imagine, Vivian and I had to shuffle many different events in our social calendars to accommodate this meeting, including our bobsledding class," Muriel said. "But, Angus, we are always here for you."

Angus smiled and shook his head. "Thank you, Muriel, we knew we could count on you," he said. Then he paused and his face assumed a more serious mien. "This is quite important, and we must insist on your absolute discretion. In fact, 'discretion' seems too weak a term. What we really need is your commitment to secrecy."

"Angus, dear, we live in a seniors' residence in a small town on the Ottawa River," Muriel replied. "Who would we tell?"

"A fair enough point, but when you hear our story, I think you'll understand the need for complete confidentiality."

"You have my commitment," Vivian said. "It's business as usual for me, anyway."

"Of course, I will keep this to myself, and I know Lindsay will, too," Muriel added.

"I've already been keeping it to myself, Grandma," Lindsay said, catching my eye.

"Well, if we're the last to know, no need to keep us in suspense any longer. Dish it, already," Muriel urged.

"Aye, let's get to it. Daniel?"

I took over then. This was at least the third time I'd described the events of the past week, and I like to think I was getting better at telling the story. I covered everything, including our initial encounter with Fleming, our meeting with Koskov, our useless briefing with Bradley Stanton, the threats to the building, our complete rejection by Coulombe, CSIS, and the RCMP, the misleading MI6 Madrid briefing, our utter failure to find anything at the Champlain Centre — the whole sordid story.

You could tell from the changing expression on Muriel's face just how shocking a tale it was when you heard it for the first time. But Vivian sat quietly, leaning forward slightly, nodding now and then. She asked a couple of thoughtful questions and shook her head in dismay, or perhaps disgust, at a few points in the story. She was not happy that the Spanish security forces had done nothing more than weld down some of the sewer covers in the area of the President's residence.

"Astonishing incompetence! A welded sewer lid would not have saved them from a C-4 explosion beneath their feet," she said. "They're lucky the Chechens botched the detonator."

"I really thought you'd find something buried in the building," Lindsay said, shaking her head. "All the signs point to it."

"It must be there, somewhere," Muriel added.

I just shook my head and concluded the briefing by describing my floundering attempts to identify Chechens in Canada. "It'll take too long if my only search parameter is 'Chechens in Canada,' and I haven't been able to find anyone yet, let alone a Chechen separatist in Ottawa with malevolent intent and a background in explosives," I said. "We have to—"

"Narrow the field and shortcut the search," Vivian interrupted.

"Exactly! Any ideas?"

We all looked at Vivian. After a pause, she nodded once, then spoke.

"Thank you for a most thorough briefing. If heard only in fragments, it is an almost unbelievable story. When stitched together, as you have done so beautifully, it becomes not only believable, but almost inevitable. That journey from the impossible to the certain is one I've made many times during my career. I have the same feeling now."

"Are you telling us you think this tale rings true when it's all put together?" Angus asked hopefully.

"This Fleming friend of yours did the heavy lifting," Vivian said. "Without her analysis, this would all be unfolding right in front of our blind eyes."

"MI6 has some explaining to do," I said.

"Oversight of intelligence agencies has been a perennial problem, particularly in Britain," Vivian said. "The leaders at MI6 have considerable power and autonomy—a dangerous combination if they lose sight of their role. I suspect this Acton fellow has decided he's in charge of payback for Russia's sins on British soil. And as for the arrogance of the RCMP and CSIS thinking they have all the relevant and available intelligence and ignoring yours, well, that's unfortunately quite an old story, too."

"So, what do we do now? How do we stop this?" Lindsay asked.

"I agree with you that an explosive device at the Champlain Centre remains the most likely tactic," Vivian said. "A surface-to-air or even an air-to-air missile to bring down Pudovkin's plane are highly unlikely scenarios in Canada."

"But we've found nary a firecracker in the building, and we've looked everywhere," said Angus.

"What about the grounds immediately above and below the building?" asked Vivian.

"The site supervisor reported that the RCMP has already swept the entire property with metal detectors and will do so again twice more before the meeting," Angus said. "It's standard operating procedure."

"And there's security at the site 24-7," I added.

"May I see the email threat, please?" Vivian asked. On my phone, I opened the image of the note with the cut-out magazine letters and showed it to her. She concentrated on it for a few moments.

"Curious wording," she said. "I think the author has English as a first language, and may well be British."

"How can you tell?" Lindsay asked.

"It's not a brilliant deduction. Rather simple, really. I shouldn't think 'flutter' is a word that anyone with English as a second language would often employ. I suspect Brits use the word more often than we do, but that's more a hunch than a certainty."

"Bradley Stanton thinks the threat is likely from the same people behind the Society for Public Architecture," I said. "But he's more celebrated for his temper than his intellectual gifts."

"Bringing us back to the practical," Angus started, "Vivian, how do we, as you put it so well, shortcut the search for this sleeper cell? What can we do with the clock ticking?"

"Rather than search for all Russians or Chechens who have arrived in Canada in the last two years, my suggestion would be to focus right now on the building contractors. They have access to the site and will be the last ones there before Pudovkin arrives. Don't worry about the caterers or floral arrangers. Their products are too easily checked upon entry, and they surely will be. Look instead at heating and air-conditioning technicians, window installers, the concrete contractor, building materials suppliers, plumbers, the cleaners, painters, and even the landscaping company."

"That's my girl!" Muriel cheered, patting Vivian's hand.

"Brilliant!" I said. "That's definitely narrowing the field."

Wow. Vivian's suggestion bowled me over, yet at the same time it made so much sense.

"But Daniel, we don't have the contractors list," Angus noted.

"I know. But Infrastructure Canada has it, and I think I know how we can get it without arousing suspicion."

We talked for a few more minutes, but we already had our marching orders. Angus rose to his feet.

"Right, then, this has been a fine start to our little adventure. We'll get cracking on the contractors. Now, I know I don't have to remind any of us, but this is very sensitive information. Thank you all for helping us."

"I don't have a lot on my plate right now so I'm happy to advise from the wings," Vivian offered. "Do let me know what you find, and I'll keep thinking on it. I may want to see the building at some point. Can that be arranged?"

"Aye, we'll take you there ourselves," Angus replied. "And we'll try to work around your bobsled practice."

That evening, I crafted an email to Bradley Stanton and hit Send. Then I called him.

"Kind of late on a Friday night for a call, isn't it, Danny boy?"

"Sorry about the hour, but I just wanted to touch base on the thank-you reception for the Champlain Centre contractors," I said.

"What reception?"

"You know, I've mentioned it a couple of times in the last few weeks. I sometimes wonder whether you're listening to me."

"That's because I don't listen to you all the time. I'm always multitasking, solving other problems, when you're speaking to me. It's how I can be so effective and efficient."

"You know, Bradley, if you stop listening to me so you can do something else, it's not really multitasking," I said. "But I will give your 'not listening' technique a try sometime."

"You're welcome," Bradley said. "So, hit me with the reception idea again. But just the highlights, it's late."

"It's very simple. We want to host a reception in a few months or so, when everything has died down, to thank all of the workers who busted their asses to get the Champlain Centre finished in time for Pudovkin. It's an easy good-news hit for the PM."

"Fine. Let's make sure the media is there."

"Of course. But Infrastructure is too busy to organize it and I know the PMO is, too. But I think it's important, so Angus and I will organize it."

"Fine. Go ahead. Are you looking for the Order of Canada for your efforts?"

I had to hold my tongue and temper. This was vintage Stanton. "Very nice, Bradley. I just need you to cut and paste the email I've written for you and then send it to

Hilary Brooks over at Infrastructure. Given the short time available, I have to get started on the reception. So, I need the power of the PMO and your omnipotent name to get the contractors list quickly from Hilary. She'll respond faster to you."

"Fine."

"Um, it would be great if you could do it now and copy me, so it's waiting for her in the morning."

"*Fine!*"

"Thanks, Bradley. The carpet layers and landscapers will really appreciate it."

Hook, line, and sinker.

I'd never once mentioned a contractor thank-you reception to Bradley. How could I have? I'd just come up with the idea that evening. But I knew I could play Bradley and his ego, and it worked just as I'd anticipated. My little plans don't always work. In fact, my batting average is probably below .500. But I was confident about this one.

Five minutes later, Bradley's email to Hilary popped into my inbox. I scanned it quickly to make sure he hadn't changed it. Silly me. Bradley never changed my writing. I had to give him credit for knowing his own limitations. His great strength was being both a brilliant political organizer and a total asshole at the same time. Writing was not his thing.

Just to keep things moving, I forwarded Bradley's email to Hilary with the following note:

Hi Hilary,

*Hope you're well. Sorry about the late email on a
Friday night. The Champlain Centre looks amazing
both inside and out. Angus and I were there today.
Congratulations. Further to Bradley's email and the
PM's desire to host this contractor reception, PMO
didn't want to add to the burden you're already shouldering by dumping the event on you. So, Bradley has
asked Angus and me to take the lead, given our role
in organizing the Pudovkin meeting. And we're happy
to do it.*

*I'm hoping you can have one of your staff send me
a full list, with contact information, for any contractor involved in any aspect of the construction of the
Champlain Centre. The sooner the better as the PMO
has asked me to give them updates on a weekly basis.
The PM seems to like this kind of event and I'm keen
to get started ASAP. Thanks for doing this.*

Daniel

It was a rare warm and clear night. Lindsay and I sat in
Adirondack chairs on the dock, holding hands and watching
the light of the moon shimmer across the water, until after
midnight. Just before my head hit the pillow, I checked my

email. Hilary was a hard worker who really had no off switch, so I wasn't surprised to see a response from her.

Hey Daniel,

No worries, and thanks for taking on the reception. We really have no extra bandwidth right now so I'm grateful you do. You'll have a list in your inbox by 9:00 Monday morning at the latest, and hopefully sooner. Now go to bed!

Hil

Yes! Now we were moving.

CHAPTER 5

True to her word, Hilary emailed me her list of contractors on Saturday morning. With time pressing down on us, I sat at the boathouse kitchen table right then and banged out a letter on my laptop for Angus to send on behalf of the Prime Minister. It thanked the companies for their extraordinary efforts to complete the Champlain Centre and announced a special thank-you reception to be held later in the year. The letter asked each company for a list of employees and their respective years of service. This, I wrote, would help facilitate personalized invitations to each worker involved in the build.

I put the letter on our minister's-office letterhead and read it over a few times, tweaking lines here and there. It wasn't a masterpiece, but it would get the job done quickly, and that was the goal. Then, using the list Hilary had provided, I spent about an hour setting up a mail merge that would personalize each letter. Finally, I drafted a quick introductory email using the subject line *Urgent email on behalf of the Prime Minister*, before batching and sending them. Even though we weren't necessarily interested in every one of the suppliers, I decided to send it to all of them just to cover my . . . let's go with *bases*.

I was hoping contractors would respond quickly because I'd invoked the Prime Minister's sanction. When you have the power of the PMO, you use it. And it worked. I suppose the speed and number of responses weren't necessarily driven by the prestige of the Prime Minister's Office. It's also possible that the contractors felt indebted to the federal government for throwing buckets of money at them to finish the building in record time. Or maybe folks just really liked a party. Whatever the explanation, when Angus and I arrived at the office Monday morning, there were already nine responses, and they continued to flow in for the rest of the day.

Angus left for a Cabinet committee meeting in Centre Block—he was a member of the Global Affairs and Public Security committee—and I cleared my decks and dug into the employee lists.

While there were dozens of companies working on the Champlain Centre, I focused on the kinds of contractors Vivian had noted as our most likely suspects. I was looking for those whose services or products lent themselves to, you know, planting a bomb inside the building. As luck would have it, many of the contractors I'd earmarked as priorities had sent in their lists that morning.

I quickly found a groove. I'd scan the names of employees in search of those that sounded even remotely eastern European, or Russian, or what I thought might be Slavic — as if I really knew — or just different enough to warrant a closer look. I love Ottawa, but it's not a big destination city for immigrants (the cold winters alone might explain this), which meant that I didn't come across many names that merited closer attention.

Whenever I identified a prospect, I'd first pump the name into Google to discover its regional or national origins. It really helped that Google in general, and Wikipedia in particular, served up lists of common names by country.

When I found employees with names that originated anywhere behind the old Iron Curtain, I'd dig a little deeper. This meant first assessing their social media footprint. Did they have a Facebook page? Were they on Twitter or Instagram? Did they have a LinkedIn account? This gave me at least a sense of who they were. Finding someone who'd "liked" a Chechen independence Facebook page or tweeted a death threat to Pudovkin would have really narrowed my search, but I had no such luck. But I did come across some potential candidates.

I found a Ukrainian man who worked at the company contracted to do the interior and exterior painting at the Champlain Centre. But he'd been with the company for more than thirteen years, so he didn't fit the profile of a recently arrived immigrant.

I looked at a Russian landscaper, but he'd been in Canada for over twenty-two years. Same for him.

I identified a woman from Georgia—the country on the Black Sea, not the Peach State south of our border—who worked at the company contracted to handle catering. Not only had she been employed there for nine years, she likely had not yet set foot in the Champlain Centre, and probably wouldn't until the day of the Pudovkin visit—as Vivian had suggested. Nope. She was out of the running.

Knowing that Eugene and Tatyana, our Chechens code-named after lovers in a Pushkin novel, had arrived in Canada two years ago, I was beginning to see that including employees' years of service on the list was a masterstroke, if I do say so myself. It became an important way to filter candidates.

Then I came across a man with a name that is common in Belarus, on Russia's western border. He'd worked for the window contractor for the last two years, so the timing worked. But a quick look at his Facebook page, cross-referenced with an online birth announcement in the *Montreal Gazette* archives, confirmed that he'd been born in Canada. So he was off the list.

This kind of thing happened about six more times. It became relatively easy to exclude candidates—but then I hit one that wasn't so easy to exclude. Not easy at all.

Red Pine Steel, based just outside of Ottawa on the road to Rockland, was the designated contractor for almost all of the Champlain Centre's steel fabrication requirements. This included everything from cosmetic products like decorative railings and fireplace fixtures all the way up to structural steel needs like beams, girders, and HVAC unit mounts. It was a big contract, according to the public procurement records I'd called up on my screen. The only name on the Red Pine Steel list that caught my eye was Anzor Dudiyn, though I had no idea of its origin. My Googling told me it wasn't Russian, Ukrainian, Georgian, Polish, Latvian, or Estonian. This could have gone on for a while, so I decided to shortcut the search and go right to the Wikipedia listing I'd found of Chechen names. Wikipedia has everything.

And there they were. Both Anzor and Dudiyn made the cut in the inventory of common Chechen names and surnames. I felt my breathing change all on its own, and my heart rate jumped. My mind raced with the thought that maybe, just maybe, I was onto something, or someone. But I needed to check at least one more box first. I turned back to the Red Pine Steel employee list to find that Anzor had been employed by the company for, yes, *two years*. That's when my stomach muscles tightened up.

I took a few breaths and forced myself to calm down. Believe it or not, I set Anzor aside for a few minutes and checked my email. I needed a moment to process it all. There were only three more contractors I wanted to check, and all three of their lists had arrived while I'd been working my way through the others. There were four potential names on those lists, but one by one, I confirmed they were in the clear: all four employees with eastern European–sounding names turned out to be first-generation Canadians with more than two years of service with their companies. Done and dusted. Now I could focus on the one lonely viable candidate auditioning for the role of Eugene in our drama. Anzor Dudiyn of Red Pine Steel.

My deeper investigation didn't start off well. The man had absolutely no social media accounts, not even a seldom-used LinkedIn profile. Relative to most of us in this digital world, Anzor was a ghost. I was disappointed, until I realized that his utter absence from the online space was completely consistent with hatching an assassination plot that could change the face of geopolitics.

So I took a different approach. I looked up the online presence of Red Pine Steel and found a robust profile on the traditional platforms. I clicked to the company website first, but it was focused on marketing and customer service, with no photos of employees, save for some headshots of senior management. Anzor was apparently not a senior player with the company.

Then I found a Red Pine Steel employee Facebook page that seemed more promising. There were photos of various company social gatherings: staff birthdays, fundraising events, Ottawa Senators hockey games, Christmas parties.

Many, though not all, of the photos had captions identifying the employees in the shots. How convenient. I hunkered down, zoomed in to enlarge the images, and scrolled through each photo one by one, carefully reading the captions. In the more than three dozen images, I found exactly one photo of our man Anzor Dudiyn, standing with a group of guys at last year's Christmas party. They were laughing and raising drinks in their hands. That is, everyone was except Anzor. Instead, he stared right at the camera with a look of surprise. His right hand appeared to be in motion, likely on its way up to cover his face. If the photo had been shot a half-second later, you might not be able to identify him. But he was too late, and you could clearly see his clean-shaven face and dark, cropped hair. He looked of average height and weight, and he was wearing coveralls like the rest of the men in the photo—they must all work on the fabrication floor, in the middle of the action. He appeared to be in his late twenties or early thirties. He looked a little scared.

Hell, I was a little scared. Or maybe a lot scared. If I was right, I was looking into the eyes of a cold-blooded killer who was prepared to sacrifice innocent lives—including perhaps our Prime Minister's—to advance the sovereign interests of his people. It gave me chills.

Now, maybe I'm reading too much into this, I thought. I wondered if I was distorting the evidence to fit our theory. But Anzor's posture in the photo, his facial expression, his moving hand—they all gave him the look of someone who didn't want to be seen or photographed, and who certainly didn't want to be identified.

I dug a little deeper online, trying to find any references at all to Anzor Dudiyn. I came up empty, except for that one Christmas party photo. I wondered if he even knew it was posted on Facebook.

I needed advice on what to do with this discovery, but Angus was still not back from his meeting. So I called Muriel, gave her an update, and asked her if she could have Vivian call me back urgently. Four minutes later my phone rang.

It was both Muriel and Vivian, calling me from Vivian's room. I quietly gave them a full account of my morning and ended with the story of Anzor Dudiyn, or at least the parts that I could put together. I texted Vivian a screenshot of the Facebook photo.

"You've done very well to uncover this, Daniel," she said excitedly. "It's just the kind of thing our analysts spend their time doing. And you did it on instinct. Excellent and well done."

"Well, thank you," I said. "My misspent youth watching spy movies and pretending to be James Bond has finally paid dividends. But what do we do now?"

"The next step is clear. We need to find out more about our young Chechen steelmaker."

"I've already scoured the internet using all the tricks I know, and still only came up with this single, solitary photo," I replied. "There's nothing there. He's not there."

"Daniel, I'm not talking about armchair online research," Vivian said. "I mean we have to observe the man in the flesh, in the moment. See where he lives, what he does, and where he goes. We need to look for corroborating evidence to bolster our case."

"Well, that sounds like I need to pass this on to the RCMP or CSIS. That's what they do, isn't it?"

"If you think they'll respond favourably and do something about it, then by all means you can reach out to them," Vivian said. "But from what you've told us . . ."

"They aren't going to lift a finger," Muriel chimed in. "And you know it, Daniel. In Coulombe's book, Angus and you are radioactive. We are on our own."

"Further, they aren't about to pull officers off of security preparations just because a guy with a Chechen name works at a steel plant in Ottawa," Vivian added.

"I guess not," I said. "Then what exactly do we do?"

"Are you familiar with the term 'stakeout'?" Vivian asked.

"You mean sitting in a car, consuming warm coffee and stale doughnuts, bantering with your partner, and waiting until something big happens so they can break for a commercial?"

"Close," she said. "There's usually a lot more waiting around, but even the cop shows get the fundamentals right. Do you have your car with you?"

"If you mean my bright-red, less-than-understated Mazda CX-5, then yes, I do."

"It'll do in a pinch," Vivian said. "Drive to this Red Pine Steel facility. I've just checked online while you've been speaking—they have over 150 employees, so they must have a large parking lot. Shift change will likely be at four o'clock. If we're lucky, this Anzor fellow will be coming off his day's work. Park in a more remote part of the lot but still amongst the other cars, and in a position that affords a clear view. Keep your head down and watch the doors for the workers leaving. Look for Anzor. Snap a few shots on your phone but only if you can do it discreetly. You are not to wait by the plant door with a digital SLR camera and tripod, holding a sign with his name on it."

"I was planning to stand out front and hail him by name with a megaphone," I joked.

"Just be discreet and try not to make eye contact with him," Vivian continued. "If he starts to look your way, look somewhere else, but do it naturally."

"Okay, then what?"

"Presumably, he'll get into his own car, probably alone," Vivian explained. "It would be very helpful to know where he lives. So, when he starts to drive out of the lot, let at least one other car pull in behind him, maybe two, before you slide in line after that. Always put at least one car between you and our Chechen friend. And don't do anything to draw attention to yourself or your car."

"You mean don't play AC/DC at full volume with the windows down, violently bobbing my head to the heavy metal beat?"

"That is but one of many examples of things not to do when shadowing someone in a car. Others include sustained horn honking, undue revving of the engine, squealing your tires, and driving with the hood open and your head out the window."

"Hmm, that's a lot to remember, but I'll try my best."

"Just try to blend into the surroundings. And one more thing. If Angus or Lindsay are available, it's better to have someone else with you. It draws less attention if there are two of you in the car."

We hung up a few minutes later. I felt better about the assignment after my little tutorial with a former senior CSIS operative, but I was still nervous. Angus wasn't back yet and likely wouldn't be for a while longer. But if I was going to make it to Red Pine Steel for shift change, I didn't have much time to spare. I rearranged my afternoon, though other than planning the details around the Pudovkin meeting, there was nothing else pressing. Then I picked up my phone and dialled.

I met Lindsay at Carleton University about twenty minutes later. She slid into the car and kissed me, and I knew

I'd made the right call to have her join me. On the half-hour drive to Red Pine Steel I brought her up to speed on my fruitful morning playing Find the Chechen. She was very impressed. I was, too, but let modesty reign. We approached our destination just before four o'clock. I was relieved to see that there was no security gate at the parking lot entrance, and we were able to drive straight in behind two other cars, likely filled with workers about to start the four-to-midnight shift. I found a spot towards the back of the lot that was still close enough to the plant entrance that I felt sure we'd recognize our man. I turned off the engine and showed Lindsay the photo of Anzor on my cellphone. Then we slid down in our seats and watched.

A few minutes later we heard the whistle signalling shift change, just like in the *Flintstones* cartoons I watched as a kid. Within the minute, workers streamed out of the building and headed for their cars. We searched the crowd for Anzor, but it was chaotic for a few minutes. We thought we might have missed him. Finally, the flow dwindled and a group of four men emerged and sauntered into the parking lot, kibitzing with one another. I looked past them and right into the eyes of Anzor Dudiyn.

I wasn't ready for the fear that enveloped me in that instant. Without warning, my heart pounded, my hands trembled, and my throat tightened. I was looking at a man capable of violence on a significant scale, a man planning to kill many just to ensure he killed one. I slid down in the driver's seat.

"Are you all right?" Lindsay asked. "You look shaky."

There was a logical explanation for my shaky appearance: I was just a few notches shy of terrified. I took a deep breath, pointed to our man in the parking lot, and pulled myself together.

"Meet Eugene," I whispered, without intending to.

"Eugene?" Lindsay asked.

"Yes, I forgot to mention that according to Fleming, the code names for the Chechen couple sent to Ottawa are Tatyana and Eugene."

"What, the lovers from the Pushkin novel?" Lindsay asked. She did not seem frightened at all, which helped calm me down.

"One of the reasons I love you is that you know the characters in a Pushkin novel," I said, feeling more myself, but still on edge. "Just so it doesn't get confusing, let's refer to him as Eugene," I suggested. She nodded.

We both watched as Eugene walked through the parking lot. He was far enough away that we weren't worried about him seeing us, yet my pulse was pounding. I snapped a few discreet photos with my cellphone, then managed to drop it on the floor beneath the steering wheel. Smooth move.

I'm not sure if you've ever tried to pick up something off the floor of the driver's side of your car when you're sitting in the driver's seat, but you need much longer arms than humans generally sport. If you happen to be a Cirque du Soleil contortionist, you'll be fine. But my flexibility is so limited that when I drop my car keys, I have to kneel on the floor to pick them up. I'm like a Tyrannosaurus Rex trying to cut his toenails. I just can't reach.

I managed to just touch my phone by leaning down and squishing my face against the steering wheel. A car horn nearby gave a long and loud honk that was quite annoying and completely put me off reaching my keys. In fact, I forgot what I was doing in the first place. Lindsay lowered her head below the dashboard and tapped my shoulder. She may have been saying something, but the car horn blasting nearby drowned her out. I then realized that the blaring horn wasn't exactly nearby; it was directly under my squished face. I lifted my head far enough to stop the horn but not so far that our man Eugene could see us. I also noted, for future reference, that Lindsay easily retrieved my phone from her passenger-seat position.

I snuck a peek through my side window and was relieved to see that our quarry wasn't scanning the parking lot for the obnoxious driver and his horn. He climbed into a beat-up, rusted-out silver Ford Taurus sedan. I had owned a Taurus wagon of the same vintage and condition until recently—in fact, it had been our campaign headquarters for Angus's first election, even though you could see the road whizzing by beneath your feet through holes in the rusted floor. Eugene threw his lunch bag on the passenger seat and started the engine. Luckily, two guys in a black Ford F-150 pickup truck were leaving at the same time. Right on cue, Eugene pulled out of his spot, with the pickup gliding in right behind him. I started up my Mazda and pulled in behind the pickup.

I followed the two vehicles as they turned west on Highway 174 towards Ottawa. In what seemed like no time, we were hitting the outskirts of the city. By that time, we'd lost the F-150 but had managed to put a few different cars between Eugene's Taurus and us, so I was certain he had no idea he was being tailed. I looked over at Lindsay. She seemed completely relaxed, while I was sweating and wondering how much longer my stomach could keep churning before rejecting—or rather, ejecting—its contents. I tried not to think about it and instead focused on my tailing technique.

"Vivian gave me some tips on how to follow another car discreetly," I said. "The trick is to keep at least one other car between us and Eugene."

"I can see that," Lindsay replied. "Very impressive."

By this time, we were tooling along King Edward Avenue in Ottawa's Sandy Hill neighbourhood. A souped-up white Camaro was now between Eugene and our Mazda. I was glad the Camaro driver was not shadowing the Taurus, because between blasting hip hop and racing his engine at stoplights, he wasn't doing it right. I was staying a safe distance behind him but could still track the Taurus ahead.

"You never want to get so close that you arouse suspicion," I added.

"Got it."

Just then, the Camaro pulled a dramatic and abrupt U-turn right in front of us.

"Can you believe this guy?" I said, turning to glare at the driver. "Without so much as a turn sig . . ."

"Daniel!"

I snapped my eyes back to the road to find Eugene's car stopped dead right in front of us. And I mean *right* in front of us. I slammed on the brakes, eliciting a deafening and seemingly endless screech from the tires as we finally skidded to a stop. It would have been much better if our brakes, and not Eugene's beat-up Taurus, had finally stopped us, but no such luck. Fortunately, it wasn't a huge impact. No airbags deployed, no personal injury lawyers materialized at the scene. But there was no escaping the fact that I had just driven into the back of the very car I'd been discreetly following while trying to blend in and not attract attention.

On instinct, Lindsay jumped out to survey the damage. On instinct, I sat behind the wheel, scared to face Eugene. But I knew I couldn't just let Lindsay deal with him. I quelled the knee-knocking vibrations in my legs and got out of the car to join her.

There was not a scratch on our car, but the Ford's bumper now seemed rather ill-suited to its role. It was deformed by the blow, and the rubber strip that had once nicely adhered to the chrome was hanging down and resting on the pavement, you know, where the rubber meets the road. Damn. Our Eugene eventually opened his door and slowly got out. Somehow, I stepped in front of Lindsay, in case he was about to attack. But he didn't appear to be angry at being rear-ended. He just seemed uncomfortable. He was looking down at the ground, only occasionally lifting his eyes to us.

"Are you all right?" I asked, my voice shaking.

"Yes, I'm fine, I'm very okey-dokey."

I had trouble processing that I was actually talking to Eugene. I felt like I was occupying someone else's body. "I'm so sorry, I was distracted by that white car behind you when he pulled a U-turn with no warning. Are you sure you're all right?"

He did not strike me as an international terrorist bent on assassinating Vladimir Pudovkin. He just seemed scared.

"Please, I am fine, everything is fine."

Lindsay and I exchanged puzzled glances.

"By the time I looked back you were stopped right in front of me."

"Please. Don't worry. Is my fault. I stopped too fast."

"But you had to stop," Lindsay said, putting a concerned hand on his shoulder. "There was an old woman and her shopping buggy in the middle of the road. You had to stop."

He slipped out from under her touch.

"I don't know this 'buggy' word. But is my fault. And see, no damage," he said, pointing to his clearly damaged bumper.

"Well, your bumper wasn't always shaped like that, and the rubber part wasn't always dragging on the road," I said.

"I think it was. I do. Is fine. Is my fault. Please, I must go."

He seemed to be growing more anxious as a small crowd gathered on the sidewalk. His eyes darted this way and that. Then he turned and slipped back behind the wheel.

"Wait, let me give you my insurance information," I said, holding his door open and reaching for my wallet.

He shook his head and pulled on the door. "No, no, no. Is fine. Is my fault. Thank you. Thank you. Bye-bye."

Several cars behind us were starting to honk, so I released his door and he yanked it closed. He pulled away as soon as the way was clear. Lindsay and I got back in my car and began driving again, keeping an eye on Eugene's in front. We let him get about a block ahead of us and watched as he turned right on Somerset East. We slowed down to give him time to get ahead. The honking behind us started up again, so we made our turn onto Somerset East and luckily could still see the Taurus far up the road. We followed him when he turned left onto Chapel and watched as he pulled into the driveway of a small, rundown bungalow. I quickly parked a block away and hoped he wouldn't look down the street and see us when he got out of the car. Thankfully, he didn't; he just walked into the house.

"We now have an address," I said, taking note of the house number.

We sat there a bit longer and even inched the car closer so we could be the last in a line of seven parked vehicles. You know, blending in. I'm pleased to report that I didn't hit any of the other cars when parking. By this time, I was feeling more like myself and was starting to breathe normally again. I wasn't petrified anymore, just scared silly.

A short time later, we watched in our mirrors as two men, followed a little further behind by a woman, walked off Somerset East onto Chapel on the other side of the street from our car. The two men walked past the house with the Taurus—now a little more beat-up—in the driveway, and continued up the street. But the woman, who looked to be in her late twenties and was wearing a puffy blue coat and jeans, turned at the driveway without even glancing at the Ford's damaged bumper and entered the house.

"Hello, Tatyana," Lindsay said as I snapped a photo.

"Wow, I think we've found them," I said. "I can't believe it. I think we've found them!"

Lindsay reached over and patted my thigh. "I gotta say, Eugene certainly wanted no part of exchanging names, numbers, and insurance info."

"If he's who we think he is, that makes sense."

"Okay, but we're only halfway home," Lindsay said. "Now we need to know more about Tatyana."

"If I may channel the Hardy Boys for a moment, I think we have to figure out how she spends her days," I said. "We already know where Eugene works."

"Well, I'm driving Muriel into the city tomorrow for a doctor's appointment in the late morning. Why don't I bring her in a little early and we'll have our own grandmother-granddaughter stakeout and try to find out where Tatyana goes?"

"I like that you'd be using your car. That strikes me as good tradecraft."

"Plus, I don't think even the most suspicious spy would suspect an eighty-three-year-old and her granddaughter," Lindsay said.

"Maybe wear a ball cap and sunglasses. Eugene *did* see you."

A while later, I dropped Lindsay back at Carleton so she could pick up her car and go to dinner with a high school friend in the ByWard Market. I drove straight back to Cumberland and hoped Angus would be home. My mind and body were utterly spent from being so tense for the last hour or so. Fear is exhausting.

It turned out Angus was home, and as soon as I was in his house, I dropped into my favourite chair in his living room and started talking.

"Lad, you've had a perfectly productive and successful day," Angus said after I had briefed him. "Good on you, lad. I cannae believe you actually put it all together and found Eugene and Tatyana. There cannae be any doubt. Everything lines up. I'm gobsmacked and offer my hearty felicitations! I just wish I'd been with you for it all, and not rotting away at meetings that seem to accomplish nothing."

"Thanks, Angus. I wish you could have been there, too," I replied. I was glad I hadn't mentioned the horn-honking incident in the parking lot.

"Now, despite this great and extraordinary leap forward, for which you're to be congratulated six ways from Sunday, let me return to one part of your yarn to see if I've got it straight," Angus said.

Uh-oh. And here we go.

"To review, you were following our man from a safe distance so he wouldn't know he was being tailed, and at some point, you thought, *I think it would be better if I drove into the back of him?*" He was laughing now.

"It was an accident!" I said.

"Precisely! A car accident!" Angus retorted.

"It could have happened to anyone."

"I don't think it ever happened to James Bond or, what's the other guy's name you like?"

"Jason Bourne."

"Right, Jason Bourne. Have you told Vivian and Muriel?"

"Of course. I called them on my way home. It's Communications 101. Take control of the message. Don't let others set the context and tone. I'd much rather tell them myself in my own way than have you tell them in your decidedly less sympathetic way. Much better positioning for me."

"And how did our espionage advisor, Vivian, respond?"

"Well, after I explained the whole story and assured her that we weren't compromised, she laughed a little."

"You say she laughed a little?"

"Okay, she laughed a lot. There were tears. She had to hang up. I phoned back to make sure she hadn't choked, but she was okay by then."

"Grand. Just grand," said Angus. "Seriously, Daniel, all my jibes aside, that was a fine piece of work you did today, fender-bender or not. You've put us much closer to resolving this. Were you not a wee bit frightened?"

I faked a pensive look, as if the idea of being scared had never occurred to me.

"Well, I guess I was a little anxious," I eventually admitted. "It helped that Lindsay was there with me."

"Well, you made great progress today," Angus said. "But there's more to do. Now that we have a bit more evidence to make our story marginally more plausible, I was thinking I should try to have another word with Koskov."

"You mean to push him a little further on all this?"

"Aye. I dinnae think he'll listen, but I do feel obligated to try without unduly tipping our hand."

I dictated Koskov's number from my cellphone, and Angus dialled.

"Ambassador, it's Angus McLintock," Angus started when Koskov answered. "I have you on speaker here, if that's satisfactory, as I'm with my Chief of Staff, Daniel Addison. You may remember him from our London meetings. I do hope I'm not interrupting your dinner."

"Of course, not, Minister. How can I assist you?"

"Well, I'll not take up too much of your time. But I did want to ask again about the possibility, remote as it may be, of an enemy of President Pudovkin attempting to make some trouble when he is in Ottawa."

We could both clearly hear Koskov's heavy sigh, even with his Russian accent. "Minister McLintock, as I said when we were in London, there is no concern, and is certainly no concern of yours," he said firmly. "We are very good at security. It's one of our, how do you say it, specialties. There is no problem at all. Let us move on to other topics."

"Mr. Ambassador, I was reading recently about the tension between Moscow and Chechnya. It seems that many Chechens want an independent nation-state, and they see President Pudovkin as an obstacle to that dream."

"You must stop, Minister McLintock. You must. You are talking internal business of Russia and allies. Is not right. Is wrong. You look at motorcade security and leave other matters to us. They are no concern for you."

Angus looked at me. Using hand motions, I urged him not to let Koskov off the hook that easily but to take another run at him. My hands seem to be very articulate, as Angus jumped back into the fray.

"But Ambassador, if something happens while President Pudovkin is on Canadian soil, then it seems it would very quickly become our concern," Angus persisted. "Do you not consider Chechen separatists to be a threat? I can surely understand why they might think it advantageous to do something when the President is outside of the safety and security of Moscow."

"Farmers and peasants are not threat!" the ambassador snapped. "Not in Chechnya. Not in Russia. And not in Canada. Leave to us. I insist. Am I being loud and clear, Minister McLintock?"

"Aye, you are, Ambassador. I hear you, as you say, loud and clear. Thank you for taking my call. We will talk again in the coming days about last-minute details. I appreciate your reassurance. Good night."

Ambassador Koskov hung up without saying another word.

Angus turned back to me. "Well, I did my best, laddie, but he was not at his most effervescent and forthcoming this evening. In fact, I found him to be too sensitive and cantankerous by at least half."

"Well, we had to squeeze him a bit," I replied. "If he was being truthful, they don't seem to be troubled in the least by any domestic concerns in Chechnya. But you certainly pushed his buttons at the end there."

"Aye, I seem to have touched—or perhaps even pinched—a nerve. You might say he reacted as if I'd just driven into the back of the ambassadorial limousine."

"Okay, how long is it going to take for me to live this one down?"

"Well now, it's hard to say, but I think it's a wee while yet."

CHAPTER 6

"Daniel, the eagle is in flight," Lindsay said when I answered her call around 7:10 Tuesday morning. I was already at work, sitting at my desk in our Centre Block office.

"Oh, right," I replied. "Um . . . remind me again what we decided that meant?"

"For heaven's sake, Addison, get in the game!" Muriel snapped. "It means the banged-up silver rust-bucket is on the move."

Lindsay had picked up Muriel early for her doctor's appointment and headed to Ottawa to find a parking spot with a view on Chapel Street. They were in Lindsay's blue

Honda Civic, a ubiquitous model that was perfect for inconspicuous tailing. There had even been two other Civics already parked on the street. Muriel was excited to get in on the adventure. Then again, she frequently told us she was excited when she went to the bank, and every other time she ventured beyond the walls of the Riverfront Seniors' Residence, regardless of the reason.

"Got it," I said. "Excellent. Okay, bring me up to date."

"Well, right now, Lindsay dear is focused on following the silver car. She's keeping her distance so that she doesn't accidentally drive into the back of it."

"Hilarious, Muriel. Thank you for that. But what happened before?"

"Oh, we arrived just before seven and found a spot a tad down the street from their hideout," Muriel said. "Then, even though I'd been told there'd be doughnuts, we ate fresh fruit that Lindsay kindly brought, and drank coffee from a thermos. Just your average, run-of-the-mill stakeout, minus my favourite cinnamon crullers."

"Good to know you're hydrated, caffeinated, and unlikely candidates for scurvy," I said. "Then what?"

"Just before we called you, the young man, I gather we're calling him Eugene, came out of the house and started his car. But he just sat there, waiting. A minute later, the lovely and talented Tatyana emerged and got in the car with him. When they drove away, we followed a couple cars behind them, heading downtown."

"Excellent. I was worried Tatyana might take the bus, which would have made following her difficult," I said. "So where are you now?"

"We turned left on Laurier and have just now crossed over the canal into Centretown."

"Careful you don't get caught at a traffic light and lose them."

"There's now only one car between us, so I'm hoping we can stay with them," Lindsay said. "Okay, we just turned right on Bank Street, now heading north."

Their route had me wondering about their destination.

"Do you think they're going to Parliament Hill?" I asked

"We'll know in just a second or two," Lindsay said. She paused for what seemed like an excruciatingly long time. "Okay, we're at Bank and Wellington now and he's going straight across. Wait, you're right! He just turned in at the gates that lead onto Parliament Hill. I've just driven past the gates and pulled over. I can still see them in my rear-view mirror."

Despite my best efforts, I could only come up with one reason for Eugene to be driving Tatyana to Parliament Hill at the start of a workday.

"Wait, Tatyana just flashed a pass and the security guard waved them in. But I can't follow," Lindsay reported.

"My gosh, she works on the Hill. It's the only explanation," I said. "It would really help to know where they're going."

"Okay, I've put on my hazards. Grandma, you stay with the car and tell anyone who asks that I've gone to get your medication. That ought to buy us enough time."

"Don't worry, dear, I can easily play the agitated senior anxious for my meds."

Lindsay left the car and hurried on foot to keep the Taurus in sight, breathing heavily. "Shit, I've lost it," she said. "No, wait, I've got it again. He's driving up behind Centre Block."

"There's an employee entrance back there," I said. "Yep, I'm pretty sure Tatyana works in Centre Block. Unbelievable."

"Okay, the car just disappeared behind Centre Block. I'm sitting down on a bench just next to West Block, and I have a pretty good view. There's only one way back, so I'm going to wait."

"Great job, Linds. You're a natural," I said. "When he drives back past you, be careful he doesn't recognize you."

"He won't. I took your advice. I'm wearing Muriel's Tilley hat and her largest sunglasses, from about 1976. I look a little like Jackie Kennedy on safari, maybe not as elegant. I don't think you'd recognize me, so I'm quite sure Eugene won't."

"Can you send me a selfie? I'd like to see that."

"Oh, here he comes . . . and there he goes. He was alone in the car . . . Hang on. He just turned left onto Wellington. So, he's probably headed to work for his 8:00 a.m. shift. The timing is perfect."

I paused for just a moment to let this revelation sink in. It was shocking to think that Tatyana, a suspected member of a Chechen sleeper cell bent on assassinating the Russian President, might actually work in Centre Block, the very seat of our democracy. It was gutsy and outrageous. I was reeling. But I had no time for reeling.

"Okay, over to me," I said. "I'm already in Centre Block, so I'm going to head downstairs to see if I can spot Tatyana. I can't believe she works in Centre Block. That's crazy! Thanks for this, Linds. Love you. Gotta go."

I hung up and, before I could change my mind, grabbed a couple of stuffed but unimportant file folders and made my way downstairs to the basement towards the employee entrance, a tightness in my stomach. With my House of Commons pass hanging around my neck, no one gave me a second look. I patrolled the area, keeping my eyes peeled, but there was no sign of her. Maybe she worked in landscaping and was already outside.

I was about to return to our office when I decided to make one more circuit through the network of corridors in the west end of Centre Block's basement. I'd just started down the last hallway when a cleaner's cart appeared around the corner in front of me. Then, everything began unfolding in slow motion. The cleaner pushing the cart emerged into view and it was none other than Tatyana, wearing a green smock, with her ID badge prominently displayed, as required. Without her puffy coat, I could now see she was lean, like an athlete. Unless I turned around right then, we were going to meet in the middle of the corridor. Now what?

I was nervous—okay, perhaps scared. But we had to move this forward. So I ignored my instinct to turn on my heel and hightail it out of there. If we really had cracked the code and figured it all out, there was a violent Chechen separatist with malevolent intent walking towards me. Why would I walk towards her? But I swallowed hard and did just that.

I've been a bit clumsy for my entire life. I don't know why, but if there's a stray bucket, or a banana peel, or a pile of dog crap in the immediate vicinity, chances are that one of my feet, sometimes even both of them, will find it. So, as Tatyana was about to pass me, it felt quite natural to drop my burgeoning files and watch them fan out across the floor, covering an impressive patch of real estate. In fact, I may not have even done it on purpose, though that was my plan.

I crouched down, blocking her path, and started frantically collecting papers at a pace that matched my quickened pulse.

"So sorry about this," I said. "I'll just be a minute."

"I can help," she said, and immediately started gathering paper, too.

She had an accent that sounded a little like Natasha in the *Rocky and Bullwinkle* cartoons. We both finished picking up the papers around us and stood up at the same time. She handed me the thick wad she'd retrieved. She wasn't smiling. Her face was nearly expressionless, though she did seem a little on edge.

"Thank you so much for your help. I don't know what happened. It was like the file folders just leapt out of my hands," I said in a tremulous voice that sounded like I was perched on the edge of an anxiety attack.

She nodded but said nothing and looked like she was about to start moving past me.

"Um, I've worked here for several years and I don't think I've ever seen you," I said.

She looked past me down the hall before replying.

"I worked two years in Confederation Building. But just few weeks ago, moved to Centre Block. I like it better here."

"Elina Shishani," I said, reading her nametag. "That's an unusual name."

"Not where I come from. Is . . . eastern European." She snapped a glance behind her down the corridor before turning back to me. "I must get to cleaning."

"Right. Thanks again for your help."

She nodded and walked on, and when she rounded the corner and was out of sight, I very nearly sat down on the floor to gather myself. Instead, I leaned against the wall and breathed deeply. I checked my phone and saw a calendar notice flash on my screen. Uh-oh. I was about to be late for a meeting with Bradley Stanton. Not only had I forgotten the meeting was happening, I'd forgotten what it was about.

I rushed down the corridor as fast as one is permitted to in Centre Block and snagged an elevator. I had just enough time in the elevator to consult Wikipedia and confirm that Shishani is—wait for it—a common surname in—wait for it—Chechnya. Holy shite.

I whizzed by the receptionist in the PM's Centre Block office with just a harried nod. He knew me and knew Bradley's schedule, so he waved me through without a word. Bradley's door was open. I darted in and sat down. Bradley was at his desk, his sleeves rolled up and his jacket hung on the back of his chair. He was buried in what I saw was a standard issue-briefing book. I assumed it was on the upcoming G8 summit in Washington. Bradley looked tired and cranky, which was pretty much how he was all the time.

"Sorry I'm a few minutes late. I was helping an aging Senator pick up some files she dropped downstairs," I blathered.

"Don't care. And all Senators are aging," Bradley said without looking up. "So?"

I'd been hoping he'd give me a hint as to what this meeting was about. No such luck. So I went for a skate.

"Yes, well, so, um . . . let me bring you up to date on the Chechen assassination plot," I began. "We've made considerable headway in identifying the sleeper cell. We've actually tracked them to a house on Chapel in Sandy Hill. One of them works at Red Pine Steel near Rockland, and the other, believe it or not, is a cleaner here in Centre Block." I just carried on talking and mulling over what we knew. You know, taking stock.

"I get why he works where he does. Red Pine Steel is a contractor to the Champlain Centre. But why does she work here? Now, if Pudovkin were going to speak in the House of

Commons it would make sense, but he's not. So, what's up with that? Maybe she—"

"Get out of my office," Bradley interrupted, still not looking up from his briefing book.

"Pardon me?" I asked, returning to the moment. Now Bradley looked up at me, and he was angry. Yes, no doubt about it.

"I said, get out of my office. We're supposed to be discussing the PM's talking points for the Pudovkin meeting. And you were supposed to send them to me yesterday so that this meeting might be marginally useful."

"Oh, shite. Sorry, Bradley. I totally forgot about this meeting, and what we're supposed to be talking about," I stammered. "There's a lot going on with, you know, the whole Chechen thing. I've been distracted."

"No, you've been an idiot," Bradley said. "Have you even written his lines?"

"You mean for the Pudovkin meeting?"

"No, for his stand-up debut at Just for Laughs. Of course for the Pudovkin meeting! It's on Saturday! That's in four days!"

What a screw-up I was. I don't know how I could have forgotten about the PM's remarks. I was mortified.

"Right, um, I'm just cleaning them up and need a bit more time to make them, you know, flow a little better."

"Get out of my office, take your head out of your ass, and stop whatever you're doing on this action movie fantasy.

And get me a draft of those talking points by tomorrow morning, or I will kick your ass whether you've removed your head from it or not!" he snapped.

"Well, I can tell you about what I have in mind for the talking points," I said, perfectly capturing the dictionary definition of "lame."

"Not interested. Just send them to me by the morning and be back here tomorrow at one o'clock, ready to edit."

"Will do," I said. "I'm on it. Can we talk for a bit about the sleeper—"

"Stop right there," he growled. "Leave my office right now. I've got better things to do than prolong this conversation, like crocheting a tea cozy for instance. So, get out of my office, stop with the spy games, do your fucking job, and let Coulombe, CSIS, and the RCMP do theirs! Now, in case you're not grasping my message, GET OUT!"

I had nothing. I'd messed up. I got out, fast, and slunk back to my office. On the way, I privately pledged to fulfill Bradley's anatomically challenging request with regards to my head.

Clearly the PMO was not interested in what Tatyana and Eugene had planned, despite the mounting evidence, so I'd have to try door number two instead. It was always going to be a long shot, but I tried anyway and called Coulombe's office.

"Hi, Suzanne, it's Daniel Addison calling."

"Hi, Daniel," she said. "Hey, I just heard about your blowout with Stanton."

"What? How did you hear about that? It literally just happened five minutes ago."

"You know how fast news travels in this place. Hope you're okay."

I then remembered that the door to Bradley's office had been open while he tore strips off my hide. Half the Hill likely knew about it, and no doubt the social media channels were smoking with the story.

"I'm fine, Suzanne," I answered. "Actually, to be completely honest, I'm not really fine. But let's just go with 'I'm fine' for now, because I soon will be. You know, Bradley and I go back a long way. But thanks for asking."

"Good. So how can I help?"

"I'd really like a word with the minister if he's there," I said, already knowing the response. "It's important."

"I'm awfully sorry, Daniel, but the minister is just meeting with a guy from the British High Commission."

"Understood. What about Jocelyn?"

"I'm sorry, but she's in the same meeting," she said. "Oh, hang on, she's just stepped out."

Suzanne covered the phone, but I could still hear her mumbling something to Jocelyn. I couldn't hear what Jocelyn said, but that didn't matter. I heard the tone of her response and that was quite enough. Then I was put on hold . . . for a while.

"What do you want?" Jocelyn asked when she eventually picked up the line.

"I thought for sure you wouldn't pick up," I said.

"Same here, but I thought it might be more entertaining than the meeting I was in."

"Okay, then. I wanted to report that there have been some significant developments in the situation we briefed you on last week," I started.

She didn't say anything, so I barrelled ahead. I gave her the pared-down version of the story but included all the key points, including identifying Eugene and Tatyana and where they both worked, and that they both had opportunity and motive to mastermind this assassination attempt. Still, she said nothing and asked no questions, so I kept talking. As I was succinctly revealing that one of the Chechen sleeper-cell terrorists actually worked in Centre Block, I thought I could hear some faint but familiar music playing in the background.

"Wait. Are you playing Scrabble on your phone?" I asked. "I know that music."

"Yes. It helps build my English vocabulary," she admitted matter-of-factly.

"Oh, well, I have a few choice English words I can share right now, if that would help."

"Do not speak to me like that," she said sharply.

"But you're not even listening to what I've been saying about the Chechen sleeper cell? Jocelyn, this is important."

"Oh, sorry, Daniel, but no, I wasn't listening, I was playing Scrabble. Don't worry, I never listen when you're talking.

It's kind of an office policy," she casually explained. "I must get back into this meeting. But thanks for calling."

"But I haven't finished briefing you yet."

"I think you have."

Unbelievable, I thought as I hung up.

I took some time to write a briefing note to Emile Coulombe and Jocelyn on what had transpired in the last day or so, and sent it off. Paper trails, even of the electronic variety, would help protect Angus and me when the wheels fell off.

Then, before it completely fled my porous mind, I sat down and banged out the PM's draft talking points for the Pudovkin meeting, based on the general agreements we'd negotiated with Ambassador Koskov. I'd been writing for the Prime Minister since long before he ascended to the top job, working hard to strike the balance between substance and rhetorical flourish that the PM liked. I read it over a few more times, polishing as I went, and then emailed it to Bradley.

Angus had already gone to the House for Question Period, even though no questions were expected to be sent his way. The opposition had learned the hard way not to target Angus. He always had a way of responding that unintentionally made him look noble and honourable while his opposition critic came off as petty and lightweight. So, after a while, they just stopped asking, which was fine with Angus and doubly fine with me. It cut down on the need for a daily

Question Period briefing. Nonetheless, I turned on the TV to watch the fun. The Prime Minister and the Minister of Infrastructure were getting hammered on the Champlain Centre's newly added spider legs. The Prime Minister gave a few reasonably strong answers, leading with the need to manage taxpayers' money responsibly and prudently. Then the Infrastructure Minister took a few body blows on the incompetence of the geologists and engineers who had signed off on the original design. On the fourth round of opposition questions, the Global Affairs critic asked the Prime Minister about the upcoming Pudovkin meeting. With no warning at all, the PM referred the question to Angus, since he was the minister responsible for planning the encounter.

Given Angus's propensity for saying exactly what was on his mind, with no concessions to political nuance, I immediately began hyperventilating.

He stood to respond. I noted that he was wearing a reasonably neat grey suit and tie to compensate for his manic hair and beard. "Mr. Speaker, I thank the honourable member opposite for his question," he began. "For many months now we have been planning for this meeting in the, shall we say, provocative and truly unique Champlain Centre."

The opposition benches hooted and hollered until the Speaker was forced to rise and call the House back to order. When your default position is transparent honesty, sarcasm is very difficult to disguise, if Angus tried at all. The House eventually settled so he could continue.

"We have had long and fruitful discussions with the Russian ambassador, and we're hopeful that progress will be made on several fronts, including a trade negotiating framework, academic exchanges, cultural exchanges, and global warming research, particularly as it affects a region of mutual interest, the high Arctic." He then sat down. There was no supplementary from the opposition critic, so I calmed down. The Speaker recognized the opposition critic for Public Safety.

"Mr. Speaker, my question is to the Honourable Minister of Public Safety," he began before turning to face Emile Coulombe.

My ears perked up and I raised my eyes to watch the exchange on TV. At least the question wasn't directed to Angus.

"The *Ottawa Citizen* reported this morning that a note using cut-out letters from magazines was recently sent to the Prime Minister and several Cabinet ministers, threatening to destroy the Champlain Centre if the government does not stop the ugly spider-leg redesign. The threat came from what appears to be a shady underground group called the Public Architecture Militia. Can the minister tell us if this report is true and what the government is doing about it?"

Coulombe rose to his feet. "Mr. Speaker, I can confirm such a letter was received, and I can assure Canadians that we are taking it very seriously. The investigation is ongoing, and we will get to the bottom of it. Those responsible will be found and punished."

The government side of the House banged their desk tops in support.

The opposition critic was on his feet again. "Supplementary, Mr. Speaker. Can the minister tell this House if he is aware of any security threats against President Pudovkin that might come into play during his visit? And further, what steps has he taken to ensure the security and safety of the Prime Minister, President Pudovkin, and their respective entourages during their time together here in Ottawa?"

I wondered where that question had come from. Were there rumours about some kind of attack? If there were, I hadn't heard them, let alone spread them. I texted Jocelyn Massé immediately to let her know that we had nothing to do with the question. I doubted she would believe me, but it was the truth.

Jocelyn texted me back with *I don't believe you*. Right.

Emile Coulombe turned and glared at Angus before responding in his usual confident, know-it-all tone. "Mr. Speaker, we have no security concerns about the President's upcoming visit. We have been working very closely with Russian security and law enforcement advisors to ensure that everything unfolds smoothly and safely. The member opposite need not worry, and neither should President Pudovkin. This is Canada."

When Angus returned to our office, he collapsed into his desk chair.

"Good job answering that unexpected question," I said from the guest chair across from him.

"Well, it wasn't exactly a challenging query, now was it?"

"No, I guess it wasn't, but I did just want to mention that your disdain for the new Champlain Centre design was quite obvious by the tone and substance of your response. That's why the opposition started their ruckus. Now is certainly not the time to showcase cracks in the Cabinet."

"Ye gods, Daniel, I just referred to the redesign as provocative and unique. I think any fair-minded observer would agree that I was standing on pretty safe ground with that."

I sighed.

"Angus, I'm just trying to protect you," I replied. "On a happier note, I have important news. We have found Tatyana."

He snapped to attention. "The stakeout bore fruit, did it? You're a miracle worker, you are. Tell me all."

So I did, giving him a full report.

"You mean to say she works in this very building? And you actually exchanged words with the lass?"

"Well, I spoke to Eugene yesterday, so I didn't want Tatyana to feel left out," I joked. "Besides, I needed to get close enough to read the name on her pass. Her very Chechen name, I hasten to add."

"Well, we're going to owe Lindsay and Muriel more than our gratitude if this plays out the way it might. They did a brave and good thing today."

"True, but if I were Eugene or Tatyana, I would not want to mess with Muriel. Besides, we could not have stopped her from going if we tried. Vivian was quite miffed that she couldn't join them. But with three in the car, blending in would have been a tall order."

"Aye." Angus looked hard at me and something in his expression changed. "You know, lad, I have to keep reminding myself that what we're fooling with here is very grave indeed. We've got one gentle hand on a rattlesnake's tail. But that's not nearly enough. We've got to get a solid grip on the serpent's neck, or Mr. Pudovkin may not be the only bloke in trouble."

"Addison. Sit your sorry ass down," Bradley said when I entered his office the next day. "Are you finally ready for the meeting we should have had yesterday?"

"I'm ready. And sorry about yesterday," I said as I sat down. "Have you looked at the talking points?"

"I just did. Good job. Late, but good," he said. "Just remove the LGBTQ references and I think we'll be good to go."

"Why do you want them out?" I asked, confused.

"Three reasons I can think of. One, LGBTQ issues are not on the meeting's agenda. Two, we're trying to build a constructive economic relationship with Russia. And three, I said so."

He looked up at me when he made this third point. Bradley and I often butted heads over my softer, lefty social policy predispositions. He didn't really care about left or right. He was more pragmatic and just wanted our discussions with the Russians to go smoothly.

"I know it's not on the agenda. That's why I just touched on it as something we'd like to talk about at future bilaterals."

"Danny boy, you know Pudovkin. He's not exactly a social progressive on this issue. We're trying not to piss him off. Leave those lines in and the PM might as well shove a red-hot rainbow poker up his Russian ass. It will not end well."

"So, we just shy away from important human rights issues so we don't offend him?"

"No. We start by nurturing a positive economic and trade relationship with Russia. We need their markets. Then we can lead by example and push Pudovkin when we've built up enough capital in the relationship."

Bradley's position was not completely devoid of thought, but it always pissed me off when equity issues were pushed aside in the name of expediency.

Just then the Prime Minister stuck his head into the office.

"Daniel!" He'd always liked me, even after I'd abandoned him on the eve of a federal election the previous fall. Nice man, though not known for his backbone. "Good to see you."

"Thank you, Prime Minister, good to see you too, sir," I said, standing up. "When do you leave for the G8? It must be soon."

The PM looked at Bradley.

"Prime Minister, we're leaving in about two hours. Your 737 is fuelling up now." Bradley was in suck-up mode.

"Right," the PM replied. "I assume I'm all packed?"

"You are, sir," Bradley said.

I took my chance. "Prime Minister, Bradley and I were just discussing including a single fleeting reference to LGBTQ issues when you're speaking with Pudovkin."

"I'm all for it," he said enthusiastically. "It's about time!"

"Prime Minister, we talked about this before," Bradley cut in, glaring at me. "Our first priority, after the easy academic exchanges and research agreements, is to set the stage for a future trade deal. We don't want to kill all the work the Minister of Foreign Affairs and the Minister of International Trade have done in the last two years by telling Pudovkin we want him to join the rainbow coalition."

"But we *do* want Russia to join the rainbow coalition," the PM said.

"Exactly," I chimed in.

"Yes, and it would be just peachy if they fully disarmed and stopped their hegemonic incursions into Ukraine," Bradley replied. "And one day that time will come, but it'll be after we've inked the trade deal and opened up the markets for Canadian commerce. Right?"

"I guess so," the PM said, folding like a pup tent in a tornado. "I know, I know, discretion is the better part of valour, and all that stuff."

"I agree with you, Prime Minister," Bradley said. "Good call."

"Since you're both here, Coulombe briefed me this morning on security for the Pudovkin meeting," the PM went on.

"He says everything is fine and well in hand. Nothing to worry about. Slam dunk. Easy peasy."

"Did Coulombe really say 'easy peasy'?" I asked.

"Well, no. I added that. But we're fine on security."

"Well, I'm not so sure about—" I started.

"Prime Minister," Bradley interrupted, "I know you've got calls to make to the other parties on the immigration bill before we take off for Washington. We should let you go."

"Right, right. Minority government means so many more phone calls to the opposition. But I guess it's better than actually being in opposition," the PM said before leaving.

Bradley stood at his desk in silence, his index finger raised to me (I took some comfort in the fact that it was his index finger), until he heard the PM's door close.

"Jesus, Addison, do not try to freelance your demented conspiracy theories to the PM ever again. Everything goes through me. That's the law and you know it," Bradley said. "Coulombe, Massé, and several others from CSIS and the RCMP have been bending my ear about what you've been doing. Are you insane? Following people? Making wild accusations against hardworking immigrants? It's time for this to stop."

"Bradley—"

"Shut up! I'm not done." His voice dripped with vitriol. "I am commanding you to stop your asinine assassination rantings and ravings, and return your focus, and the Scottish hairball's, to making sure the Pudovkin meeting comes off without a hitch. Those croissants better be flaky and the sparkling water fizzy. Do nothing else. Is there anything else I can do to make my position on this matter clear?"

"No, I've pretty well got it," I said. "So, on the remarks, I'll soften the LGBTQ references and get them back to you." I wouldn't even call that a nice try.

"Addison. You. Will. Remove. All. LGBTQ references. In. The. Remarks. PERIOD. FULL STOP!" he shouted. "Now. Please. Leave!"

It's in all caps because that's exactly how he said it—like a drill sergeant humiliating new recruits.

Late that afternoon, just before Angus and I left for a thirtieth-year anniversary reception for a Liberal backbencher, I had an idea and made another call.

"Celine Michaud," she answered.

"Hi, Celine, it's Daniel Addison."

I'd known Celine for many years. In fact, she'd been my administrative assistant for a time, back in my Leader's office days. She was now the executive assistant to the parliamentary secretary to the Minister of Public Safety, but that didn't mean she was a fully indoctrinated Coulombe insider. Parliamentary secretaries and their staff seldom were insiders. But she did hover on the periphery.

"Hi, Daniel. I'm just leaving for the reception we're both probably going to, so can we talk there?"

"This won't take long, and it's not really reception banter," I said. "I'm trying to figure out just how much Emile

Coulombe hates Angus and, by extension, me. Can you shed any light on that? Just between us, of course."

"Hmm, do you really want to know?" She said this with a gentle reluctance that reminded me why I liked her.

"That's what I was afraid of."

"No one from the department, RCMP or CSIS, is supposed to be seen even talking to you, let alone helping you," she whispered. "Jocelyn has made that very clear. The only reason they're not more hostile with you is that they know the PM likes Angus."

"Well, I'm not sure I can see how they could be any more hostile," I said. "But thanks for being straight with me, Celine."

Twenty minutes later I saw her across the room at the reception, and we nodded and raised our glasses at one another. Angus hated these political receptions, and I can't say they were on my ten most cherished activities list, either, but unfortunately there were about four of them each week. I'd persuaded Angus to go anyway, stressing that his attendance in support of his colleagues was important, even if we showed up for the bare minimum. That night, we stayed just long enough to ensure all the important people saw us, then we slipped out into the night. Once again, I drove our ministerial car with Angus in the passenger seat. We talked all the way home about what our next steps might be. Neither of us was sure.

I parked in front of Angus's home and agreed to join him to watch the news and have a drink. I could see the light on in the boathouse and was keen to get home to see Lindsay, so I wouldn't stay long. Angus poured himself a shot or two of Lagavulin and I had a Coke, my usual, and we turned on the television. Midway through, the newscaster captured our attention:

> A Carleton University professor was taken into custody today on suspicion that he is behind the threat to blow up the soon-to-be-opened Samuel de Champlain Centre on behalf of a group known as the Public Architecture Militia. The threat was received last week by the Prime Minister and several members of his Cabinet. The threat stems from the redesign of the Centre with reinforcing braces that make the building look like a giant spider. CSIS worked with police investigators and confirmed the threatening emails had originated from a Gmail account opened using the professor's Carleton email address.

"Well, that was stupid on his part," I said. "So easily traced."

Then they cut to video of the professor getting into a police car. Just before he disappeared into the back seat he said, "This is a set-up. I've been framed. I'm a tenured professor, for God's sake. Why on earth would I do this?"

"Now, that is an excellent question," Angus said.

DIARY

Wednesday, May 7

My love,

What an intrigue we've stumbled into. I'll wager you never thought I'd be dabbling in an assassination plot. Now, dinnae worry your heart. We're being cautious and careful. Young Daniel has done much of the heavy lifting himself and seems to have identified the two perpetrators, members of a Chechen sleeper cell in Ottawa, of all places. It was rather ingenious how he managed it, guided by an experienced, now retired, former career CSIS operative, Vivian Kent, who lives at the seniors' home in Cumberland. She's a friend of Muriel's and is just as sharp.

Still, I'm missing something. It gnaws at me, this feeling that something lurks just a hair beyond my understanding. It's there, waiting for me to grasp it. Waiting for me to see it. May the scales soon fall from my eyes.

I've no idea how this will all unfold, but it has made life interesting this past week and has kept me from lamenting your absence, which I do often when nothing else occupies my mind. But you know that already, love.

AM

PART

NO.3

CHAPTER 7

I decided to work from our House Leader's office in Centre Block for the next little while, as it was closer to the Champlain Centre. It also allowed me to keep an eye on Tatyana. In the days since our encounter, I had managed to catch sight of her several times, as I roamed the halls a little more than usual. She always looked tense, working hard and pushing her cleaning cart in front of her. I tried not to let her see me and I never approached her. Dumping over-stuffed file folders twice in the span of a few days could set off alarm bells. With Pudovkin's visit so close, she was probably anxious, stressed, and on the lookout for anything out of the ordinary. "Paranoid" might be the efficient way to sum it up. So, I was very careful.

I arrived at Centre Block before Angus the next morning, to find a brown envelope waiting for me on my desk. My name and address were handwritten in jittery cursive, and I could feel something small but solid inside. Weird and worrying. I closed my office door and opened the envelope with great care and caution. After all, it could have been anything. Letter bomb? Anthrax? Confetti burst? Muriel's apple jelly?

It turned out it was none of the above. Instead, it was an old-style Motorola flip phone and nothing else. When I flipped it open, as one does, it was already turned on, fully charged, and a text was on the screen.

Leave your office and walk outside to somewhere clear of the building that is quiet and not crowded. Text me when you're there.

I didn't know who it was, but I didn't hesitate. I pulled on my jacket and walked straight out of Centre Block towards the Ottawa River Pathway, which runs along the shore just behind the Library of Parliament. Save for a few joggers, there were few people on the trail. I walked as quickly as I could without looking odd, then found a quiet spot off the beaten path, sat down on a bench, and texted that I was ready. Was it more vitriol from Team Coulombe? Maybe Bradley had found a new and creative way to torment me? Was Angus just messing with me?

The phone vibrated. I tried to be cool, but anyone watching might have thought I'd just been electrocuted. I waited until I landed back on the bench before answering.

"It's Daniel Addison," I said in a voice that only kind of sounded like mine.

"Can you speak freely where you are, without being overheard?" asked the woman with the English accent. And I knew.

"Fleming? Is that you?"

"No names. Can you speak freely where you are without being overheard?" she repeated.

"Um, yes." I looked around. "It's quiet where I am. No one is near me. Go ahead."

"You've made real progress. Well done. But there's more to do if Eugene and Tatyana are to be stopped."

"How do you know we've made progress?" I asked.

"I just do. Without being too cliché, it's my job," she said. "We don't have much time. Talking on cellphones is seldom a good idea. Just listen carefully. The evidence used to detain the professor was manufactured to make it look like he's prepared to do much more than just advocate for aesthetic public architecture."

"Manufactured? How do you know?"

"That isn't important. What is important is that you trust me and accept what I'm saying."

"Right. Understood."

"The trumped-up arrest is a well-executed distraction to give the sleeper cell some air cover so they can more easily complete their mission. The Society for Public Architecture founder's email will have been hacked and the threatening message sent without his knowledge."

"*How* do you know this?"

Fleming sighed but said nothing.

"Okay, okay. I know, trust you, it's your job, et cetera, et cetera. Got it."

"Now, listen. You must find a really strong cybersecurity expert to examine the email threat. Check the IP addresses carefully and dig deeper into the opening of the Gmail account. On the surface, everything will conveniently point towards the professor. But it's too convenient and too neat. Look underneath and you'll find the truth."

"Okay, we'll try," I said. "Angus received the email threat, too, so we have it."

"Good," she replied. "Can you find a techie who can dig into this and really get underneath?"

"We know someone who probably knows someone," I replied, thinking of Vivian.

"That's usually how it works. The point is, this is a carefully constructed ruse wrapped in a lie. The professor now killing time at the police station almost certainly threatened no one."

"When I saw him on the news, he certainly, well, professed his innocence, and looked quite sincere doing it."

"Sincerity works best when it's true," she said. "All right, that's it for now. Keep the phone handy, and fully charged, but don't use it except when I text or call you. Clear?"

"Yes. Okay, we're on it."

When I got back to the office, Angus was waiting for me, so at my suggestion, we went for a walk so I could fill him in on my call with Fleming. We walked to our favourite part of Centre Block: the Library of Parliament. The sliding wooden doors opened to admit us to the round, high-ceilinged room lined with three levels of beautiful wooden shelves, in all its breathtaking splendour. Mere words will never do it justice. We climbed to the third level and sat down at a small table in an alcove. There was nobody around us, yet we still spoke in hushed tones. I described the whole flip-phone call from Fleming, and what she'd reported and suggested.

"This whole thing is getting very complicated," I said after my update.

"Aye," Angus agreed. "Wheels within wheels."

The phone rang twice before she picked up.

"Hi, Vivian, it's Daniel. Am I catching you at a bad time?"

"Well, I can't say I have much going on today," she replied. "Shuffleboard was mercifully cancelled this week, but I might gaze at the fish tank for a while this afternoon."

"It'll get better, Vivian," I said.

"I know it will. Now, don't fuss about me. This is just recreational bellyaching. What's up, and what can I do?"

"We're hoping you might be able to help us on something," I said. "Do you happen to know a private and reliable cyber-security expert who can do some forensic email sleuthing?"

"As a matter of fact, I do. When I saw the news about the Carleton professor, I thought you might be in need of some help."

She always seemed one step ahead of us.

"That's great. Thanks so much," I said. "We have the email, so I just need someone to dig into its origins and hopefully find out where it really came from."

"Call Newton," she said, and gave me a local phone number. "A really good person I've used before, and a proven leader in the cybersecurity domain."

"Newton? Is there a last name?"

"Maybe that is the last name," she said, before falling silent.

"Okay, I see what you did there," I said. "We'll just go with Newton."

"Excellent decision. Just say that Harpo sent you."

"Harpo?"

"Yes, Harpo."

"No last name?"

"What, like Marx? Wrong Harpo," she said. "No last name. Just Harpo."

"Got it."

I didn't wait long after hanging up with Vivian before reaching out to the mysterious and talented Newton. About half an hour later I went for a walk on the front lawn of Centre Block, where I would not be overheard.

"Yes, hello, I'm trying to reach Newton," I said when a woman's voice greeted me on the phone.

"Damn, you found me."

"So, you're Newton? The cyber-famous Newton?" I asked.

"Damn, you found me."

I don't know why I assumed Newton would be a man—I mean, other than the typically male name and the many movies that depicted computer geeks as nerdy young Bill Gates clones with pocket protectors, elevated belts, taped glasses, and pimples. I was happy to discover that Newton was a she.

"Well, um, Harpo told me to contact you about an urgent job."

"You want me to excavate an email trail to figure out where it really came from," she said.

"Right, but I thought I'd be the one to tell you that."

"Harpo briefed me already," Newton explained.

"Oh, okay, I guess. So, can you do it? And I'm a little unfamiliar with the payment arrangements."

"If it's for Harpo, it's on the house," she said. "Just send me whatever you received, and I'll try to work my magic." She gave me an email address to use. "It's a Gmail account, right?"

"Right."

"I'm assuming Newton is a code name of some kind," I said, trying to make conversation. "It seems a little ironic that a tech genius would take the code name of an early-nineties computer product that was a complete bust."

And no, I don't know where that came from, either. Maybe it was because I'd just read an article about the ill-fated

Newton on the plane back from London. Or it could just be my well-established propensity for saying the wrong thing. If I wasn't putting my foot in that stray bucket, I was putting it in my mouth.

"Listen, the Newton failed only because it was a decade ahead of its time. The iPad exists today only because of the Newton," she said with a sharp edge to her voice. "Now, do you want me to look at the email or not?"

"Sorry, I didn't mean to . . . um . . ."

"Venture into a realm you know little about?" she suggested.

"Yes, that's exactly where I was going," I said. "I'd be really grateful if you could look at the email, and I promise to keep my observations to myself in future."

"Ah, I'm just screwing with you. The Newton was well before my time, and it bombed big-time. I go by Newton because of my father. He was a physicist who often said, 'All roads lead to Newton.' That's where I got it from."

"Oh. Good to know."

"I'll call you when I have something."

I reported all of this to Angus when I returned to our office.

"This little affair is moving at a blistering pace," Angus said. "I dinnae know if the threatening email is part of the assassination plot, but if it is, Fleming's distraction theory rings true."

"Well, if Newton is as good as Vivian says, we may know sooner than later."

"Aye, and even that could be too late."

Angus and I had to attend a long and boring meeting in Centre Block for the rest of the afternoon. It was so long and boring that I honestly can't recall what it was about, and may not have been able to tell you while I was actually in it. I suspect it had something to do with our legislative agenda for the coming two months, before the House broke for the summer. But my mind—and I assume Angus's too—was elsewhere. As the snooze fest was winding down, I felt my phone buzz in my pocket. There was no caller ID. I stepped out into the corridor, which was deserted.

"Daniel Addison."

"Hi again, it's Newton."

"Great. Thanks for saving me from the meeting I've just stepped out of," I said in a voice just slightly louder than a whisper. "Did you have any luck?"

"I did. You were right to be suspicious," she said. "It's true the email was purposefully made to appear as if it had come from a Gmail account linked to the IP address of the Carleton professor. This would make it very easily traced back to the prof, as it quickly was."

"And you don't think that makes much sense," I suggested.

"Right. Even someone who is not super smart or cyber-savvy would not be so careless when setting up a supposedly untraceable Gmail account. So, the conclusion is that whoever is pulling the strings behind all of this wanted the email to be easily traced."

"But that's not the end of the story, is it?"

"Nope. I dug more deeply into the Gmail account. Behind several formidable firewalls, I was able to find the actual source email domain of the person who opened the Gmail account, if you're still following me."

"I'm with you, I think."

"I don't know the actual source email address, but deep in the code, I found the domain, which really narrows the search by a big margin."

"Okay, the suspense is killing me," I said.

"Well, I can't identify exactly who set up the Gmail account, but I know where they work."

"I assume it isn't Carleton University."

"Correct. But get this—the person behind this has a British High Commission email address."

"What? The British High Commission? You're kidding," I said, stunned. "You must be wrong."

"I wish I were. You don't often see a major industrialized nation messing with the lives of citizens of trusted allies. I've certainly never seen it."

"What's your level of confidence in your findings?"

"Very high."

"Holy shite."

I briefly paced outside the meeting room, trying to assimilate in my scrambled brain what Newton had just revealed. This was becoming very real, very fast. I thought of Fleming and what she had put on the line to start us off down this path. Clearly, she was right to suspect her own boss's motives and actions. I figured this could mean MI6 was directing the show, and someone at the British High Commission in Ottawa was in the cast.

I stepped back into the meeting and signalled to Angus that we had to leave.

"Mr. Chair," Angus said, standing up, "I apologize, but I must depart for another urgent meeting related to the Pudovkin visit. Forgive me, but 'tis beyond my control. But do please carry on. I'll catch up afterwards."

Everyone nodded sympathetically as Angus gathered his papers and joined me outside. While I was tempted to start talking on the way, I waited until we were back in our office before recounting the stunning news about the British government's complicity in framing a Canadian university professor. While the Carleton prof arrested might be annoying when he got on the topic of public architecture, he was completely innocent of sending what amounted to a bomb threat to the Prime Minister and his Cabinet. It was outrageous that a foreign government and trusted ally was operating clandestinely against Canadian citizens on our soil.

"We have to contact Fleming," Angus said.

"But she told us not to text or call on this flip phone," I reminded him.

"Well, then I suggest we immediately text her on the blasted flip phone," Angus said. "This is a critical development that could bc linked with the Pudovkin visit. So get those pudgy texting fingers working, lad."

"You know it's about 11:00 p.m. in London."

"Aye, Daniel, I'm aware we live in a world of time zones, but I think she's going to want to hear this."

"Okay, okay," I said as I texted her.

Fleming called a few minutes later. I put it on speaker turned down low.

"What's happened?" she asked before even saying hello.

"It was not the professor who opened that Gmail account," I said.

"I know that. It was I who told you."

"Yes, right, but a deep dive into the back end of the email reveals that the Gmail account was set up by someone whose IP address makes him or her an employee of the British High Commission in Ottawa."

"Idiots. Bloody imbeciles." She paused and sighed deeply. "Idiots!"

A thought occurred to me and I spoke before thinking, an event with far too many precedents to mention.

"You could have orchestrated this," I said, realizing that she had all the information to make it happen.

"What! Don't be absurd!" she snapped. "I've been doing everything in my diminishing power to stop it! I would never have reached out to you if I'd wanted a clear playing field to mess with the lives of innocent Canadian professors."

Angus gave me a withering look.

"Of course, it's absurd, Ms. Fleming," Angus soothed. "Daniel was just examining all of the options, even the ludicrous ones." He made it clear with his wildly gesticulating hands that he wanted me to jump back in and make amends.

"Right. Totally absurd," I agreed. "Sorry, I didn't think that one all the way through."

"Indeed," said Fleming. "But this news certainly confirms my worst fears that my immediate supervisor has gone clean off the rails and is out there operating beyond his MI6 mandate, and well beyond any parliamentary oversight."

"Just to leave nothing to chance, are you telling me that MI6, an intelligence agency of our closest ally, is behind this subterfuge?" Angus asked. "The Queen is still on our coinage in Canada!"

"Minister McLintock, this is absolutely not a sanctioned MI6 operation," Fleming said firmly. "Kendal Acton is operating on his own and using MI6 assets and resources to do it. He wants to do everything in his power to see the assassination attempt succeed. Acton only has one operative in the High Commission in Ottawa. It's a chap named Thomas Maynard and he's clearly doing Acton's bidding, despite the consequences."

"He'd lose his job over this," I said.

"Daniel, lad, if we don't make a hash of it all, the whole lot of them, from Acton all the way down, will not just lose their posts," Angus said. "They can look forward to being locked away in the Tower of London for a spell."

"But what's the point of framing the architecture prof?" I asked. "Won't Pudovkin just cancel his little meeting with our PM if there are any security issues, like, say, a plot to blow up a very ugly building?"

"That's just it," Fleming said. "That's why the professor's arrest is so important. It takes him off the street and closes down the idea of blowing up the building. Your RCMP will search the Centre yet again and still find nothing to back up the professor's threat. That ends the security risk, once and for all."

"But the risk is not over," I said.

"No, it surely is not," agreed Fleming. "This elaborate ruse was undertaken to make sure the meeting proceeds as planned. The battlefield will then be clear, allowing our Eugene and Tatyana to complete their mission."

"And all the while, MI6 has CSIS and the RCMP wrapped around their trigger finger," Angus said.

"Not all of MI6, Minister McLintock."

"But what about the innocent professor languishing in jail even as we speak?" I asked. "Shouldn't we share the email analysis with the police so he can be released?"

"I wouldn't advise that just yet," Fleming said.

"I agree," said Angus. "While it is obviously wrong to incarcerate an innocent man, having him out of the play clears the air, greenlights the big meeting, and allows us to catch our Chechen friends in the act."

"Now you're thinking like a ruthless intelligence agent," Fleming said.

After we hung up with Fleming, I immediately dialled another number on my own cellphone.

"Who are you calling now?" Angus asked.

"Coulombe's office." I clicked to speakerphone.

"Minister's office."

"Hi again, Suzanne, it's Daniel calling."

"Yes, I know, Daniel. We've had caller ID since the nineties," she said with a laugh.

"Oh, you're right. Anyway, I'm hoping you can do me a favour, off the record."

"I'll try. What do you need?"

"The other day when I called, you said the minister was meeting with someone from the British High Commission. Can you tell me the name of the Brit?"

"Daniel, you know I'm not allowed to do that. It was a confidential meeting, and, well, we're not supposed to have any dealings with your office anyway."

"I understand completely, Suzanne, and I wouldn't want you to do anything that would make you feel uncomfortable."

"Thank you for understanding, Daniel."

"But how about this?" I persisted. "You don't have to give up the guy's name. Instead, I'll say the name. If I've got the right guy, hang up immediately without saying a word. And if I'm wrong, just say 'Goodbye,' and hang up."

There was silence on Suzanne's end.

"Okay, let's play Name That Diplomat," I said in my best game-show-host voice. Then I paused before making my play. "Thomas Maynard."

Suzanne hung up fast without a word.

"Bless the lass," Angus said.

I banged out a quick text on the flip phone to tell Fleming that Thomas Maynard had met with Emile Coulombe earlier in the week.

"Angus, by the way, did you really use 'greenlight' as a verb in our call with Fleming?" I asked. "I never thought I'd see the day."

Rather than call Muriel and Vivian, we decided to drop in on them on our way back home. I texted Lindsay to tell her about the meeting. She didn't want to miss the gathering, so she jumped in her car and headed over to the Riverfront Seniors' Residence, too. A little while later, Angus, Muriel, Lindsay, and I assembled again in our little corner of the lounge. Vivian was the last to join us, scootering over and parking adeptly to round out our cabal.

"Apologies," she said. "I was doing my weight training."

"You lift weights?" I asked.

"I surely do," she replied proudly. "I find it helps my arthritis, strengthens my aging muscles, and kills some time, which is a good thing around here. You should lift some weights, too. It's very good for you."

"Yeah, well, I don't know if you've noticed this, but the problem with lifting weights is that they're just so heavy," I said.

The group seemed divided on whether I was kidding or not. I wasn't. But we had more important things to discuss, like the British High Commission framing an innocent Carleton professor, possibly with the help of an MI6 operative named Thomas Maynard.

"And guess who paid a visit to Emile Coulombe earlier this week?" Angus asked.

Muriel inhaled sharply. "Who? Master Maynard?"

"In all his duplicitous glory," Angus said.

"But we're still left with that one critical unanswered question," Vivian said, keeping her voice at low volume. "And if we can't figure it out, all of your excellent amateur sleuthing and tradecraft may not be enough to thwart our Chechen couple."

We all waited but Vivian said nothing more.

"And that critical unanswered question is?" I asked.

"Oh, sorry, I thought we all knew," Vivian said, looking around the group.

"Where's the bomb?" Lindsay suggested.

"Precisely!" Vivian said. Lindsay looked pleased with herself, and I once again realized I was dating out of my league.

Vivian still had the floor. "Exactly how are Eugene and Tatyana planning to bring the house down? That is the pressing question."

"We've looked everywhere in the building and found nothing. Nothing. There just isn't any place to plant a bomb," I said.

"It cannot be a coincidence that Eugene works for the steel contractor and may very well have been on-site," Lindsay continued.

"Absolutely right, Lindsay," Vivian said. "We must see the building."

"I echo Daniel's view," Angus added. "We've examined the entire facility, the public spaces, the employees-only areas, the physical plant, the electrical rooms, the crawlspaces below the floors and above the ceiling tiles, and even the grounds around the building."

"Then there's only one other possibility," Vivian said. "The bomb is not in the building." She paused. "The building *is* the bomb."

We fell silent as her pronouncement settled over us. Then, I watched as Angus's eyes suddenly widened, and he jumped up, hopping from one foot to the other in excitement. We were startled, as were the others in the lounge.

"Vivian, bless that brain of yours, that's it!" he shouted.

A chorus of shushes came from the other residents, invoking the "no boisterous play" rule. I may have shushed him, too. Angus sat back down and leaned in close.

"Something has been taunting and teasing me since our last visit to the Champlain Centre," Angus explained. "'Twas when I was on that hydraulic Skyjack. It was there. It was right there, but I just couldnae grasp it. Something was not sitting right, and it eluded me until this very moment, courtesy of Vivian's wise words. Daniel, we must return to the Centre, pronto!"

"'Pronto'?" I said. "There's a word you don't hear every day."

"Aye, and you'll hear a whole stream of colourful new words from me if you dinnae stop parsing my vocabulary!" he said. "Now, let's be off. This cannae wait."

"I'm going with you," Vivian said. "I can help."

"Well, then I'm coming, too," Muriel said. "After all, I introduced her to you all."

We all turned to Lindsay.

"Well, if Grandma goes, I go," Lindsay piped in. "She needs me."

I looked at Angus and he looked at me. We were both making the same calculation in our minds. *Do we tell them they can't come and suffer the many painful and long-lasting consequences, or do we just cut our losses and acquiesce?* I could tell we'd both reached the same conclusion.

"So be it," Angus said. "But we must go now."

I ran out to the parking lot to bring our ministerial Buick something-or-other—I'm not really a car guy—around to the front entrance. We all squeezed into it, loading Vivian's scooter (which conveniently collapsed into three separate pieces) into the trunk. Going together in one car would make our entry to the building site a little easier.

At that hour of the evening, the traffic to Ottawa was light. Whenever I looked in the rear-view mirror, Angus's sizable cranium and chaotic corona of hair were all I could see. He seemed calm, even serene.

"Angus, we need to make a call right now to our dear friend Bradley," I said. "These new developments just might bring him onside." It was time, once and for all, to bring others into the fold, to persuade the doubters that this plot was real and to enlist their help. Battling skepticism and contempt wouldn't be easy, but it had to be done. We needed help in high places.

"Aye, I suppose it's unavoidable."

"I think it would be better if you took the lead in briefing him," I suggested. "He's unlikely to hurl obscenities at you."

Angus heaved a heavy sigh but agreed. "Give me a moment to map out the clearest and shortest path to enlightenment. So much has happened since we last spoke to Lord Stanton." The car was silent as Angus developed his approach. "Ready" was all he said a minute or two later.

I dialled Bradley from my cellphone using the car's hands-free system. It rang twice before he picked up.

"Danny boy, I just can't escape you, even when I'm at the G8," he said when he answered. "I haven't got a lot of time. I still have to tie the PM's bow tie for the dinner."

"Thanks for taking the call, and we'll try to be brief," I said in my most ingratiating tone. "I'm with Angus and you're on the speaker. Now, Bradley, we've known each other for a very long time. We haven't always gotten along, and some might say we've never gotten along. But I have always respected the need in public life for your special gifts, and I hope you feel the same way about my different but also important abilities."

"Is this going somewhere, Addison?" Bradley said.

"It is, Bradley, and very soon. I just want to ask you, in recognition of all we've been through together over the years, to listen with an open mind to what we have to say, because we truly believe that lives are at stake here, including the Prime Minister's."

Before Bradley could protest, Angus jumped in. "Mr. Stanton, I like to think I'm a reasonably intelligent and sentient member of the human race. And I'd say, contrary to occasional circumstantial evidence, young Daniel here is, too." He smiled at me. "I'm just kidding, lad. You do have a Ph.D., after all." He turned his attention back to Bradley. "And, I know, Mr. Stanton, that you have not risen to your lofty station by being a dullard and a simpleton. So, let us agree that we all have at least above-average cerebral acuity."

"I'll grant you that, Minister," Bradley said.

"Then I implore you to bear that in mind when I tell you an extraordinary tale and provide the documentary evidence to justify our collective belief—and fear—that it is all true and about to happen."

"Understood."

"Thank you. Now, this is no trifling matter, I assure you. This has profound national and international security ramifications and warrants your full attention and concentration."

"I hear you, Minister, and I promise I'm ready for you to start," Bradley said, with just a scintilla of exasperation edging his voice.

"Very well. But we have tried to share this story with you once before, some days ago, and you were not receptive. Now we possess much more evidence, information, and understanding than we did then. I assure you, this evening we stand on very solid ground as we try to tell you a second time." Angus paused to lend some gravity to his opening. "Mr. Stanton, one thing has not changed since we spoke last. We still are not able to identify the source that set us on this path, but it is critical for you to accept that the person has a long and enviable career in this field. This did not start with troubling graffiti on a bathroom wall. It began with careful and deep analysis and has since been strengthened by evidence emerging now almost on a daily basis. So please do us the honour of listening carefully to everything I'm about to say."

"Again, Minister, I accept what you're saying," Bradley said impatiently. "You've set up your story at some considerable length and I now encourage you to tell it. The PM's tie will not tie itself."

I could see Muriel and Lindsay exchange eye-rolling glances in the back seat. They both knew Bradley Stanton and his special interpersonal gifts.

"Aye, I will. Right now."

Angus was masterful. He remained calm throughout. He was efficient in telling our tale, emphasized the key evidence at each important juncture, and skillfully pre-empted questions with timely conclusions. When he was finally finished, about twenty minutes later, I was more convinced than ever. In fact, I was terrified with how all the pieces, precious few of which we had identified a week and a half earlier, now fit together so well. What had started as a theory now seemed like a fait accompli.

"Mr. Stanton, you've kindly listened, or at least you've been quiet. We are driving to the Champlain Centre to confirm the final piece of this puzzle. Have we persuaded you that our fears are justified?" Angus asked.

There was a very long pause and a very deep sigh.

"Jesus," Bradley said in a voice I barely recognized. "Pudovkin lands in Ottawa in thirty-six hours."

"Thank you, Mr. Stanton," Angus replied. "That's just the reaction we were hoping to elicit. We'll call you back within the next hour or so from the Champlain Centre."

CHAPTER 8

"That was a tour-de-force performance, Angus," Vivian said after we'd hung up. "You make a very powerful case."

"I second that," Muriel said. "I spend my days with my body almost constantly racked with tremors. But after listening to that call, I'm shaking a lot more than I usually do."

"Well, we'd be nowhere without Vivian's insight, contacts, and advice," Angus said. "So I guess it's fitting that you're with us. We could use the on-the-ground expertise."

When we reached Nepean Point, we saw that the protestors had dwindled to a handful. I'm sure it's tough to get picketers out on the line on a Thursday evening. The on-site security team helped part the raging waters—or, by then, the babbling brook—and we drove through the gates. Brenda, the head security officer, didn't even ask to see our passes. She knew who we were.

We drove in, around the bend, and up to the front door beneath the great concrete awning. The landscaping in the last two days had transformed the property. Tulips, daffodils, and plenty of other common spring flowers that I could not identify, bordered by surgically edged, freshly laid grass, gave the place a finished and classy look. The whole site finally looked worthy of receiving a world leader.

We piled out of the Buick. Well, Lindsay, Angus, and I piled out; Vivian and Muriel eased out carefully with our steadying hands. Angus quickly reassembled Vivian's scooter after my first three attempts failed.

I succeeded in getting Vivian seated on her scooter on my first attempt, and Lindsay had Muriel on her arm. A bright-red carpet led from the car to the doors, as if we were attending the Oscars. We started moving agonizingly slowly, led by Angus and Vivian. Unfortunately, Muriel's Parkinson's was acting up and she was having trouble getting her legs moving. She was locked in place with her legs twitching but failing to respond to her commands. Lindsay looked at me and nodded. That was my cue, and I knew what to do—I'd done it before. I walked over and lay down on the carpet directly in front of Muriel. She promptly hoisted her left foot, high-stepped over me, and walked very well thereafter, even catching up with Vivian. Having something, or in this case someone, to step over helped Muriel get moving again.

Inside, the Centre was nearly empty, except for some activity in the kitchen and plenty of vacuuming. Paint, broadloom, signage, lighting, fixtures, and furnishings were all done and ready for prime time. Most of the final preparations were happening outside, as a platoon of landscapers gave a final spit and polish to their remarkable efforts. When we were inside, the site manager gave us free rein, despite our unusual contingent.

With the Centre built all on one level, the entire facility was accessible. There were no stairs anywhere, so Vivian was able to explore everywhere. I tagged along. It really did look amazing on the inside, even if it was ugly on the outside — and man, was it ugly on the outside. Vivian scootered around to all of the areas you might expect to find a bomb hidden: cloakrooms, utility closets, janitorial rooms, the kitchen, the employee change room, bathrooms, and storage spaces — all the areas that Angus and I had examined days earlier. Like us, she came up empty-handed in each space.

"You seem to know what you're looking for," I said as she looked around. "Have you searched for explosives before?"

"Not often, but regrettably, yes I have," she said. "It never fails to make me queasy, like I'm a foreigner in my own body."

"But you're not finding anything suspicious?"

"Not yet, at least not in any of the obvious places. But that just makes me even more queasy. If there is a device somewhere in this concrete-and-glass maple leaf of a building, then we're dealing with a sophisticated and formidable adversary."

Finally, Vivian wheeled into the main assembly room as I trotted along trying to keep up. Lindsay and Muriel were over by the window admiring the scenery. The enormous glass panels offered an unhindered view of the Ottawa River, Hull on the Quebec side, and the ongoing cleanup of the collapsed Alexandra Bridge. The Skyjack was still in the corner of the room but would surely not be there for long.

Angus was hunched over the building's blueprints, which he'd spread out on a large round ballroom table in the middle of the room. Vivian scootered over for a closer look. Then, Lindsay, Muriel, and I made our way over and dropped into the chairs.

Angus pointed to the straight, thick lines on the blueprint. "These are the ceiling beams you can see above us." Then he flipped the big page over and pointed to similar lines on the next blueprint. "And these are the floor beams below our feet," he continued. "You can see the ends of the ceiling and floor beams sticking out a bit just beyond the windows. These beams provide the principal load-bearing capacity and run back into the rock face. If they are damaged seriously enough, the building falls into the river, sure as my hair is unruly."

"Now, that's what I call certainty," I said.

"But you said there's no bomb up on the roof or beneath the floor," Lindsay said.

"Aye, but as you can see on the blueprints, these beams are technically called Hollow Structural Sections. According to this cross-sectional view, all of them are supposed to be hollow. But I fear they are not. I just didn't see it until last evening, when Vivian opened my eyes. Or, to be more accurate, I didn't *hear* it."

"Ah, I see. Not 'the building is the bomb,' but 'the *beam* is the bomb.'" Vivian nodded. "Or the beams."

We all looked up at the ceiling.

"It's our good fortune that the scissor lift is still in the room," Angus said, walking over to the corner where the machine was parked. He climbed in, hit the Start button, and drove the Skyjack into position just under the beam he'd inspected on our last trip to the Centre. Then he raised the platform until his head nearly touched the beam. He was holding a rubber mallet, borrowed from a toolbox he'd found in the kitchen.

"Now, have a wee listen to what is supposed to be a hollow beam," Angus directed. He swung the mallet and struck the beam. A dead, dull, barely discernible sound accompanied the blow. "Does that sound hollow to any of you?"

Then, without lowering the platform, which was probably recommended in the owner's manual, Angus moved the Skyjack over until he was underneath the next beam.

He took another swing with the mallet, yielding a loud and resonant *bong*.

"So now you hear the difference," he said. "This one is surely hollow."

We all looked at one another. Vivian was calm, and Lindsay and Muriel were attempting a high-five, but I was about to lose control of my senses and perhaps some bodily functions as well.

Angus rolled a little farther, to the next beam, and swung. Again, we heard the deadened, solid thud.

"Um, Angus, should we really be swinging a hammer against a beam filled with high explosives?"

"Lad, it's merely a rubber mallet and poses no detonation threat. Am I right, Vivian?"

"Hit away, Angus," Vivian said.

Angus systematically banged every ceiling beam with his trusty rubber mallet before descending and joining us back at the table.

"Mystery solved. A hearty congratulations on this brilliant work," Vivian said, beaming. "I'm willing to bet the farm that every second beam is stuffed full of something, very likely C-4. As in Madrid."

"You mean we're all standing beneath enough explosive force to rip this building from its moorings and drop it in the river?" Lindsay asked as she grasped my already trembling hand.

"My hunch is it's worse than that," Vivian replied, and looked at Angus.

"You think the floor beams will be similarly configured," Angus guessed.

"Yes, but I suspect our Chechen friend stuffed not the corresponding beams but the alternate ones in the floor. But we should confirm."

With that, Angus grabbed me by the arm and guided me out the emergency exit. We clambered beneath the building, picking our way along the cliff face on a narrow catwalk built to allow inspections of the structure's underside. It was nerve-racking, inching along the catwalk with the Ottawa River swirling below us—well, it was nerve-racking for me. Angus seemed quite at home on our precarious perch, banging on the beams.

It turned out that Vivian was absolutely right. Every second floor beam seemed anything but hollow, and those lined up with the hollow ceiling beams. Angus explained that offsetting the C-4–stuffed beams above with hollow beams below, and vice versa, would maximize the destructive force of the explosion. Good to know.

"Vivian, you were right," Angus announced when we'd returned to the assembly room. "Assuming every second ceiling and floor beam is filled end to end with plastic explosives, is that enough of a blast to send this building to the deeps?"

"If it's standard C-4, they've built in a considerable factor of safety," Vivian said. "Stuffing every third or even every fourth beam would likely do the trick. We might only be left with a few stray black spider legs dangling from the cliff."

"Well, that might be more attractive than it is now," I joked.

"It's really quite ingenious using the beams this way, isn't it?" marvelled Muriel. "No one would ever suspect."

"It may be brilliant, but why are we still standing here, right at the epicentre of the blast?" I asked. "It just seems like a very bad idea."

"Daniel, as long as Pudovkin is in Washington, and therefore not in this building, I think we're pretty safe," Lindsay said.

"I'm not so sure, Linds. There are six residents of a certain apartment house in Madrid who may beg to differ from the afterlife."

She paused and nodded, conceding my point.

"Speaking of Madrid, are we sure the beam bombs will be detonated via cellphone, as the C-4 was to be there?" Angus asked, looking at Vivian.

"I'd say so," she answered. "Typically triggered by cellphone, usually in close proximity to ensure signal strength."

"Well, depending on their carrier, the cell service around here is less than reliable," I said. "Can you imagine them getting this far and then not being able to get a strong enough signal to pull the trigger?"

"I'm certain they've considered that and will likely be in line of sight," Vivian said. "Now, to confirm the cellphone detonation theory, we'll probably find antennae of some kind on the ends of the beams where they emerge from the building into the open air. It could be as simple as a small-gauge wire."

"Daniel, once more unto the breach," Angus said as we again left the room. This time, we climbed a concrete staircase at the southwest corner of the building to reach the roof. Angus sauntered towards the points of the leaf high above the river, as if he were strolling through a park, while I stayed back a safe distance. There was no point in both of us plummeting into the water. When he was close to the edge, he lay flat on his stomach and slid towards the precipice until his head was in fact over the edge.

"Angus, be careful," I called. "Do you want me to hold on to your ankles?"

"A nice thought, lad, but I'd much prefer to be unencumbered," he said. "It's flat here, and I'm not going any further."

I confess, I was relieved he had rejected my offer.

With that, he lowered his head over the edge and closely scrutinized the end of the first C-4–filled beam. I saw him reach his hand over the edge and run it along the corner of the beam.

"Aye" was all he said.

He shimmied his way over to the first hollow beam and repeated his routine. Then on to the next one, until he'd traversed the entire roof, while I supervised from a few feet away. A few minutes later we were back with the others.

"Right again, Vivian," Angus said. "You might have a bright future in this field."

"What did you find?" she asked.

"I found nothing on the hollow-sounding beams," Angus said. "But on each of the stuffed beams, there was a very small wire running back from the end on top of the beam. I had to look very closely to see it, as it's been painted the same colour as the beam. I'd never have noticed it were I not looking specifically for it."

"Well, we know the beams were not painted on-site. That means it was part of the manufacturing process, which points an incriminating finger at Eugene," Lindsay said. "He could easily have added the wires before the beams were shipped from Red Pine Steel."

"Exactly," Muriel said.

"We have to tell the Prime Minister and cancel the visit," I said. I was freaking out inside. We had to stop the meeting. I expected Vivian to support my abort plan, but she didn't.

"I know that seems the logical next step, Daniel, but if we do that, the Chechens will initiate their exfiltration plan— sorry, their escape plan—and they'll disappear in the night."

"So, where does that leave us, then?" I asked. "We have to tell *somebody*—the RCMP, CSIS, the Russians, the Mormon Tabernacle Choir, who?"

No one said anything.

"Wait, we know where they live," I said suddenly. "Why doesn't the RCMP just pick them up and hold them until after the meeting?"

"Until we confirm we're dealing with C-4 or some other comparable explosive, we don't really have enough to hold them," Vivian explained. "Being Chechen is not grounds for arrest."

"But we can't do nothing!" I said.

"There is another option," Vivian said. "Just play this out. We stage the meeting in this completely empty building. The PM's car and Pudovkin's car drive onto the site, underneath the great awning, and stop. They pause there, unseen by prying eyes, but nobody gets out. The cars then drive offsite, according to the protocols already developed for the meeting. From afar, Eugene and Tatyana will be watching the limos enter and exit. They will assume that Pudovkin and the PM and their respective teams have entered the Champlain Centre and are in this very room starting their formal discussions."

"Okay, then what?" Muriel had read my mind.

"Well, by then, we will already have been searching the area with an unprecedented security force and we will apprehend our Chechen friends, presumably before they trigger the C-4."

"But what if we don't find them in time?" Lindsay asked.

"Then the building is destroyed, but not a single human life is lost," Angus interjected. "In light of the eyesore this architectural abomination has become, I'd call it a win-win, or at least a reasonable trade-off."

"But it's a big fail if we don't find the perpetrators," I pushed.

"Aye, but by that stage, the RCMP and CSIS will have the entire area on lockdown. We know the Chechens will need to be close enough to detonate the beams. We know what they look like. We have to trust and hope that they'll be caught before they act."

"I don't think the Russians will agree to put their President in danger that way," Muriel noted.

"There'll be no risk to the President, Muriel. Neither Pudovkin nor any other Russian will be anywhere near this building on Saturday," Vivian explained. "The limos used by the PM and the President will have tinted windows and flags on their fenders. Remember, the drivers will be alone in the cars, and they'll be on-site for just a few minutes while their imaginary passengers disembark. Then they'll get the hell out of Dodge. I doubt Pudovkin will even leave the luxurious confines of his plush plane parked on the tarmac."

"Isn't it safer to just call the whole thing off?" I asked.

"Well, if I were the President of Russia, I'd want to maximize the chances that the plotters will be caught, tried, and punished," Angus said.

"And if this happened in Russia, who knows, they might even skip the trial and go straight to the punishment," Muriel said.

"So, we give the PM and Pudovkin those two options," Angus said. "Calling it off or safely simulating the meeting."

"Isn't there a third option?" Lindsay suggested. "Can't we just defuse the explosives, play out the meeting charade, and still catch the bombers in the act? They won't know we've defused them, and this beautiful, striking, and beloved architectural wonder will be saved."

"Excellent thinking, dear," said Muriel, as Angus rolled his eyes.

"Yes, sound thinking, but I'm afraid only in principle," Vivian replied. "If these people are sophisticated—and everything we've encountered thus far suggests they are—these beam bombs will not be easily or safely defused. They likely have fail-safe mechanisms and may even have built-in sensors to alert the Chechens through their phone if we start tampering with the fuse mechanisms."

"But I think it's worth a look," I said hopefully.

"Yes, it certainly makes sense to have the RCMP bomb squad confirm that the beams are in fact filled with explosives and, to the extent they're able, examine the fuse and detonation mechanism before decisions can be made on the best way to proceed," said Vivian.

Vivian impressed me. Throughout all of this, she was calm, steely, and thoughtful, and brought a real sense of leadership. I admired her. We'd be flailing in the dark without her.

"Well, as soon as we tell Bradley, I imagine this will immediately be put in the hands of the RCMP and CSIS. We'll be out of the play. And that's not a bad thing," I said.

"The RCMP bomb squad should be on-site at the earliest opportunity to check those beams," Vivian said. "When that happens, you're right, it'll be out of our hands. But it was fun while it lasted." She looked almost wistful.

"You must get the PM's attention," she continued. "There's not much time, and nothing short of the Prime Minister's

Office will be able to mobilize the necessary forces to manage this effectively."

"Aye, you're right," Angus replied. "It's our next call."

"Well, you'd better make it good if they're going to buy what we're selling," commented Muriel.

We left the building shortly thereafter and headed back to Cumberland. Angus and I waited until we were back at his home before I dialled the call on my cellphone and put it on speaker. We'd agreed Angus would take the lead.

"Addison, what is it? I'm in a meeting," Bradley whispered.

"Mr. Stanton, 'tis Angus McLintock. My strong recommendation is that you step out of the meeting to someplace private, for we have important news to report."

We heard a noise that sounded quite a bit like someone pushing back his chair, standing up, and striding out of the room.

"Okay, I'm out of the boardroom. I'm alone."

"Splendid. Let me try to make this as clear as possible. Please listen carefully." Angus paused and inhaled deeply. Then he spoke.

"We've just come from the Champlain Centre. You will know that steel beams, made locally by Red Pine Steel, are the building's principal load-bearing members, anchored at the south end in the cliff face," he began, his tone serious and weighted with, well, gravity. "According to the blueprints, all twenty of those steel beams are hollow. Are you with me, Mr. Stanton?"

"Yes, I am," Bradley replied, in an equally serious tone for a change. "Please continue."

"Well, we have just confirmed that every second steel beam supporting the floor and ceiling, supporting the whole blessed structure, is not hollow but filled with something. We strongly believe C-4—plastic explosives—has been stuffed in the beams by Anzor Dudiyn, a Chechen immigrant who, not coincidentally, works at Red Pine Steel."

Angus paused to let that sink in. We could hear Bradley's breathing quicken and deepen.

Angus continued. "Mr. Stanton, we have found disguised wire antennae protruding from each of the stuffed beams, which almost certainly means that these beam bombs are to be detonated via cellphone signal."

"Jesus."

"We have confirmed that if our supposition is correct, there is ample destructive force packed into the beams to send the entire building into the river, with little chance of survivors."

"Jesus," Bradley said again.

"Well, Mr. Stanton, I think we'll need more than his help," Angus replied. "And we have a suggested course of action."

"The path forward is clear. We have to cancel the meeting right now. Simple as that," Bradley said.

"There may be another option, one that will not only protect the lives of the Prime Minister, President Pudovkin, and everyone else who was to accompany them, but also apprehend the assassins," Angus said. "If we simply cancel the meeting, our Chechen sleeper cell will disappear from our shores, and we'll never be able to bring them to justice."

"Who cares if the bombers leave the country? That's a win for us."

"Mr. Stanton, please, we've come this far." Angus was using his *I mean business* voice. "Do hear me out."

"Of course," Bradley said. "Continue."

Angus carefully outlined Vivian's plan to stage the meeting with no threat to human life to maximize the odds of apprehending Eugene and Tatyana. When he'd finished, there was silence, I assume as Bradley processed the plan. Angus let him think it through.

"But why would we go to all that trouble and risk?" Bradley eventually asked.

"I understand your concern, Mr. Stanton," Angus replied. "But we believe the risk, though it can't be eliminated, can at least be minimized through this approach. At the very worst, the building could be destroyed, which might very well elevate the Prime Minister's standing in the polls. As well, there is a side benefit. President Pudovkin will be very grateful if we thwart his assassination and apprehend the Chechen separatists behind the plot. It could enhance our influence and help us build an even more constructive and economically beneficial relationship with Russia."

There was more silence on the other end of the line. We could hear Bradley breathing. We could almost hear him thinking. Finally, after what seemed like a very long time, he spoke again.

"I'll talk to the Prime Minister and offer both options. Have you briefed Coulombe yet?"

Angus looked at me and I jumped in. "No, and we think it should not come from us," I said. "The hostility, even hatred, towards us coming from his office has been a big part of our problem. We've had to figure all this out on our own because no one in Minister Coulombe's office would even listen.

"Bradley," I continued, "our suggestion is that the Prime Minister, through Coulombe, direct the RCMP to take samples of whatever is in the beams so we can confirm what we now only strongly suspect. But they should do it discreetly and quickly. No one can know, if we want to leave all our options open. The building could be under surveillance now that we're just a day or so out."

"I can't believe I'm saying this, Addison, but that sounds like a reasonable approach."

"I can't believe you're saying it either, Bradley. But I'm glad." I looked at Angus.

"Mr. Stanton, when speaking to Emile, there's no gain in revealing how you found out about this. We need quick action from him, and if we're seen to be part of this, it could retard the process."

"I agree, though I didn't think we could use the word 'retard' anymore," Bradley said.

"We've no time for a full-blown grammar lesson," Angus replied. "But the verb is perfectly acceptable. It's the noun that can be plenty hurtful."

"One more thing, Bradley," I said. "When Coulombe, the RCMP, and CSIS are fully engaged, the Russian ambassador should be brought into the fold. We think he will favour the option that includes capturing the Chechens in the act."

"Haven't you been dealing with Koskov up till now?" Bradley asked.

"Yes, but we've been pushing him a bit and may have strained the relationship. It makes more sense if we back away from all of this now that you obviously accept the plot as a credible threat. You wield much more power and authority than we do."

"Okay, thanks for this," Bradley said, in an unusual, even unprecedented spasm of civility. "Is there anything else?"

"Bradley, the most pressing priority is discreetly ascertaining what has been crammed into every second hollow steel beam in the building. Vivian says it's likely C-4," I said.

"Vivian? Who's Vivian?"

Shit.

"Um, I didn't say Vivian."

"Well, it sure sounded like it."

"Mr. Stanton, we dinnae have time for this. Please get the RCMP over to the Champlain Centre quickly but quietly, and let's find out once and for all what we're confronting."

"Addison, Minister, I'll stay in touch as this plays out," Bradley said. "Thank you for your persistence."

I ended the call.

The next night, Lindsay and I joined Angus for dinner in his wonderful home. There were bookshelves in almost every room. In the living room, all of the books written by his late wife, Marin Lee, foundational works in the feminist canon, were lined up on the top bookshelf for all to see. A silent, heartfelt tribute.

True to his Scottish roots, Angus made a big batch of spaghetti bolognese, complemented by garlic bread and Caesar salad. After dinner, the three of us lounged in the living room in a post-prandial stupor. That's when my cellphone buzzed, and I answered on speaker.

"Bradley, good to hear from you. Angus is with me," I said. "How did the G8 end up?" We had been waiting all day to get an update from him. Lindsay rose to leave but I motioned for her to stay.

"It's a bit early to tell, but the PM seemed happy by the time we landed back in Ottawa, about twenty minutes ago," he said. "I've been busy on this other little matter that you brought to my attention."

"Well, we're eager to hear what's transpired," said Angus.

"All right, Addison and Minister, let me bring you up to date," Bradley said. "Thanks to your behind-the-scenes work, we have accomplished a great deal. Let me count the ways. First of all, and most importantly, you were absolutely right. Every second beam—by the way, they're called Hollow Structural Sections. You may not have known that, Danny boy."

Vintage Bradley. But I wouldn't let him get to me.

"Actually, Bradley, I did know that. It sounds like you read the same Wikipedia article I did."

"Anyway, every second Hollow Structural Section holding the entire building up is crammed end to end with C-4. And all ten of the filled beams have detonation fuses."

"So, it is done," Angus said.

"Wow," I said. "Bradley, is Coulombe fully on board?"

"He was a little ambivalent, until the RCMP and the Department of National Defence confirmed your suspicions. But now he has the bit between his teeth. Secondly, on the strength of the evidence, including the little matter of the C-4, the RCMP were dispatched to the address you gave us to pick up the Chechens. But they seemed to have bailed out. We found no trace of them. It's now a crime scene and the RCMP is turning the apartment upside down." He paused. "So the important news is, without the Chechens in custody, the Prime Minister wants to pursue the second option, where we stage the meeting and catch them in the act. He liked that idea so much that when he spoke with Pudovkin, it was the only approach he advanced."

"Hang on. The PM actually spoke to the President about this?" I asked.

"Yep. We had a short meeting this afternoon before we flew back. The head of the FSB was also there, as was Coulombe. Ambassador Koskov joined by phone, too," Bradley said.

"How did Pudovkin react?" Angus asked.

"He was polite but clearly skeptical, and so was the FSB dude. But that changed when the PM got to the part about the C-4 stuffed in the steel beams. Coulombe was also very convincing, with slides and photos and chemical analyses. Pudovkin paid very close attention after that."

"Bradley, are you saying that Russia is on board for the fake-the-meeting, catch-the-bad-guys plan?"

"It's not final, but it's certainly looking that way. We did not report everything to the Russians, as we don't want FSB agents on Canadian soil taking the law into their own hands. The Brits are still complaining about the problems they had on that front. Pudovkin and the Russian ambassador have given the PM their assurance that we have the security lead tomorrow for the showdown."

"Well, that does sound encouraging," I said.

"In the meantime, the Mounties are still looking for our two assassins. The man did not show up for his regular shift today at the steel plant, and the woman worked all day, but her shift ended and she left before they got to her. Both are apparently off tomorrow. Seems like they may have plans."

"So Pudovkin is really coming?" I asked. "That's confirmed?"

"Pudovkin says he will land in Ottawa tomorrow morning as planned. We're going to have him taxi into a special hangar. But he will not leave the plane until we have captured the two Chechens and the threat is over."

"Well, whatever happens, it'll be done tomorrow," Angus said.

CHAPTER 9

If I'd known what the day would bring, I'd have held on to Lindsay for much longer than I did as we stood there in the driveway that morning. We eventually broke our embrace and she climbed into her Honda.

"Give Muriel a hug for me," I said, then kissed her again.

"I will. And please be careful today. I'm worried about Angus and you. Just don't do anything crazy," she said. "Make good decisions today. I want you to come home tonight."

"Linds, don't worry. We have no role today. We can't get near the Champlain Centre. We'll be outside the security cordon along with everybody else. I think we're safe.

Besides, there are eight hundred Ottawa Police, Mounties, CSIS operatives, and other security staff combing the area already. They'll find Eugene and Tatyana long before the empty limos pull up to the entrance, and probably before Angus and I show up."

"But you two always seem to find yourselves at the flashpoint of everything, the hotspot, ground zero," she said. Her tone was no longer light and carefree.

"I blame Angus for that. That never happened to me before I met him."

"Just remember, you are not an intelligence agent. You are not the hero in the thrillers you read."

"Lindsay, I know. I'm well aware of that and have no desire to be anywhere near the pointy end of this stick."

"Good. Now that the RCMP and CSIS have finally, finally, come on board, let them deal with it from here on in."

I nodded, touched by the seriousness of her concern.

"Just be safe and come home."

"I will."

I watched as she drove up the winding driveway and out of sight, on her way to Riverfront, where she was going to watch the live proceedings with Muriel and Vivian. Because we had no formal responsibilities that day, Angus and I were going to head to Ottawa, but only as spectators.

With the official law enforcement circles finally in control, I worried that there'd be a leak. This whole plan turned on Eugene and Tatyana believing they were the only ones who knew what was to unfold that day. A story in the *Ottawa Citizen* or on CBC News could render all of our work for naught. But so far, there was nothing in the media, nothing on Facebook or Twitter, nothing anywhere.

I was staying in close and frequent contact with Bradley Stanton. Believe me, that is not an experience I ever expected or desired. But he seemed to recognize that Angus and I were the only ones who had figured this whole thing out, and that without us, the Prime Minister might not have survived. It seemed to buy a little civility, if not gratitude, from him.

Bradley let me know that Pudovkin and Koskov had both landed in Canada and were now sequestered on the President's palatial jet inside a secure hangar, guarded on the outside by members of the Canadian Armed Forces and on the inside by Pudovkin's own crack security team. I was worried for Koskov. I was sure Pudovkin was not pleased that this assassination plot had developed right under his ambassador's unsuspecting nose. If Koskov were suddenly recalled to Moscow, or banished to the Russian embassy in Burundi, we'd know why.

Apparently, Pudovkin's official car travelled with him, and it would be driven to the Champlain Centre as part of our ruse. It was an armour-plated Aurus Senat, a beast of a limo developed in Moscow by an organization with the most literal name in human history, the Central Scientific Research Automobile and Automotive Engines Institute. I'm not kidding. That's what it's called.

I drove Angus into Ottawa, still in our ministerial Buick, and parked behind the Library of Parliament. Using our passes, we slipped in the back door and walked through Centre Block. It was closed to the public, so it was very quiet, with only a skeleton security staff on duty while the rest of the team had been seconded to support the search for Eugene and Tatyana. Angus and I walked out the entrance under the Peace Tower and strolled across the lawns to Wellington Street. It was a beautiful day. The sun was bright, and the clouds were white. We then turned east and eventually north on Mackenzie to get as close to the Champlain Centre as we could.

The security cordon at the Centre was even larger than I expected. A few interested observers had gathered in the hopes of catching a glimpse of the Russian President and our Prime Minister, too. From our vantage point behind the yellow police tape, we could see hundreds of security officers, some in plainclothes and others in uniform. They were everywhere and always moving, fanning out on the streets and up the hillsides and rock faces around the Centre. There was really nowhere for Eugene and Tatyana to hide. Yet . . .

"There's only fifteen minutes before the limos arrive. And by the look of the security forces, they haven't found Eugene and Tatyana," I murmured to Angus.

"Aye, 'tis a wee bit disquieting," he replied. "I'd have thought it'd be all over by now."

I scanned the area but could only see increasingly animated and agitated security teams combing the grounds around the Centre.

"Where could they be?" I asked. I turned to look back the way we'd come, and certainty struck like lightning. I don't recall ever feeling so confident about anything in my life. It was as if I were not in control. The thought simply entered my brain and I immediately accepted it as fact.

"Angus, I know where they are," I said urgently, looking back towards Centre Block. "We should have thought of it before now."

Angus followed my eyes and seemed to know, too. We turned to look at one another as all the pieces fell into place.

"Shite, lad, we should have known," he said. "We're a good ten-minute sprint away. We're almost too late. Come on!"

"Let's just tell the Mounties and let them handle it," I said.

"Daniel, can you see a single security person within earshot? They're all searching the hills up around the Centre. And who would believe us, anyway? We'll have to go ourselves." Without waiting for any more suggestions from me, he started running back the way we'd come. "Come on, lad, flap the wings on your heels," he shouted over his shoulder.

By federal regulation and city bylaw, no building in downtown Ottawa can be higher than Centre Block's Peace Tower, and the result was a perfect line-of-sight view to Nepean Point and the Champlain Centre. You would have thought, given the security usually swarming all over Parliament Hill, that it would not be a good place from which to detonate a deadly explosive device. But that day, it was the perfect spot: few security guards roamed the halls of Centre Block that day, with most of their contingent drafted for search duty around the Champlain Centre. And now we knew why Tatyana worked in Centre Block. It was a brilliant and simple plan.

I was half dead before we even hit the Château Laurier, but there was no way I could stop and rest until the sixty-something Angus did. But he didn't, so neither did I. I was surprised a man of his age and build was so fleet of foot. I, on the other hand, was more flat of foot, and fell behind with every step. Angus anxiously waited for me at the corner of East Block.

"Okay, lad, we cannae run like panicked gazelles across the lawn, because they'll likely notice from the tower."

"Well, that's unfortunate, because I was just about to kick into panicked-gazelle mode," I huffed, about to pass out or throw up, or both.

"Let's walk briskly, but don't looked concerned," Angus said. "We're just walking and talking."

We left the lee of East Block and walked across the lawn as quickly as we could while still giving the impression that it was just a typical perambulation on a typical day. When we ducked under the Peace Tower and were out of sight, we tore up the steps and burst into the foyer. The lone security officer staffing the command room, sitting in front of a large console of video screens offering views from the dozens of CCTV cameras in the building, looked up. There was a monitor tuned to CBC, showing a side view of the Champlain Centre. On the screen, two limos emerged from under the concrete awning and drove out of view along Murray Street. Uh-oh. That was not good.

"Officer Lapierre, you know who I am," Angus said, looking at the guard's name tag. It was security's job to know each MP. "This is important. We believe someone is in the Peace Tower, about to take malevolent action. Can you show us any camera images from the Peace Tower?"

Officer Lapierre looked a little startled but quickly gathered himself.

"I'm sorry, Minister, but there are no cameras at the top of the tower, just one at the base," he said. He quickly called up a view of the base and put it on screen. The shot showed an open area and the elevator that ferried tourists to the top. It was very quiet, like a still photo. The lights above the sliding doors showed that the elevator was at the top of the tower. I would have thought its resting position would have been at the bottom.

Angus was about to say something, but a flash of colour on the CBC monitor caught my eye, and all three of us turned in time to see the explosion. The ugly black spider legs broke away from the structure. The entire building shuddered and tilted. Smoke billowed. Flames flowered. And then, before our very eyes, the Samuel de Champlain Centre broke from the rocky face and fell into the river, taking a chunk of the cliff with it. Just before it hit the water, a low rumble started and grew louder as the sound and shock waves washed over Centre Block. We were frozen in place, but could feel the floors vibrate beneath our feet. The rumble and tremors seemed to carry on forever, but in retrospect, we know it lasted less than four seconds from start to finish. It wasn't the gigantic Hollywood conflagration we've come to expect, but it was still a big explosion.

"Och, crivvens, it's done." Angus shook his head. "What I've always called *that blasted building* is now just that."

I felt sick and woozy. We *knew* their plan. We'd figured it out from next to nothing. We just couldn't stop it. We'd saved the President, the PM, and many others, but not the building. A lot of people were going to be very angry. Then again, many, many more would be celebrating the death of the spider.

Officer Lapierre was stunned and just stared at the TV screen. I glanced at the Peace Tower elevator screen. Something had moved.

"Angus, the elevator is coming down!"

We watched with bated breath as the indicator lights moved all the way down, from nine to one. After a long pause the doors slid open, and Tatyana emerged, calmly pushing her cleaning cart. She wore what looked like the same smock as when I'd first met her, along with jeans and white running shoes. She appeared to be relaxed, unperturbed, unhurried. She turned and headed down the south corridor, out of view of the camera.

Lapierre read our minds and brought up the live feed from two other cameras, at either end of the corridor. "I was told no cleaning staff were to be on-site today," he said.

"She seems to be exerting herself a little too much for pushing a standard cleaning cart," I observed.

"Aye. Is there a camera in the cleaners' room where they store the cart?"

"No, sir."

"Officer Lapierre, can you call the RCMP or the police to get some backup here as fast as you're able?"

Lapierre nodded and picked up the phone.

Angus dashed out the door. I sort of dashed, too, to catch up to him.

"Angus, I know where she's going. We can't take the same route. I know a faster way."

"Lead on, Macduff," he replied.

"She'll need to take an elevator to the basement," I said. "I think we can make it there in time."

We ran along the north corridor to a stairwell in the corner of the building and ran down the stairs as fast as we could without falling. I peeked through the window in the stairwell door just in time to see Tatyana push the cart into the cleaners' room.

"Okay, it's clear," I said, and slipped out into the hallway.

Angus and I huddled just outside the door to the cleaners' room. Angus started to stand up to look through the small window in the door.

"Let me, Angus," I said. "I have a better angle, and my hair is less likely to be noticed."

I don't know why I said that. I was back to being terrified, but having Angus there somehow made it easier. I screwed up my courage and inched up the door until I could see through the window. I was just in time to watch as Eugene lifted himself out of the cleaning cart's garbage can. He was wearing black jeans, black running shoes, a black T-shirt, and a black jean jacket. He was obviously going through his black fashion phase.

"Eugene is in the house," I whispered. "He used to be in the cart."

"Right, then," Angus said, standing up and reaching for the doorknob.

"No, Angus," I hissed, as visions of Lindsay danced in my head. "Now is the time for caution, discretion, patience, and maybe even a little cowardice. The police will be here any second now. These two assassins have just blown up a building. They are killers, or at least they think they are. So stand down until the cavalry arrives."

"Sound advice, lad," he said. "Sound advice."

Then Angus burst through the door.

I'd been afraid of that. I also burst through the door, but at a much slower pace and in a manner that blended timid and tentative, laced with crippling fear. But not quite crippling enough, as I found myself in the room, standing slightly behind Angus.

In one smooth motion, Tatyana reached into her cleaning cart and pulled out a gun. I'm not good with firearms, and I can't tell you what kind it was like they do in the James Bond novels. You know, it was a Walther PPK, or it was a Kalashnikov, or a bazooka of some kind. Let's just say it was big and black and very gun-like. She levelled it at us.

Now, this would be a time when any sane individual would simply put their arms in the air and look very, very compliant. That's exactly what I did, shaking from toes to fingertips. If only Angus had joined me.

"You must be Tatyana and Eugene," he said, looking down the barrel of the big black gun.

Eugene's head snapped back and he turned his bulging eyes to Tatyana.

They argued in what I assumed was Russian. To my ear, Tatyana won.

Beyond *nyet*, Smirnoff, Sputnik, and Lada, my Russian is pretty weak. You might call it non-existent, and I'd be hard-pressed to argue. But by Eugene's reaction and the tone of their exchange, it was clear we'd found our Chechen duo, and she was calling the shots in their partnership. I hoped she wouldn't also be taking shots at us. Then Eugene looked at me, nodding his head.

Eugene then pointed at me and said something to Tatyana.

Tatyana turned to stare at me, her eyes narrowed and her head slightly tilted. She said something to Eugene that sounded like agreement, while nodding. Then she spoke in English. "We met."

"Really?" I said. "I don't think so."

"You dropped your paper in hall. I helped."

"Oh, right. I remember now. Thanks so much, for helping me," I said. "That was very nice."

"Shut up!"

"You hit my car," Eugene said.

"Wow, what a coincidence." I gave a tremulous chuckle.

"Look, lassie—I mean Tatyana—we know what you and Eugene just did. It's over now. Let's not do anything silly. Let's not take this any further," Angus said calmly.

"I said, shut up!" she snapped. She turned to Eugene and apparently gave an order.

He jumped to it, pulled a roll of duct tape out of his jacket pocket and proceeded to bind our wrists together in front of us.

Tatyana issued another command and Eugene immediately fished in our pockets and took our cellphones.

"Come," Tatyana ordered us.

She pointed the gun to the small staircase that led outside. Eugene took the lead, looking outside first and then allowing us up the stairs. We emerged in the parking lot behind the Library of Parliament, and the first car I saw was our blue Buick. The second was Eugene's beat-up Taurus. I kicked myself for not noticing it when we'd parked earlier. I looked around for any living soul and prepared to elevate my eyebrows meaningfully, wiggle my ears, cross my eyes, crinkle my nose, blow out my cheeks, anything to catch their attention. But there was no one there. Not a soul.

Tatyana hissed at Eugene.

He jerked to action and immediately opened the trunk of the Taurus. Since they had no luggage with them, I was not happy with this turn of events.

"In," she commanded. "Fast!"

"I don't think we'll both fit in there," I protested. I really did not want to get in the trunk.

"In. Now!" She pointed the gun directly at me.

"Well, now that you mention it," I said, "maybe we will fit."

"After you, lad." Angus seemed perfectly calm, normal, and natural. I checked exactly none of those boxes.

"Um, you should go first, Angus," I said. "You know the theory. Put the big stones in first? You're the big stone here."

Angus climbed in and slid as far up as he could. Then I stepped over the lip of the trunk and hunkered in. Turned out there was room for both of us after all, provided we squished into each other closer than conjoined twins. Tatyana slammed the lid down and we were in the dark. That was not a good moment for me but seemed like any other for Angus. We heard them get into the front seats and continue speaking in their language. The car started and then we were moving.

Physically, I wasn't very comfortable. My head was pressed into Angus's chest, and his beard scratched my cheek. A plastic bottle of windshield washer fluid was jabbing into my back. Emotionally and psychologically, I was slightly worse off than merely uncomfortable.

"Are you doing that shaking, lad?" Angus asked.

"No! Angus, this car is a mechanical monstrosity at the end of its life. It has so many different vibrations, I can pretty well guarantee that what you're feeling is not coming from me."

I was shaking like a paint-mixing machine in a hardware store. My heart was pounding, my eyes were watering, and I'm pretty sure I was hyperventilating. Had I not already been lying down, I'm quite sure I would have collapsed by then. What can I say? Terror just seems to have that effect on me.

When my eyes adjusted to the darkness, I realized it wasn't that dark in the trunk after all. Reminiscent of my own experience with the early Ford Taurus models, plenty of light spilled in from rusted-out holes in the lid and fenders.

"This floor doesn't feel very solid," I whispered. "It's got some give to it whenever we hit a bump."

"Aye, it's not unlike your old wagon, where you could see the road rushing beneath your bleedin' feet."

"While I'm very keen to escape, falling through the trunk floor onto the road at eighty kilometres an hour has 'out of the frying pan, into the fire' written all over it," I said. "Where do you think we're going?"

"I haven't the foggiest," Angus replied. "I'm trying to sort out whether they're going to take us with them, shoot us, or leave us in the trunk."

"I'll take door number three, please." The car suddenly turned sharply, and Angus and I got to know each other a little better.

"Did you know, laddie, that in 2002 all car manufacturers were required to install a glow-in-the-dark trunk-release mechanism inside the boot?" Angus said.

"Oddly, I did not know that," I replied. "Did you know that this is a Taurus from the late 1980s?"

"Aye, I did. Did you know that Ford has incorporated the inside trunk-release mechanism since the late 1970s?"

"Oddly, that somehow managed to escape my attention as well. How do you know that?"

"Daniel, I am a mechanical engineering professor."

"Yes, well, I wasn't aware that you needed to know about glow-in-the-dark emergency trunk-release handles to get your iron ring."

"No matter," he said. "There's lots about politics I don't know."

I somehow inched myself over onto my back and started feeling for the handle, with my hands still bound together with the miracle that is duct tape.

"Given this vehicle's advanced age, the handle may not be glow-in-the-dark, but it will have some kind of cable attached to it. It'll most likely be near the latching mechanism attached to the trunk lid."

Angus was exactly right. In a minute, I found a plastic handle attached to what felt like the brake cable on my first bike with gears.

"Dinnae yank on it now," Angus said. "I think it best to bide our time and see where we're going."

"It's so cramped in here. I'm starting to feel a little claustrophobic."

"'Tis no surprise it's cramped. Passengers generally are not supposed to ride in the trunk. Be glad I didnae have those leftover cabbage rolls for breakfast," Angus said as he suddenly shifted position.

"Hello!" I croaked.

"Are you all right, Daniel? Your voice sounds a little higher pitched than usual."

"That's because you just crammed your knee into the sensitive spot I was sincerely hoping your knee would miss."

"Ah, so that's what stopped it. Deepest apologies, lad. Happened to me all the time during my rugby days. Very unpleasant. Breathe deeply and the pain will pass."

Angus still sounded absolutely normal, as if we were in the front seat of our ministerial Buick driving home from the Hill, not bound and lying in the trunk of a rusted death trap of a getaway car. I was doing my best to appear as if I were just fine—you know, just another day with the Member of Parliament for Cumberland–Prescott. But I wasn't fine. I was terrified. Eugene and Tatyana had nothing to lose; it seemed like a faint hope that they might let us live. If Angus hadn't been smushed up against me, I figure I'd have been weeping by then.

My private little wallowing session was interrupted when Angus started humming a classic bagpipe tune he often blasted throughout his house on weekends. I'm serious. He was lying bound in the trunk of a speeding car, humming a Scottish lament. I can't remember the name of the song, but I'm quite sure the word "bonnie" was in it.

"Are you not frightened, Angus?" I asked.

"You mean because we've been abducted at gunpoint by two people who are clearly prepared to sacrifice human life to further their not entirely unjust cause?"

"Yeah, I guess that pretty well sums it up."

"Of course I'm frightened. Who wouldn't be? But I also know that, being locked in the trunk here with my wrists bound, my fear isnae useful or helpful in extricating us. Fear does not aid us. So I bury it down deep. But it's there, lad. It's there, sure as Newton's laws."

"My fear seems a little closer to the surface," I said. I tried to loosen the binding immobilizing my wrists, but Eugene deserved top marks for his tape job. It was rock solid.

"So, what's our plan?" I whispered, failing to disguise the desperation in my voice.

"We haven't enough data yet to develop a plan," Angus said. "We need more information, probably when the car stops. Then we'll make a plan, likely in a very few ticks of the clock."

"Sounds awesome" was all I could muster.

We were driving faster now, but not quite fast enough to be on the highway. We'd been on the road for about fifteen minutes when we finally slowed down and made what felt like a left turn. We could feel the car slowing. I twisted my body and pushed my face up against the fender wall where there was a small rust hole.

"I can see water. It's the river," I said. Part of a sign passed through my field of vision. It was familiar. I'd been there before. "Wait, wait, I think we're pulling in to the Rockcliffe Flying Club. Does that help our plan?"

"Aye, I suppose it does, provided they leave us in the trunk when they reach their plane."

"You think they're flying themselves out on a little plane?"

"It seems a logical assumption if we're stopping at the Rockcliffe Flying Club. I dinnae think Tatyana is here for a lesson."

I kept up my vigil through the rust hole.

"Okay, we've gone through the gates. We're driving by a chain-link fence. We just turned left around the end of the fence. I think we're now on the tarmac. I see small planes."

The Taurus slowed to a halt, so I stopped talking. We heard both car doors open, then slam shut. Through the rust hole I could just see Tatyana and Eugene quickly walking away from the Taurus towards a small plane. A typical Cessna high-wing, it was white with what I think was a red stripe.

"Angus, they're getting into a plane, just the two of them," I said.

"Tell me when the propeller starts turning and they start rolling. Then be ready to yank that handle and move."

I assumed he meant so we could then run to safety. Uh-huh.

"I can only see the pilot side, but they both just got in the plane. Tatyana put on a headset. Okay, I hear the engine, but I can't see the propeller from here."

"But is the plane moving, lad? The timing is critical."

"Not yet. Not yet. Not—yes, now it's moving!"

"Are they moving away from us?"

"Yes, they're heading away from us, towards the runway."

"Pull that handle, now!"

"But why?" I asked in a voice that quavered more than I wanted. "We're safe in here."

"There's no time, lad. Yank that handle!"

I squirmed back to my earlier position, found the plastic handle, and pulled. Then came the familiar click of the trunk unlatching, but the lid did not spring open. It didn't move at all.

"Give me some racing room, here, lad," Angus said.

I shimmied as far from him as I could, which was about four inches, and he kicked up at the trunk lid. His foot went right through it, but it opened as well. I hauled myself out by my bound hands and hid behind the rear bumper. Angus managed to muscle himself out, too, then quickly closed the trunk lid. Eugene and Tatyana were still taxiing away from us at a sedate speed. Angus briefly tried to bite through his duct tape binding but quickly gave up.

"We've precious little time, lad. All right, into the front seat with us. I'm driving."

"The faster we're away from here, the better," I offered.

That was Angus's cue to agree with me, but he said nothing. That did not augur well. We moved up our respective sides of the car, managed to open our doors, and slid inside.

"Stay down now, Daniel," Angus said.

"No encouragement needed," I whispered. "I'm down."

We were both crouching well below the dashboard and out of sight in case Tatyana or Eugene craned their neck to look back at the car.

"Hellfire and damnation, the keys are not in the ignition," Angus said. "Why would they take them? They're surely not coming back."

My head was resting just above the cupholders. I shifted my position for a look.

"The keys are here!" I said, fishing them out of the cupholder. I immediately regretted opening my big yap.

"Merciful heavens. Give 'em here, lad!" I clutched them in both hands, holding tight. "Daniel, be a good lad and give 'em here," he said in a soothing voice.

I said nothing but just closed my eyes and shook my head.

"Daniel!" he snapped.

I gave him the keys. He somehow managed to insert the key into the ignition. It was difficult performing all these mundane tasks with our wrists still constrained. I tried to bite through the layers of tape binding mine but it just didn't work, and it didn't taste great either.

Angus quickly looked up. The Cessna had made its turn from the taxiway and was just reaching the runway. He worked the key and the Taurus roared to life. Not really—it cranked over anemically and sputtered to life-support systems. "Christmas, it sounds like it's running on half its cylinders. I hope we can do this."

"Do what? Drive to the police station? Drive to the RCMP office? Drive far away from here? Because that's what we should be doing. Driving far away from here."

"Buckle up, Daniel."

"Angus?"

I struggled to fasten my seat belt and Angus did, too.

"Not quite yet," Angus said to himself, eyeing the plane through the side window. "Stay down, lad. Almost. Almost."

I took a peek and saw the plane, now on the runway, moving parallel to us and then past us as they picked up speed.

"The road out the gate and away from here is clear. Let's go!" I urged.

"We're going to go all right, lad. Now, hold on to your kilt," Angus said as he threw the gearshift into Drive and took off across the grass separating the taxiway from the runway. It was clear we were not heading for the exit. No, we were chasing after the Cessna.

"Angus, what are you doing? Angus!"

"What do you think I'm doing? Use your imagination."

"I'd rather not use my imagination. But what are you going to do if we catch them?" I asked.

"Not now, lad!" he snapped.

"I withdraw the question." His plan had become obvious. Terrifying, but obvious.

Tatyana and Eugene still hadn't seen us as we approached from behind. Angus had his foot to the floor, and we were gaining on them. I glanced at the speedometer and in short order saw that we were zipping along at 125 kilometres per hour, the car shaking so much I was seeing double. That Taurus probably hadn't moved that fast in many years, and for good reason. As we closed in on the plane, I knew what Angus was doing. I couldn't believe it, but it was obvious. It was our only option after he'd clearly rejected my "let's just drive away" alternative. With his wrists awkwardly taped together and grasping the steering wheel at twelve o'clock high, he kept up the pursuit. We were alongside the back end of the Cessna now. Angus coaxed the last bit of speed out of the aging Ford as the tail of the plane suddenly dipped and the nose wheel came off the ground. Last chance. I was paralyzed, and powerless to stop what happened next.

Angus jerked the wheel to the right and crashed into the tail of the Cessna just as it was poised to take to the air.

"Aaaaaannnnnnnngggggggguuuuuuuuuuuuusssssssssssss!" someone screamed. It was long and loud and seemed to be coming from somewhere inside the car.

The impact caused the entire front-right fender of the Taurus to crumple and fly up and over the car. I covered my face with my hands, leaving a few finger peepholes so I didn't miss anything. I watched as the plane tilted over from the blow and cut across the runway. In what seemed like slow motion, its right wing hit the tarmac and folded up like cardboard. The screaming in the car continued, but I'm pretty sure it wasn't Angus. He was still busy at the wheel, and the look on his face was calm, almost serene.

The Cessna, now on its side, skidded across the runway with a head of steam. When its damaged right wing dug into the grass, the plane flipped over on its roof, slid another twenty metres or so, and finally came to rest on the grass, leaving a deep furrow in the sod behind it.

Finally, everything was quiet, almost silent but for our idling engine. My head was aching and I noticed my chest was hurting where the seat belt had done its job when we'd hit the plane. I could also feel a fast and rhythmic banging somewhere. I quickly diagnosed it as my pulse, pounding triple-time.

Angus stared at the plane, his brow furrowed but his eyes clear and focused. We could just make out Eugene, upside down in his seat on the side closer to us. The main strut from the damaged wing was folded up across his door, so there was no way he could get out of the plane on his side.

Then, instead of finally making an escape, Angus drove the car across the grass to the other side of the Cessna. Yes, he really did. And there was Tatyana, also upside down in her seat, struggling with her belt. Without hesitating, Angus drove over the wing and nosed the Taurus in so its front bumper was pressed up tight against the door to stop her from opening it. If looks could kill, Tatyana proceeded to murder us several times over.

"Yes, lad?" Angus asked. "What is it?"

"What do you mean?" I replied.

"A short time ago you yelled my name with considerable urgency, presumably to pose a question, or offer a suggestion, or engage me in conversation. Which was it?"

"Never mind," I replied.

"Well, are you all right, Daniel?" he asked.

"Well, I banged my head on the side window when we hit, but I'm still seeing straight. So I think I'm okay, other than being just a few feet away from Tatyana."

"Good. Then let's make haste and get out of the car, now. I can tell Tatyana is a wee bit steamed in there, and she very likely still has that gun within reach."

I needed no further incentive. Our wrists still bound, we managed to scramble out and run across to the far side of the runway. With no risk of the two Chechens extricating themselves, we sat down in the grass, and everything seemed to slow down. I oscillated between damning Angus for putting our lives at risk and celebrating his (our?) bravery in grounding the escape plane. Angus has a gift for engendering conflicting feelings.

"Can you reach into my front right pocket, lad?" inquired Angus.

"I probably can, but must I?"

"I'm not looking for you to scratch an itch, I have a pocket knife there and we can finally be free of this all-too-effective tape."

I positioned myself accordingly and was able to shove both my hands, which were still trembling, into his pocket to snare the knife. We were liberated from the duct tape a minute or so later, with no blood shed.

Eventually, I began breathing normally again, and I was surprised to find my mind occupied with thoughts and images that took me far from the Rockcliffe Flying Club. Lindsay figured in most of them. Okay, in all of them. It was then that I heard the sirens. Was it the airport's fire trucks? Nope. An RCMP car screamed across the grass and skidded to a stop on Tatyana's side of the plane. The officer got out, drew her weapon, and trained it on the two Chechens, who were still desperately trying to escape their predicament.

About two minutes later, four more cars, three RCMP and an unmarked vehicle, joined the scene. The unmarked car drove over to where Angus and I were huddled in the grass on the other side of the runway. Officer Lapierre was driving. He leaned over and opened the passenger door with a big smile.

"*Félicitations, mes amis,*" he said.

I turned to Angus. "He's saying congratulations."

"Thank you, Daniel. I understood him well enough." To Lapierre, he said, "You called in reinforcements. How did you know where we were?"

"I had a CCTV feed in the parking lot, and I saw them put you in the trunk. I got the licence number and put out a general call to the Ottawa Police and RCMP," Lapierre explained. "We got lucky. An RCMP officer at the gates of Rideau Hall heard the call and saw the car go by on the Cartier Parkway. It helped that there aren't many twenty-year-old rusted Tauruses still on the road. The officer drove down the parkway but couldn't see the car anywhere. Then, when she drove past the flying club, she actually heard the crash, and then saw it."

"Her timing was perfect," I said.

"I figure we owe her at least a drink, if not the Order of Canada," said Angus. "And you, too, Officer Lapierre. We're in your debt."

"It was definitely my most exciting day in twenty-two years on the job. Before this, it was when a Cabinet minister had a few too many drinks in the parliamentary restaurant and fell down the stairs," he said with a laugh. "This is a much better story to tell. And I heard from the RCMP that no one was even in the Champlain Centre when it fell. No one!"

"No kidding," I said, relieved but not surprised. "That's great news."

I looked over and saw Claude Rosseau, the RCMP liaison to Emile Coulombe's office, walking over from the plane towards us. When he reached us, his hand was outstretched. Angus and I each shook it in turn.

"I'm sorry we didn't listen to you," he said with sincerity. "Obviously, we were wrong to ignore your intelligence."

"We don't blame you, Officer. I may not have believed us had I been in your shoes. There is no ill will whatsoever," Angus said. "We know it can be difficult working in a minister's office. Daniel tells me that every other day."

We watched as Eugene and Tatyana were put in handcuffs and seated in the backs of two separate RCMP cars. I breathed a sigh of relief, and my heart rate returned to normal sinus rhythm. It was all over.

I looked at Angus and noticed for the first time an abrasion across his forehead. He saw me looking at it and wiped it, noticing a little blood on his fingers.

"'Tis nothing. I hit my head on the blasted steering wheel when we rammed the plane. You've got a wee artifact on the side of your forehead, too, you know," he said, pointing.

The ambulance arrived a few minutes later, and Angus and I re-enacted the classic cop-show epilogue scene: we sat on the edge of the open ambulance door looking heroic while police scurried about and paramedics tended to our very superficial flesh wounds. I could almost hear the closing dramatic music as the credits rolled.

It would have been nice if this was how the whole affair had really ended. The assassination plot thwarted. The sleeper cell apprehended. Pudovkin and the Prime Minister safe. Fleming protected. Angus and I redeemed and feted by a grateful nation. Life restored to normal—or as normal as my life ever got.

Yes, that would have been nice.

PART

NO.4

CHAPTER 10

It wasn't long before the satellite trucks arrived, four of them in the span of about twenty minutes, undoubtedly diverted from the Champlain Centre blast scene. Reporters were soon doing live updates from the scene and shooting all the footage their portable hard drives would hold. The RCMP kept the media away from us. There'd be time for interviews, and likely sooner than we'd like.

Just before Officer Lapierre drove us back to Parliament Hill, I checked the glove compartment of the battered Ford Taurus and recovered our cellphones. That was a lucky break, because the prospect of replacing my cellphone was just about as traumatic as being abducted in the trunk of a rusty Ford. I had several missed calls from Lindsay, so I called her right away. She'd been watching the news and was certainly relieved to hear from me.

We spent the entire afternoon debriefing the Ottawa Police, the RCMP, and CSIS. It would have been quite efficient to deconstruct our adventure minute by minute only once, with all three security organizations in the same room. Alas, that's not how they tend to operate. Instead, we endured three separate interviews, covering nearly the same ground in each.

Though we were pressed to, we never revealed that our original source was Fleming. Suffice it to say that the now-accepted existence of the sleeper cell made it easier for us to defend the bona fides of our source and the credibility of our intelligence. Kudos and accolades were showered over us for our investigative work in identifying Eugene and Tatyana, discovering the beam bombs, and realizing the Peace Tower was the perfect place from which to detonate the bombs. The RCMP and CSIS were so impressed that several officials made us standing offers to ply our new tradecraft under their auspices should we ever tire of politics. I suspect they weren't serious.

We were just wrapping up our final briefing with CSIS when Bradley Stanton's name flashed across my vibrating phone.

"Hi, Bradley."

"Well, you sure know how to upstage the Prime Minister," he said.

"Apologies for saving his life and catching the bad guys as they were about to escape," I replied, a little—or maybe a lot—peeved.

"Addison, I'm yanking your chain. You and Mountain Man Minister McLintock have done amazing work on this. And I can't believe what you did today," Bradley said. "Sorry it took me a little while to take you seriously. You've given me so many reasons in the past not to, it just took me a bit of time. I hope to be a better listener in the future."

"Wow, thanks, Bradley," I replied, surprised at his words. "But you eventually came on board and deserve some credit for forcing Coulombe, the RCMP, and CSIS to take this threat seriously. We could not have done that on our own."

"Okay, enough sucking up. I need you and the minister to get over here to the National Press Building. The Prime Minister, Minister Coulombe, and Ambassador Koskov are nearly finished explaining why there wasn't anyone in the Champlain Centre when it dropped into the river."

"Are we being open about the whole affair?" I asked.

"There's really no choice but to reveal all. It's being positioned as a master class in bilateral cooperative intelligence and security."

"I bet Coulombe is lapping it up," I said.

"Maybe, but the PM isn't happy, and he has already asked for a full investigation into why you and Angus had to freelance the whole effort on your own until you found C-4 in those beams and the alarms started ringing."

"So where is Pudovkin?"

"He left town as soon as the Chechens were arrested," Bradley said. "He wanted to transport them back to Russia on his own plane and deal with them there."

"I don't think that's even legal," I said.

"It's not. He took off for Moscow as soon as we refused to hand them over," Bradley said. "But he was quite emotional, and very grateful for your efforts and action-movie pyrotechnics. If you ever get tired of Canada, there's probably an FSB job waiting for you in Moscow."

"Actually, I prefer winters in Ottawa. And I may be the only living person ever to have said that," I replied. "So, what do you want Angus and me to do at this newser?"

"Just get over here, and answer questions as honestly and openly as you can without making Coulombe look like the imbecilic and vindictive asshole he is. And I know that's asking a lot. For better or worse, Angus and you are already the heroes here. The story of your abduction and the crazy shit you pulled at the airport is all out there now. There's even a video, shot by some guy in the airport control tower. So I actually wasn't kidding when I said you've upstaged the PM again. He's nowhere in this news cycle right now."

"Sorry about that."

I had to talk Angus into appearing at the media briefing, but when the Prime Minister wants something, even

Angus will eventually acquiesce. So there we were, just the two of us, seated at the table at the front of the National Press Theatre, with Canadian and Russian flags behind us. Fuelling the hero narrative were the bandages on both our heads—the power of the visual. Nothing says you risked your life and survived like a bandaged head.

Angus took the lead in responding to questions and for the most part adhered to the basic strategy we'd agreed to on the drive over. "Much of the credit for figuring out the plot, who was behind it, and where they might be found at the climactic moment, goes to my Chief of Staff, Daniel Addison," Angus said. "We were together for the entire affair, including an uncomfortable period when we were literally on top of one another in the trunk of a car. I think he has a future, if not in intelligence work, at least in writing thrillers."

Everyone laughed. Of course, I was asked to comment. Angus had briefly departed from our plan when he commended my efforts. I tried to get us back on track.

"Well, the minister is trying to shift attention away from his own important role in this," I began. "It was he who discovered the explosives stuffed into the very steel beams that secured the Champlain Centre to the cliff face. It was he who, against my advice and judgement, physically confronted the two Chechens in the basement of Centre Block. And it was he who, with no thought for his own life, or mine for that matter, drove a speeding car into the side of a plane in mid-takeoff just to keep it on the ground. I'd go into battle again with Angus McLintock any day. I just hope it's not any day soon."

Everyone laughed again. I noticed Coulombe standing along the side wall with other departmental officials, but he wasn't looking our way. I had hoped the day's events might have thawed our frosty rapport, but based on his scowl, I didn't think so.

Angus closed with a comment that came as no surprise, though we hadn't discussed it beforehand. Fortunately, I was in full agreement. "Ladies and gentlemen, in light of this long and free-ranging session, Daniel and I have agreed that we'll not again speak publicly about this affair, nor will we respond to related queries in the future, except for those posed as part of formal investigations undertaken by law enforcement agencies. We are eager to return to the important work that comes with our public service. Thank you."

By the time we escaped the Parliamentary Press Gallery, the iPhone video shot by the air traffic controller on duty had gone viral, racking up over six hundred thousand views in the first two hours. It's tough to keep a low profile when you're featured in a viral video on YouTube's front page. When I finally saw it, the whole thing was much more dramatic than I'd remembered, and I'd been there. The runway collision, the flying front fender, and the flipping Cessna were all just a giant fireball short of the Movie of the Week. I broke into a sweat and my heart pounded as I watched it, as I relived it.

"Suffering saints, that looks frightful," Angus said after viewing the video. "I cannae believe I did that. I obviously took utter leave of my senses. I'm sorry, lad, for risking your skin to ground that plane. I was operating on pure instinct, anger, and adrenalin. Not a healthy combination."

On the drive back to Cumberland, my phone rang and I answered on the hands-free system. "Daniel Addison."

"Daniel, I just had to call," said the voice I knew well. "Is Angus with you?"

"Aye, I'm here, too, Prime Minister."

"Good. I don't really know how to express this, but it seems clear that I owe you both my life, not to mention the lives of dozens of Canadians and Russians who would have been in the Champlain Centre at precisely the wrong time," the PM said. "It was extraordinarily brave of you to put yourselves in harm's way. I watched the video, like so many others have, but am still trying to process what I've seen."

"Thank you, Prime Minister, but there's no need to dwell on it. The deed's been done. It's over, we're all safe. And we're eager for life to return to a semblance of normality."

"You might not escape quite so easily. The President of Russia has been fully briefed, and I'm told he has also seen the video. I don't think he'll be satisfied with writing you a thank-you note."

"Ye gods, is there no way to slip this noose?" Angus asked.

"We'll do our best to honour your wishes, but Canadians and Russians want a chance to thank you and Daniel, too, for what you've done, at considerable risk to life and limb. So, I ask you to indulge our national and international need to register our gratitude."

"Of course, Prime Minister, but anything you can do to minimize the hype and hoopla would be grand and very much appreciated."

"We understand each other, Angus, and I'll do my level best," the PM said. "Further, I've asked a very smart retired B.C. Supreme Court Justice, Paul Wilder, to complete a quiet but thorough, objective, and fast investigation into the whole affair, including why CSIS and the RCMP were asleep at the switch, and MI6's role, too. I need his report quickly to strengthen my hand when dealing with the British PM. He has a lot of explaining to do. So, I'm afraid you'll be party to that undertaking as well. Again, gentlemen, I thank you and, without being melodramatic, the nation thanks you."

We said our goodbyes and I ended the call.

"Pomp and puffery! I cannot stomach it," Angus said after I hung up the phone. "Can we not just carry on as we did before? This is going to dog us for weeks, maybe months!"

"Angus, you saw the video. It could be years," I replied. "How did you expect the world to react? We just stopped the assassination of the Russian President. And without us, Eugene and Tatyana would have succeeded. That is an indisputable fact, supported by the building now resting on the bottom of the Ottawa River. It's naïve to think it's now over—this is an international incident that will be on the front pages of every newspaper in the world. Sorry, but if you really wanted to avoid all of this, walking into the cleaners' room to face Eugene and Tatyana probably wasn't the right decision. And ramming their plane didn't help much, either. Angus, the world is safer because you acted, but there are consequences, and we're about to find out how far-reaching they'll be."

Angus said nothing, which usually meant he was thinking about what I'd just said and finding some truth in it. Or, he may have just stopped listening and nodded off.

Five minutes later, we arrived at the Riverfront Seniors' Residence to see Vivian and Muriel, and Lindsay, who was still there from that morning. We'd just locked the car and started across the parking lot, which was surrounded by maple trees with buds ready to burst, when my phone buzzed again. I reached for it but realized quickly it wasn't my cellphone that was ringing. I fished the burner phone out of my coat pocket. I'd completely forgotten it was there.

"Hello, Fleming?"

"Yes, I'm here. Is Mr. McLintock with you?"

"Yes, standing right next to me. We're in the far corner of a parking lot, just the two of us. You're on speaker. No one is around, so you can speak freely."

"Two points. First, you did it. You stopped them," she said, though she didn't sound very happy. "I didn't expect you'd have to do it all on your own, and in such spectacular fashion. But somehow you did it."

"Aye, it was not how we saw it unfolding, but necessity demanded it," Angus said.

"Second, and more to the point, you betrayed me, and I want to know why."

Angus and I looked at one another, stunned. "We did nothing of the sort," Angus protested. "Our lives were made much more challenging because we would not reveal the provenance of our intelligence and thus could not effectively establish its credibility and legitimacy. It's why young Daniel and I were still on our own today for the finale. We never once gave you up, Ms. Fleming. You have my word on that."

"That's what you claim, but gentlemen, I have been fired, detained, and confined to my own home. I will soon be charged under the Official Secrets Act for unlawfully divulging information to you both. It is not yet in the public realm and may never be, but a stint in prison is not unlikely. There is no escaping the truth. You betrayed me, and despite how you saved the day, I'm livid and filled with regret for ever reaching out to you in the first place. You failed me."

Angus and I just looked at each other again, this time in shock and horror.

"We did not," I said. "We have been extremely careful this entire time. All I can think of is that someone at your end figured it out and blew the whistle, because we did not."

"I don't think so. There's no other explanation!" she snapped. "You promised not to give me up, yet you did. You stopped Tatyana and Eugene, and I'm grateful for that, but at a very high cost that I shall be paying personally."

"Ms. Fleming, we were not the source of your misfortune. If the Prime Minister or the Minister of Public Safety were with us now, they would both confirm that we never gave you up, as you put it. They were very angry with us for keeping your confidence, but we did."

"But I told you to wait a bit before acting. You'd just come from London. They put it together. Guessed it was MI6, and then you gave in and gave me up. They had you."

"No. No, that's not what happened. We had meetings in Rome, Berlin, and Paris, and reminded everyone about that. Angus even mentioned a recent trip to Washington to help throw them off your trail."

"But they knew the name Fleming. The only time I've used that alias in twenty years was when I gave you that name in the pub," she said. "I should never have chosen that name. Acton discovered that I used Fleming in the field two decades ago, and they already knew my theory, so the net closed on me quickly."

"We've never uttered the word Fleming in anyone else's presence since we met that night in London," Angus said. "We would never betray you, regardless of the stakes."

She was silent for a time. "Hm. Just a minute. If what you say is true, perhaps you didn't betray me knowingly. I should have thought of this," she said. "Listening devices."

"What? You think our conversations could have been bugged somehow? This isn't a movie," I said.

"No, it's not a movie. This is very, very real. And I'm looking at prison time because I tried to do the right thing and help an ally, as we are obligated to do under at least one multilateral intelligence-sharing agreement!"

"All right now. All right," Angus said gently. "Let's think this through."

"We cannot discount the notion that your conversations were bugged," she said. "If you are telling the truth, then it is the only possible explanation."

"There's no question. We're telling the truth. It's all I know how to do," Angus said. "So how do we proceed?"

"Do not under any circumstances go to your own intelligence service. They are one of the few entities that could employ listening devices. They cannot be trusted, particularly now, when we know our MI6 official, young Mr. Maynard, was in to see your minister. Do you know anyone outside of official channels who might help?"

I looked at Angus, and we both nodded. "Yes, I think we do."

I was horrified at this turn of events. We had done everything in our power to protect Fleming.

—

As soon as we stepped into the lounge, Lindsay set new land-speed records in at least a few seniors' homes when she shot across the floor and jumped into my arms. She said nothing as she squeezed me tightly. Her eyes were also squeezed tightly, but not enough to stop the few tears that drifted down her cheeks. "You're safe," she whispered. "That's all that matters."

"Linds, I'm fine. It was really not that bad," I said.

She pulled away and looked at me. "Daniel, I've seen the video."

"Oh," I said. "The one from the airport?"

"Yes, that one."

"Oh. Well, it looks worse than it was," I said. "Really."

"Is that right?"

"Linds, I'm fine, and so is Angus."

She said nothing and hugged me again.

When we made our way over to join Angus, Muriel, and Vivian, it was clear that the whole hero narrative hadn't quite reached Cumberland yet.

"What was in your head, Angus?" Muriel said, right up in his face. "It was a plane, speeding down a runway. We do have ways of tracking flying objects. They couldn't have gotten far. But no! You have to crash a car into it."

"I know, Muriel, dear, I know," Angus said. "I was there."

"Crashing a plane? It was insane, Angus. You both could have been killed," Muriel continued.

"If it's any consolation, there were several moments leading up to the climax when we might also have been killed, but that's not the point," Angus said. "The point is, we are safe. We are home. It is over. And the plot was foiled."

"And we're safe," I added.

"I just said that, lad."

"I know. I just thought it warranted reinforcement."

While Muriel was angry with us, Vivian sat beaming throughout this exchange. "You, gentlemen, made me so proud today," she said.

"Vivian!" Muriel snapped.

"Yes, yes, Muriel, I know," Vivian said. "You should never have gone that far and put yourselves at such risk. I agree. But you stopped them. In their tracks. You stopped them. Well done."

At their insistence, we retold the whole story, from our drive to Ottawa that morning right through to our return to Cumberland. Angus softened some of the points and tried not to dwell on the more dangerous aspects of our day—you know, like the big black gun.

As Angus fielded questions, I caught Vivian's eye and nodded towards the window. We both moved over to gaze out at the river.

"Thanks for all your advice and support through all of this," I said. "I'm quite sure that without it, there would have been a different outcome today."

"Yes, well, without my meddling, you might not have spent your day bouncing from one life-threatening situation to another."

"Well, it seems we're not quite finished with this caper," I said. "Our friend at MI6 who first briefed us in the pub has been betrayed, fired, and detained, and will soon face charges that could put her in prison. Not exactly a happy retirement. For obvious reasons, she blames us."

Vivian did not look surprised. "But surely neither you nor Angus breathed a word beyond our little circle. You certainly didn't give her up."

"Of course not," I said emphatically. "So, Fleming feels the only other logical explanation is that some of the conversations Angus and I have had were bugged somehow."

"Call Newton," she said. "She's a full-service operative and can sweep for listening devices."

"But where should she look?"

"Does the RCMP still sweep ministers' offices periodically?" she asked.

"Yes, and our government-issue cellphones are checked now and then, too."

"I figured as much. I think it's worth checking Angus's home and that boathouse apartment of yours that Lindsay speaks so fondly of. But if I were trying to listen in on your conversations with Angus, the best place to plant a listening device would be your ministerial car. You commute together often and, ironically, you probably feel safe, secure, and able to speak freely on those drives. Am I right?"

"Shite. It's where we do most of our talking. And recently, our driver hasn't been with us, so it's been just the two of us, no inhibitions, no reticence. Holding nothing back," I said. "Shite."

"It would explain a lot," said Vivian.

"Who's behind it, though?"

"Come on, Daniel. It should be obvious. Who has access to your ministerial car?"

"Shite."

"Newton actually lives out this way. Give her a call. Don't forget to mention Harpo," Vivian said.

"By the way, I've been meaning to ask, what's the significance of that code name, anyway? Are you a big fan of the Marx Brothers?"

"Hardly." She rolled her eyes. "Reading it backwards might give you a clue."

"Riiiight." I smiled. "I like a code name that's not random."

"Not much about this line of work is random," she replied.

"The scoundrel," Angus said when I told him about my conversation with Vivian. "I'll drive the Buick home. You go with Lindsay, so we're not tempted to talk in the car."

"I'll contact Newton and get her here in the morning, if she's around. And no talking around your house or the boathouse until Newton has swept them."

"Aye."

Lindsay drove, and held my hand much of the way home.

"We can talk in general terms about today in the apartment, given that it's all over the news," I said before getting out of her car. "But nothing sensitive until we determine that there are no bugs."

"Then let's cook that frozen pizza and head for the dock," Lindsay said. "It's a nice night."

I felt weird being inside the boathouse knowing that someone could be listening to everything we were saying and doing. I wanted to look under the bed, inside the light fixtures, and behind the paintings. Those were the kinds of spots I'd seen bugs placed in movies. But I figured I'd leave that to the professional.

Twenty minutes later, we took our pizza down the dock and sat in the two Adirondack chairs facing the peaceful river. There was a lovely breeze and we could hear the water lapping on the shore. We pushed our chairs close together so our fingers could interlace on the broad, flat arms, and I could feel the stress and trauma of the day drain out of me. At that moment, there was no place I'd rather be.

The pizza failed to match the other idyllic elements of the moment. After my first bite, I checked the crust to make sure I'd separated the cardboard box from the actual item we were supposed to eat. I had but was only convinced upon physical confirmation.

Lindsay turned in her chair to face me, fixing me with an unwavering gaze. Uh-oh.

"I was just thinking back to our conversation this morning, before I left for Grandma's," Lindsay said.

My spidey senses were tingling. "Right, I remember a really nice hug," I said, steeling myself.

"I remember more about our actual words," she said. "I remember imploring you not to do anything crazy and not to make bad decisions. I remember asking you to be safe and come back home."

"And here I am, back home safe and sound," I said. "Mission accomplished."

"I remember reminding you that you aren't an action hero . . ."

"Lindsay—"

"And I remember reminding you that CSIS and the RCMP, who know quite a bit about this sort of thing, were on the job now, so you and Angus could back off, withdraw, and start acting like an MP and his Chief of Staff again."

"Linds—"

Then she began squeezing my hand really tightly. "Then Muriel, Vivian, and I watched as the Champlain Centre exploded and landed in the river."

"I know, I know—"

"And you didn't call. I didn't know where you were. I didn't know if you were safe. You didn't call."

"Yes, but there's an explanation for—"

"Of course there's an explanation for it," she said, in a severe tone of voice she'd never used with me before. "You didn't call because you were chasing Eugene and Tatyana through the halls of Centre Block and accosting them in the basement. Oh yes, that's when Tatyana pulled a gun on you. A *gun!*"

"Lindsay, please—"

"I'm not finished yet," she said, clenching her teeth. "And you didn't call me after that whole gun thing because they took your phone, tied you up, and piled you into the trunk of a beat-up car."

"Yes, but it felt like she was driving very carefully."

"Not funny, Daniel, and I'm not done yet here. Not by a long shot."

"Sorry. Carry on."

Her voice was getting louder. "And *then* comes the moment when you were finally safe. The bad guys were in their little plane and moving away from you. That's right, they were going in the other direction. So, it was time for another decision. Do we escape with our lives and alert the professionals? You know, CSIS, the RCMP, the police, airport security, the CIA, maybe the Avengers? Yes, that sounds like the prudent, safe, and *mature* decision to make. But wait, instead, *why don't we drive the car as fast as it will go and crash into the plane just as it's taking off?* Yes, let's do that."

"We weren't going that fast," I said.

"I watched the video, several times."

"Right."

"Almost there now. Stay with me," she continued. "So, the plane is on its roof and you are still in a damaged but functional automobile. It was the perfect time to zip across the airport, out of the gate, and to safety. Seemed like a good decision to make after a whole slew of very bad decisions. But hang on, I think we have time for *one more* colossally bad decision. What about driving the car right up to the door of the plane where Tatyana—you know, the one with the big gun—is seated, and almost certainly crazy angry at you for stopping her escape? Excellent choice."

Lindsay finally stopped. It's hard to speak when you're on the verge of tears.

"Lindsay, please," I began. "I'm sorry. You make it sound like Angus and I carefully weighed all the factors at each of the many critical moments in the day's events and calmly and coldly, in possession of all the facts, with lots of time to consider the consequences, decided to make the most dangerous call possible at each juncture."

"Well, that's how it appeared to the person who loves you, and was waiting for you, and worrying about you, and watching crash videos starring you," she said, her voice cracking.

"I'm sorry. I understand that now," I said. "But it wasn't like that. You may not believe me, but when we were outside that room in the basement of Centre Block, with Eugene and Tatyana on the other side of the door, I pleaded with Angus that it was the time to retreat, to let the RCMP take it from there. Angus even agreed. But the RCMP wasn't there. Angus was. And he went through that door. That was really the key moment."

Lindsay was quiet but still holding my hand, which I took to be a positive sign.

"I could have turned and run for help at that moment, and left Angus there alone with two people who had come very close to killing their own President. Maybe I should have. But I didn't. If something terrible had happened to Angus after I bailed on him, I'd have to live with that for the rest of my life."

Lindsay squeezed my hand.

"After that, everything happened so fast. And short of wrestling the steering wheel from Angus, I was kind of just along for the ride. And as you know, that's generally what life with Angus is all about."

Lindsay then stood up and sat on my lap, her arms around me and her head on my shoulder.

"When it was over, and the RCMP cars were surrounding the plane, and we were safe, seeing you, and holding you, and talking to you was all I wanted to do. That's when we recovered our phones and I called," I said softly.

"I've spent the last several hours switching back and forth between being so proud of what you did and so angry at you for doing it and risking what we have." Her voice was almost a whisper.

"What about Angus?"

She had the grace to laugh. "Oh, I haven't even started with Angus. This was just my warm-up," she said. "But when I hear you explain it all . . ."

"You're moved and overcome with new understanding and empathy."

"No, I'm still angry," she said. "But I wouldn't have left a friend in that basement room, either. I would have followed you into the fire, and I know you would have followed me. I get that. And I'm glad you were so brave to stand with Angus, even if it wasn't the safest call."

"I've heard that traumatic events can force a new perspective on those who have lived through them," I said, looking into Lindsay's eyes. "I understand that now. It's clearer to me tonight than it was this morning just how much you mean to me, and that what we have is what I want."

"I was thinking the same thing as I watched your car slam into the side of that plane on YouTube." She smiled. "In the end, you're safe, you're home, and we're together."

"That's all I ever want," I said. In a Hollywood rom-com, that would have been the moment for the couple to kiss. I try never to miss those opportunities.

"Staying on the topic of being together, how goes your thinking about next September? Are you leaning towards one school over the others?"

"I keep going back and forth," she replied. "Every day a different school seems like the right choice. Oh, I don't know. It's a big decision—and a difficult one."

"Linds, you know I'll be wherever you end up. So take me out of your figuring and make the right call for yourself.

I'm going to be where you are anyway, for as long as you'll have me."

I felt and heard her deeply sigh as she nestled in closer. She squeezed my hand again. We stayed like that on the dock in happy reverie for the next hour.

Later that evening, my personal cellphone buzzed. The call came up as unidentified, so I quickly stepped back outside and down onto the dock, away from the prying ears of potential bugs.

"Daniel Addison."

"Newton."

"Thanks for calling."

"No worries, and yes, I can sweep for unauthorized listening devices," Newton said.

"I see you've already spoken to Harpo," I said. "Do you think you could come by first thing in the morning to, you know, sweep Angus's house and my apartment, which is at the same address, and take a look at our phones and cars?" I asked.

"How about seven o'clock?"

Ouch. I didn't expect that early. "Yep, that works," I replied. "Thanks so much."

"No worries. It shouldn't take too long."

If the boathouse was in fact bugged, whoever was listening later that night would have heard two people very happy to be safe, home, and together.

DIARY

Saturday, May 10

My love,

When last I wrote, I told you not to worry your heart, that we were being careful and sensible. To be fair, we had a slight departure from this cautious path. I'm to blame, but before you start to chiding, all ended well, and despite the fiery destruction of a building that deserved its demise, no hands were injured or lost. I did bump my head a wee bit, but 'tis nothing.

I reckon you watched events unfold, so you know I was a tad impetuous and took action that in some quarters might have been considered reckless at best, and idiotic at worst. I tend towards the reckless camp. Yet it all ended well. We stopped those responsible for the plot, and I even got to ram a nearly airborne getaway plane with a car at high speed. What's left to experience, I ask you?

As is his custom, Daniel was a stalwart co-conspirator with only an occasional quivering bottom lip, to which he was justifiably entitled. He deserves the credit for deducing that the Peace Tower was the assassins' deadly perch. Nearly one thousand security forces were searching high and

*low for them, but just not high enough. Young
Daniel cracked the code. Aye, it's true, I should
have seen it. But that's what Daniel does: he
fills in my many gaps, and I hope I plug a few
of his. Together, I'd hazard, we're a potent team.
But we're not done yet. An injustice in London is
imperilling the good feelings today's events brought.
So, we're not quite clear of the woods just yet.*

*I fear the next few days will be filled with micro-
phones, lights, sycophants, and fulsome praise,
and I cannae abide the lot of it. But I'm safe,
Marin dear, and still in your thrall.*

AM

CHAPTER 11

Angus and I were waiting on the front steps of his house when Newton came down the driveway the next morning at seven o'clock sharp. She was not what we were expecting, but the way the previous three weeks had unfolded, we weren't surprised in the least. Firstly, she arrived on a bicycle. It was a small bike—likely designed for an adolescent—but it was big for her, and she had added blocks of wood to the pedals so she could reach them. Behind her bike she pulled a two-wheel trailer of sorts, presumably bearing her equipment. She also wore a bike helmet that rode down low and almost covered her eyes. It was capacious to say the least. It would have fit André the Giant's gargantuan head with room to spare. She pulled up to us and, while still moving, swung her right leg up and over the seat and executed a perilous though practised descent from the bike. There she stood, thin and sinewy, and all of about four foot eleven, wearing green cargo pants, a black T-shirt, and a grey fleece tied around her waist. Tiny little hiking shoes were on her feet. She held her index finger to her lips and motioned us further along the driveway as she pushed her bike and trailer rig. We silently followed. When we were about halfway between the house and the boathouse, she stopped and turned to us.

"Gentlemen."

Up close, I guessed she was in her early forties, though it was hard to tell. She doffed her punch-bowl helmet and hooked it on the handlebars before shaking out her hair, which was curly brown with streaks of grey. There was no discernible style—it was just curly all over.

"Good morning," I said. "Newton, I presume."

"Correctamundo," she said. "Sorry about the little walk, but until I've cleared the house, we should not be talking anywhere near it."

"Makes sense. I'm Daniel Addison." I offered my hand.

"I figured. Nice to see you in person and not just on YouTube," she replied, and shook my hand. I winced. She not only had André the Giant's helmet, but she had his grip, too.

"And this is the Honourable Angus McLintock," I said.

"Angus will do," he said, shaking Newton's hand. He winced, too.

"Oh, I know you both. Most of the country knows you now. You had quite an adventure yesterday."

"Yes, well, we're hoping there'll be fewer days like that in our future," Angus replied.

"I thought you were awesome. You kicked some serious Chechen ass," she said. "I mean it. Over the years I've worked with hundreds of—well, let's call them operatives—and your performance yesterday was one of the most impressive I've ever seen."

"Beginners' luck," Angus said humbly.

"Maybe, but I wouldn't want to mess with you, beginner or not."

"Anyway . . ." I nudged, eager to get going.

"Right, let's get moving," she said. "I'll start with the house and the apartment, though I doubt we'll find anything there. Then I'll check your cellphones, personal and government, and any landlines. We'll finish up with your cars. It'll take me an hour or so. You can talk out loud as you normally would. It would be weird if you didn't—it might set off alarms for whoever might be listening. But don't say anything that's sensitive—not in the house, the apartment, or near the cars—anywhere, really, until we know what we're dealing with."

Lindsay was still sound asleep, so Newton started in Angus's place while we sat on his back deck overlooking the river, munching on toasted bagels. There was a soft and rolling mist on the water near the shore. It wouldn't last for long before the sun asserted itself. It looked like it would be a beautiful, clear Sunday.

"All clear," Newton reported a little while later on the deck. "I checked all the rooms except the basement. I didn't find anything. You can talk in there till your heart's content. That's how my mother would have put it."

I went over to the boathouse to rouse Lindsay from her sleep, which is not nearly as straightforward as it seems. This particular morning it involved executing a rather complicated set of actions we'd come up with together, including playing different ringtones from my iPhone, whispering into her ear, and gently prodding her shoulder blades with one hand while slowly exposing her bare feet to the chilled morning air with the other.

Ten minutes later Lindsay and I were sitting on the dock together. She was clad in sweatpants and a hoodie and cradled a coffee in her hands. Newton started in our apartment and then swept Angus's workshop below. Twenty minutes later, she joined us by the water.

"Newton, this is Lindsay," I said, and friendly nods were exchanged, which alone severely taxed Lindsay's faculties so soon after waking up.

"All clear up top and below," Newton said. "And may I ask, *what* is that vehicle in the workshop?"

"Oh, that's *Baddeck 1*," I said. "It's the hovercraft Angus designed and built."

"Oh, yeah! I remember now. He flew up the frozen river and saved the day, right?"

"That he did."

"Very cool. Okay, phones next."

"They're all up at Angus's house."

I left Lindsay on the dock, still semi-conscious, and led Newton back up the hill. Angus stood guard over all our phones, which we had lined up on a table on the deck. Angus and I stepped inside, because it seemed bad form to watch as Newton undertook what was probably a secret and perhaps proprietary procedure. A few minutes later, she joined us in the living room and handed back all of our personal and government phones.

"Nothing. All clear," she said. "I'll do all the cars now and that should just about do it. I'll need your car keys. I like to have the engine idling when I sweep the cars. Sometimes the listening devices are programmed to start when the car is running."

Newton started with my CX-5 and then moved to Angus's Camry. She was leaving the big Buick for last.

"What happens if she finds nothing?" I asked Angus.

"Then we're back to being the rogues who betrayed Fleming," he replied grimly.

Twenty minutes later, Newton was done.

"Your own cars are clear," she said. Then she paused. "But I got a hit on the government car. Three hits, to be more precise."

Angus and I looked at each other with our mouths open.

"Can you make more sense of that for those of us who are espionage neophytes?" Angus asked.

"There are three bugs, three listening devices, planted in your Buick," Newton said. "One is in the rear-view mirror, a common and very good central location to cover off the front seat, and the other two are in the back seat, hidden below those hooks that hold your dry-cleaning, one on either side."

Even though Vivian had mentioned this possibility, still I was stunned, and by the look on Angus's face, he was a tad taken aback, too.

"You're telling us you actually found three bugs—functioning, operational listening devices—in our government car?" I asked. Until that moment, I had blocked out the suggestion that this was possible.

"Exactly. Yes, you have clearly understood the two very simple sentences I just spoke."

"I can't believe it," I said, ignoring her sarcasm.

"I don't know for sure, but it looks like a domestic job," Newton said. "It's a government car, so tough for foreign agencies to get to. And the devices themselves are the same kind CSIS has used in the past."

Angus just shook his head, looking angry and sad at the same time.

"So, Vivian was right. The official car of a minister of the Crown has been bugged by our own intelligence agency," I said in disbelief.

"In my experience, CSIS operatives would never do something like this on their own authority," Newton said. "They're being directed."

Again, Angus and I looked at one another, drawing the same conclusion.

"This takes a simple falling out, a professional difference of opinion, a petty feud, and hoists it onto a whole new and frightening plane," Angus said.

"What a complete asshole" was how I put it.

"Yes, but now you have the upper hand," Newton said. "You know about the bugs, but the person listening doesn't know you know. That puts a completely different spin on things."

I nodded, the wheels in my head turning.

We thanked her profusely and offered her payment of various kinds, including cash, single-malt scotch, and left-over spaghetti, but she would hear none of it. As before, she claimed it was a favour for Vivian—sorry, *Harpo*—and that she was happy to do it. She packed up her gear, donned her mega-helmet, climbed up onto her bike, and pedalled down the road. By then it was about eight thirty.

"I have an idea," I said when Angus closed the door.

"I figured you might."

If Emile Coulombe had in fact ordered the bug infestation in our ministerial car, his days as a member of Cabinet were numbered—provided we could prove it. Deniability was a precious resource for politicians, and Coulombe would certainly have left himself an escape route.

It took Angus and me a good hour to map out the plan. I believe they call the approach a "sting operation." But we couldn't do it alone. After we ran the plan by Lindsay, she was on board in an instant. She put a call in to Muriel, who we hoped would be a co-conspirator.

We needed a venue that was well known and accessible but private. I called someone I'd known for a long time: Gina, the manager of Mamma Teresa's on Somerset, a famous restaurant frequented by politicians and power brokers for decades. They had a separate bar and private dining area on the second floor that would serve our purpose well. Gina agreed to let us use the private dining area at noon. With our venue in place, we had to deal with the most important part of the operation.

"Addison," Bradley said when he answered my call. "You and your guy are dominating my morning media clips yet again. Your minister has an uncanny gift for drawing attention to himself."

"Good morning to you, too, Bradley. And Angus considers it a curse, not a gift," I replied. "He hates it, as difficult as it might be for you to understand that."

"Yeah, well, you've completely pushed the PM's great performance at the G8 not just off the front pages but out of the media entirely. Congratulations!" he snarked.

"Bradley, we just stopped the assassination of President Pudovkin and likely the death of the Prime Minister too. Surely that's more important."

"Addison, we're thankful for your role, but that's old news now, overtaken by your airport *Mission: Impossible* exploits."

"Bradley, we don't have time for this," I said. "There's a final piece in this little melodrama, and we'd like to bring down the curtain on it this afternoon, with your help."

"Jesus, Addison, it's Sunday."

"I think you're going to want to hear this."

I heard Bradley pause, then sigh deeply.

"Okay, okay. I'm listening."

"Courtesy of an independent security contractor, we just learned this morning that Coulombe has planted listening devices in our ministerial car. Three of them. This explains how and why our original source was betrayed, fired on the eve of her retirement after a long and storied career at MI6, and committed to house arrest, and now faces the prospect of imprisonment under the Official Secrets Act."

"That is a serious allegation. How do you know it was Coulombe?" Bradley was serious now.

"Because it makes all the pieces fit perfectly in a very complicated puzzle," I replied.

"Saying that does not constitute proof. Coulombe is many things, but stupid isn't one of them."

"You're right, Bradley. And that's why we're setting a little trap to give us the indisputable proof that he's behind this."

I told Bradley about Thomas Maynard, the MI6 guy in the British High Commission in Ottawa, and his meeting with Coulombe. On the strength of that news, Bradley agreed to contact the Ottawa Police and have the hapless and wrongly accused Carleton professor released. After I'd finished explaining the gambit Angus and I had cooked up, and Bradley's role in it, we had him hooked. I knew he'd love the idea of being in the room when a deserving jackass plummeted from his pedestal. Of course, there remained a slim chance that Angus and I had made one extrapolation too many as we analyzed and interpreted all we'd learned in the past twenty-four hours. But I buried that negative thought down deep and focused on the plan.

We reviewed our scripts one last time, and then, shortly after eleven, with Angus at the wheel, we pulled out in the Buick and turned towards Ottawa. Lindsay left five minutes later to pick up Muriel. It took me a few minutes to figure out where to hold my iPhone so it could capture, in living colour, the performance we were about to give. In the end it seemed easiest to brace the phone against the passenger-side window. I hit the big red button on the screen, and we began.

"I still can't believe it," I said.

"Aye, neither can I," Angus replied, per our script. "Emile and I have never really seen eye to eye, but to do this is as unbelievable as it is unconscionable."

"Clearly the PM is taking it seriously, calling a meeting on a Sunday. I've never heard of a gathering like this."

"Why would he convene it at Mamma Teresa's, of all places?"

"The PM says it's too sensitive to discuss on the Hill and that Coulombe has eyes everywhere and would find out about it. So meeting off-site makes sense. Bradley is even driving the PM in his own car, without security, to keep a lower profile. I don't think that's ever happened, either."

"Poor Emile. He won't know what hit him," Angus said. "Lad, are you watching the clock?"

"We're fine. The meeting's at noon. We'll make it in good time. Mamma T's doesn't open until five, so we'll have the private dining room upstairs to ourselves."

"I dinnae think he can survive this, poor wretch."

"Angus, he brought it on himself, and he deserves whatever the PM has in mind for him."

"Aye. I still dinnae think he can survive it."

I ended my video recording and pocketed my iPhone. We moved on to chat about other things, including reminiscing about the airport adventure of the day before, just to keep it all sounding natural and realistic.

We arrived at Mamma T's at 11:35 and parked in the lot kitty-corner to the restaurant. I recognized Bradley's car right away. We went around the back of the restaurant to the deliveries door, which was open. Gina met us inside.

"Gina, hi," I said, leaning in to kiss her cheek.

"Good to see you still in one piece, Daniel. You're a hero."

"That would be my partner." I replied, pointing to Angus. "Gina, this is Angus McLintock."

"Is this a Comic-Con Ottawa meet-up?" she asked. "Are there more superheroes coming?"

"Alas, no." Angus shook her hand, bowing slightly. "Thanks so much for giving us the room."

"We really appreciate it," I said. "It's important, and very, very hush-hush."

"No problem, Daniel. I have plenty of work to do anyway. I'll be tucked away in the office near the front. Your secret is safe."

"Would you mind unlocking the front door? We're expecting at least one, perhaps two, more guests anytime now," I said. "As soon as they're in, you can lock it again."

"Sure."

We walked up the stairs to the private dining room and bar. Sure enough, Bradley Stanton was lolling in the chair at the head of the table. He was dressed casually. It was a Sunday morning, after all. The Prime Minister's security chief, Murray Cochrane, was leaning against the bar.

"Addison, Minister, good to see you, as always," Bradley said. "I sure hope something happens here. I'd still be in bed otherwise."

"Well, if it's any consolation, Mr. Stanton, we, too, hope something happens here. I'm not sure of our next steps if we end up passing the time here by ourselves. This is our only plan."

I stepped behind the bar and propped my phone up against the draught-beer tap, then checked to see if the camera view was wide enough to take in the whole table. It was. Then I walked out of the private dining room and over to a window on the west side of the restaurant. As planned, Lindsay's car was parked on O'Connor close to the intersection, a spot strategically chosen for its good view of the corner and down both Somerset West and O'Connor. They weren't looking my way, but I could clearly see Lindsay in the driver's seat with Muriel next to her. If I squinted, I could even make out the cellphone in Lindsay's hand. Just then, her text arrived. *In position* was all it said. It was 11:55.

Back in the dining room, Bradley was talking quietly on his phone. He moved the phone from his ear, pushed a button, and laid it on the table in front of him. Murray Cochrane was still leaning on the bar, and Angus was standing beside the table. I made my way back behind the bar and stood beside the beer tap.

"We're all set here," Bradley said, pointing to his phone. "We know the drill."

"Greetings, Prime Minister," Angus said.

"Hello, Angus," said the PM through Bradley's phone. "This is very troubling indeed, if your suppositions are correct. I confess a large part of me hopes that no one else joins this meeting."

"Well, Prime Minister, if he doesnae show up, our mystery remains unsolved," Angus replied. "The truth is all we're seeking here."

"Agreed. But the truth isn't always easy to accept."

"Aye, Prime Minister, you're dead right, there. But it remains the truth."

That's when we heard the footsteps approaching. It did not sound like Gina calmly climbing the stairs to see if we needed anything else. No, it was more like a stampede of water buffalo thundering across the savannah. My heart pounded. I pushed the Record button on my phone.

The door flew open and banged against the wall, and there stood Emile Coulombe, cutting a fine figure in his sweatpants and a collared golf shirt, perspiring and panting from the exertion of it all. Jocelyn Massé appeared in the doorway a few seconds later, in jeans and a black sweater.

"Minister, I'm very sorry to see you here," Bradley said, shaking his head. "Please come in and sit down."

"I'll stand. What's going on here?" he snapped. He and Jocelyn walked into the dining room, and Angus moved over to close the door behind them.

"Minister, what brings you here this morning?" Bradley asked.

"A strong suspicion that these two are up to no good," Coulombe said, pointing to Angus and me.

"Minister, I must ask you, how did you know we were here?"

"That's not important," he replied. "What is important is that I am being set up and framed by these two."

"Why do you say that? What do you mean? And please, be specific."

"I mean whatever they have said about me is a lie, and I will vigorously defend myself." Emile seemed close to frothing at the mouth.

"Again, Minister, I must ask you, how did you know we were meeting here this morning, and that Minister McLintock and Addison were involved?" Bradley spoke in a severe, almost chilling tone.

"I—it's—it's my job to know," he stammered. "I have a ministerial mandate to know."

At this point, Bradley nodded to Murray Cochrane, who approached the table and sat down.

"Minister, as the Prime Minister's security chief, I've been part of planning this little event this morning," he began, looking straight at Coulombe. "Minister, based on the evidence, the only way you could have known about this meeting, and that it somehow involved you, was if you eavesdropped on the carefully scripted conversation that you recorded this morning via three listening devices secretly planted in a federal Cabinet minister's official car. There is no other explanation."

Coulombe flinched, then shook his head vigorously. Jocelyn's face was ashen.

"Minister, this is outrageous, unprecedented, and potentially criminal behaviour," Bradley said before Coulombe could speak. "The Prime Minister knows about this and, in fact, has been listening in via speakerphone. I suspect he has something to say. Prime Minister, you have the floor."

"Emile, I can barely contain myself. I'm shocked, disappointed, and as angry as I've ever been," the PM said. "I expect your resignation within the hour, attributed to personal reasons, while we figure out how to handle this to protect the government and our relationship with a key ally. Mr. Cochrane will escort you home so you can draft your letter. You are well advised not to open your mouth about this to anyone until we've sorted through the myriad communications problems you have single-handedly created. I also expect you to disclose to Mr. Cochrane the full extent of your illegal eavesdropping operations." He paused, and for a few seconds, his heavy breathing was all we could hear.

"Bugging a fellow Cabinet minister's car? Good God, Emile, what were you thinking?"

In a split second, Coulombe crumbled. His shoulders sagged and his face drained of colour to a deathly pale. "I will say nothing without my lawyer," he replied, looking at the floor.

"Well, I don't care if you say nothing more right now, but you will draft and deliver your resignation letter within the hour, or I will announce your firing and the reasons for it," the Prime Minister said sternly.

Coulombe turned and left the room, Jocelyn and Murray following close behind.

"Are they gone?" the Prime Minister asked.

"Yes, sir, they are," replied Angus as he closed the dining room door again.

"I don't know what to say, Daniel and Angus, except that you have done exemplary investigative work to bring the truth to light. Without you two, we'd never have known, and Emile Coulombe would still be out there violating the sanctity of Cabinet and the rights of ministers. On behalf of Canadians, for the second time in as many days, I thank you both for your diligence and intelligence in support of the national interest."

"Prime Minister, I'm quite sure I speak for young Daniel when I say we were just doing what we considered to be right and just. You should expect that from any elected member."

"Thank you, Prime Minister," I said. "But while you're on the line, Angus and I will want to talk to you about our MI6 contact, whose life has been turned upside down simply because she acted honourably when surrounded by unscrupulous colleagues. We think we have some leverage now with Downing Street that might help our friend. Without her, the plot that was foiled yesterday might actually have succeeded."

"By all means, Daniel," the Prime Minister said. "Set it up with Bradley."

The gathering broke up after that. Before we left, Bradley was generous in his comments about our morning's work. I wondered if we finally might be overcoming the central issue that had always divided us—that Bradley just didn't much like me, and I didn't much like him. But time would tell.

Lindsay and Muriel were still sitting patiently in the Honda Civic parked out front.

"He made quite an entrance when he arrived," Lindsay said through her open window, as Angus and I stood on the sidewalk. "He screeched to a stop, two wheels on the curb in a no parking zone, and flew into the restaurant."

"His face was the colour of a freshly boiled lobster, only more vivid," Muriel added. "You should have seen it."

"We actually did, about ten seconds after you saw it," Angus said.

"We knew you'd been successful when he appeared a few minutes later, a mere shell of his former, aggressive self," Lindsay said.

"I'll say," Muriel said. "He looked utterly defeated."

"For good reason," I said. "Did you manage to record his arrival and exit?"

"The whole thing," Lindsay said. "He was in too much of a hurry to notice when he pulled up, and seemed oblivious to everyone and everything when he came back down. I'll upload it and send it to you when we get back."

"Thank you both for efforts far beyond the call of duty," Angus said. "We couldnae have done all this without you. We're both in your debt, and frankly, Canadians are, too."

"Ah, that's enough of that," Muriel said. "This is the most fun I've had since the campaign."

I kissed Lindsay through the open window, bumping my head on the door in the process—but it was worth it. She pulled away to drive Muriel back home.

I slid into the driver's seat for our return trip to Cumberland. The day had seemed long, yet it was still not even one o'clock. Following Newton's instructions, Angus, screwdriver in hand, proceeded to remove and disable the three listening devices, all of which were hardwired into the Buick's electrical system, suggesting it was a time-consuming job that could not have been done by anyone other than CSIS personnel. It was nice to be able to speak freely, without fear of being recorded.

"Thank goodness he was listening," I said as we drove along Highway 417 to connect with 174. "By the time we reached Mamma T's, I was having doubts we were right."

"Aye, the stakes were high. But our man Emile came through. It was a stunner, though, when he burst into the room. I could scarcely believe my eyes, yet the airtight logic of it all made it inevitable. 'Twas very strange."

"And we have it all in high-definition video," I said. "Okay, shall we call her?"

"Aye."

I pulled out the burner phone and handed it to Angus. He opened it and hit the Dial Last Call button. It rang twice before she answered.

"I hope you have good news, gentlemen, because I'm a little short of that commodity right now."

"Hello, Fleming," Angus said. "We're pleased to report that we do have glad tidings to convey."

"My ears, mind, and heart are open."

"I'll give you the headlines and then let Daniel provide the more detailed briefing. To start, you were absolutely correct. There were no fewer than three state-of-the-art listening devices hardwired into my ministerial vehicle—the one Daniel and I used frequently in the last few weeks. When alone in the car, we've spoken often of this entire affair, mentioned your name on more than one occasion, and, if I'm not mistaken, we've even called you while driving back home. In light of the cozy relationship Minister Coulombe has with Mr. Maynard of the British High Commission, it is no wonder your boss of dubious distinction, Mr. Acton, tied all of this back to you."

"It's the perfect storm, and I seem to be huddled in its eye," she said.

"Through a brilliant trap that Daniel cooked up and that we just finished executing," Angus continued, "the less-than-Honourable Emile Coulombe's illegal eaves-dropping was completely exposed, in front of the Prime Minister, no less. Coulombe will resign from Cabinet within the hour. Finally, the Prime Minister has agreed to meet with Daniel and me to discuss how we can help restore your good name in your own country. MI6's role in creating false evidence and working to ease the path of our Chechen friends gives us great bargaining strength with your government. So, we are optimistic that your reputation in MI6 will soon be justly rehabilitated and rendered even more lustrous."

"Be still my galloping heart," she said, clearly pleased. "This Coulombe chap actually admitted to bugging your automobile?"

"He didn't officially confess it, but the proof that he knew of it, and made use of the information gleaned therefrom, is bulletproof," I said.

"Gentlemen, it seems you were equal to this task, even if we got off to a bit of a rocky start. I'm grateful for your efforts on my behalf, but the charges I'm facing are daunting, to say the least."

"Fleming, we're dealing directly with the Prime Minister, who will soon be dealing directly with your Prime Minister. We are hopeful, even optimistic, that we can make positive strides to absolve you of any wrongdoing. Canada owes you a great deal. Because of you, our Prime Minister is still alive."

"I leave it to you, gentlemen, and have learned not to doubt your abilities."

Back at home, Lindsay arrived at the same time as we did, and within ten minutes, she was hunkered down at our kitchen table with books and papers strewn everywhere, making final revisions to her thesis.

"Thanks for all you've done in the last two weeks," I said, standing behind her and rubbing her shoulders. "I'm sorry it's taken you away from your paper."

"I wouldn't have missed the excitement for anything. It was amazing to be part of the sting today, and Grandma was thrilled. But I do need to get this done."

"Understood. I'll get out of your way and see you later."

I grabbed a can of frozen lemonade from our freezer— which is where we like to keep our frozen lemonade—and climbed back up the hill to Angus's.

"Lunch?" I asked when he answered the door.

"Just tackling said same," he replied, walking back to the kitchen.

He was making a couple of grilled ham and cheese sand- wiches in a cast iron fry pan. I made another two, and in under ten minutes we were eating on the deck. For some who live on the river, the stunning vista can fade and even disappear through constant exposure. But not for me, and not for Angus. We'd spent hours in that exact spot talking over important and not-so-important issues, our eyes fixed on the glory of the river.

"Two ideas have struck me since arriving home from our latest coup," Angus said, "and I've already put one in motion."

"Do they involve resting, undisturbed, for extended peri- ods of time?" I asked hopefully.

"We've plenty of time for indolence later, lad."

"Somehow I knew you were going to say that."

"First, I'm hosting a thank-you dinner this very evening for the three women in our lives who have helped us through the odyssey of these recent weeks. Without Muriel, Vivian, and Lindsay, we'd quite possibly be planning a state funeral for the Prime Minister right about now."

"Dinner is a great idea. Happy to co-host and co-prepare," I said. "What are we having?"

"I've been thawing a standing rib roast in the fridge for three days now. I pulled it out when I got home, and it's currently resting in the sink on its way to room temperature. And we've got plenty of spuds, some brussels sprouts I picked up at the market a few days ago, and enough carrots to tide us over."

"I'm very good at making gravy," I said. "Except for that time when I mistook icing sugar for flour. And that other time I mistook cornstarch for flour. Other than those two incidents, I'm very good at making gravy."

"I'll make Marin's famous coffee cake for dessert. It's a snap, if I avoid your mistake with the flour."

"Should I call Muriel and Vivian?" I asked.

"I'm way ahead of you, lad. I called them about two minutes before you rapped on my door. They're pumped and primed. You have only to persuade the lovely and talented Lindsay to make the ascent from the boathouse."

"She's knee-deep in her thesis right now, but she has to eat sometime, right?"

"I'll just go and get the beast in the oven. It'll need about two and a half hours."

I looked at my watch. "So we should be back here by four?"

"Ah, no. I'm going to use the timer to start cooking the roast at three thirty, for you and I will not be here then. That's where idea number two comes in."

Angus refused to elaborate on his second idea until after he'd pressed garlic cloves into the beef and covered it with tinfoil. He set the timer and slid the roasting pan into the oven.

"We'll have plenty of time to rustle up the vegetables upon our return," Angus said. "Now, follow me, if you would."

We walked back down the path towards the boathouse, ignoring the staircase that led up to the apartment and instead heading to Angus's workshop on the ground level. When inside, he swung open the two large doors at the north end, revealing the wooden boat-launch ramp sloping down to the river. It didn't take a genius to figure out where this was going. Even I got it.

"Now, look at the river, Daniel," Angus said. "There's not a lick of wind, and the water is calm and untroubled." I looked out at the water, then back at him. He was leaning against *Baddeck 1*, the two-seater hovercraft he had built with his own hands and his own innovative design. He was stroking the hull with pride in his eyes.

"I propose a jaunt up the very placid river for a quick look-see at the erstwhile Champlain Centre. I want to see what's left."

"We're going to get wet, aren't we?"

"I cannae deny that until we get the craft up on top of the water, there will be a wee bit of spray. But the modest moisture will be more than offset by the thrill of flying over the surface."

"It's so loud, too," I said.

"Come on, lad, 'tis the perfect day and ideal conditions. And we'll be back in a couple of hours, refreshed . . ."

"And soaked."

"Ye gods, lad. It'll be thrilling!"

"All right, all right, I'm coming."

CHAPTER 12

Baddeck 1—named after the small town in Cape Breton where Alexander Graham Bell, one of Angus's heroes, designed and built the HD-4, the hydrofoil that set the water-speed record in 1919—was famous, at least in certain circles. When Angus was in opposition after his first shocking electoral victory, the minority Conservative government tried to pull a fast one. To help ensure their budget passed in the House of Commons, the Tories violated tradition—but not the House Standing Orders—when they called an unexpected vote on the budget in the midst of one of the worst snowstorms in Ottawa's history. Many MPs were stranded and not able to reach the House of Commons to vote, which is exactly what the government wanted. Angus, who was not on House duty but in Cumberland at the time, foresaw this subterfuge. Now, I don't want to give away too much of the story, but let's just say that Angus and *Baddeck 1* saved the day, and Angus became a folk hero. So you can imagine how his Cessna takedown was fuelling the mythmaking machine.

I helped Angus guide the hovercraft on its wheeled dolly down the ramp and into the river, then we both climbed into the cockpit, which was really just a bench seat. Angus took his place behind the wheel, while I provided ballast and balance next to him. I won't go into detail about the innovative design, as I barely understand the basics, but what I do know is that a single snowmobile engine drives a single multi-bladed fan to generate both lift and thrust. When the engine is throttled higher, a portion of the air being forced down is redirected through horizontal ducts to provide the thrust that propels the hovercraft. Okay, that's my limit, and may be more than you wanted to know.

"Are you ready, Daniel?"

I already had my fingers in my ears, so I lip-read and nodded yes. Angus stabbed the starter button on the dash, and the engine mounted directly behind us roared to life—and "roared" is a significant understatement. As Angus increased the power, the spray commenced. It was like repeatedly driving through a car wash in a convertible with the top down, minus the soap and the big spinny brushy things. I suddenly remembered and made a mental note that I had to arrange for Roy Fitzsimmons to take a ride in *Baddeck 1*.

We moved forward and picked up speed as Angus guided us out into the channel. At one point, I could feel the hovercraft suddenly accelerate, and as it shot ahead most of the spray mercifully stopped.

"It's not exactly warp factor 7, but we just surpassed hump speed," Angus shouted.

"Hump speed?" I shouted back. "Has an illicit ring to it."

I should have known better. When Angus is in *Baddeck 1*, he is no longer an MP or a Cabinet minister. No, he reverts to a fully actuated engineer, loaded for bear. As soon as I asked about hump speed, I realized my mistake.

"Illicit? Only to your salacious ears. It just means that at low speeds, the hovercraft, instead of rising above the water, pushes the water down, creating a rolling wave at the front," he shouted. "Eventually, we get moving fast enough that we get up over that wave or hump, and then we're actually flying above the surface. It's a fascinating reality of hydrodynamics."

Oh, yes. Profoundly fascinating, even riveting. I listened, nodded, and furrowed my brow to simulate deep thought. But I was really focused on the fragment of cheddar cheese lodged in Angus's beard just southwest of his all-too-active mouth.

Other than learning—or not learning—what I needed, but didn't want, to know about hump speed, it was a smooth, if loud, voyage up the river. I could see on the speedometer that we were moving at just over thirty kilometres an hour. I know that doesn't sound very fast, but when you're flying a foot above the water, it feels like a blistering pace.

It took us about an hour to reach Nepean Point. As Angus slowed the hovercraft (unlike most similar vessels, *Baddeck 1* had excellent manoeuvrability even at slow speeds, thanks to Angus's unique design of the integrated lift/thrust system), we saw little on the water to reveal that an entire building had dropped into the river. There was some flotsam, including insulation, fabric (probably curtains), and soggy boxes that had once held coffee filters and crackers, and a few stray steel beams were sticking up out of the water, bent and twisted. I noticed that they were the hollow beams—I doubted there was anything left of the ones stuffed with C-4. I could also see two of the black spider-leg braces emerging from the river. But beyond these visible remnants, the rest of the building had been consigned to the deep—or the shallows, in this case. If we looked straight over the side of *Baddeck 1*, we could see hulking grey shadows and shapes where the Champlain Centre had come to rest, but it was difficult to discern any recognizable parts of the building. The blast had completely torn it apart.

We lifted our eyes to where the Centre had stood only forty-eight hours earlier. A few of the upper spider-leg braces clung stubbornly to the cliff face, but the rest of the site was essentially destroyed, with only a scar running from one side of the property to the other. It was fresh and raw and looked like the immediate aftermath of a major landslide.

I looked to the right of where the Centre once was and noticed a large group of people assembled at the main driveway. I pointed it out to Angus. They were pumping placards and chanting, but we could hear nothing over the noise of our engine. You'd think they could take a break from the daily ranting and rallying now that the offending structure was gone, but perhaps not. Angus hit the kill switch to silence the roar. We settled down and floated on—no longer over—the water.

When we could hear the crowd, it became clear instantly that the tone had changed from the earlier protests. There was no anger this time; in fact, this was a celebration. This was jubilation. Soon the strains of their chanting reached our ears.

"Ding-dong, the witch is dead! Ding-dong, the witch is dead!"

Angus laughed and joined in the chorus.

Above us there was cheering and dancing and all manner of frivolity to mark the literal fall of the Samuel de Champlain Centre. It was the largest crowd I'd ever seen at the building site. A few of the revellers looked down at the river, saw us, and promptly identified Angus, thanks to his hair—the hovercraft helped, too. On a good day, his mane was crazy and wild, but after an hour racing over the Ottawa River, our heads buffeted in the slipstream, the chaos on Angus's head and chin had reached new extremes. He was instantly recognizable, likely from a mile away. That's when the standing ovation started, accompanied by a new chant.

"Angus! Angus! Angus! Angus! Angus!"

I wouldn't give them full marks for creativity, but they scored off the charts for energy and enthusiasm.

"Sufferin'! I cannae take much more of this." Angus smiled and gave the adoring crowd a gentle wave. "Time to bolt."

He does not do well with adulation. He never has. I don't think I'd mind it so much, but I seldom have the chance to find out for sure.

He hit *Baddeck 1*'s Start button again and instantly the voices above were drowned out, just as Angus had intended. We took a last look at the hollowed-out cliff that used to support the cantilevered, leaf-shaped building, then Angus pointed the nose of *Baddeck 1* to the east and throttled up towards, you know, hump speed.

An hour later, around four thirty, we arrived back at the dock, soaked to the skin. We muscled the hovercraft back onto the dolly and clipped the winch cable to the front cleat. Then Angus slipped up to the workshop, turned the winch crank, and hauled the hovercraft back up the ramp and into the workshop. Water dripped off her and gathered on the floor, eventually to evaporate.

I went back to the boathouse to check on Lindsay, who was still hard at it, then changed into dry clothes and hustled up to help Angus in the kitchen. When I stepped through his front door, the aroma of the roast beef nearly knocked me over. It smelled amazing and reminded me of Sunday night dinners growing up. I prepared the brussels sprouts. That means I cut the hard little knob off the bottom and spread them out on a cookie sheet with a little olive oil, and into the oven they went, on a rack above the beef. That was it. We got the rest of the dinner ready, then Angus set the table in the dining room, where there was yet another river view. He even broke out the "good silver" to mark the occasion.

At six thirty, I drove over to Riverfront to pick up Muriel and Vivian. They'd gone to some effort to dress up a bit and were buoyant about the night out. By the time we arrived back at the house, Lindsay had surfaced; she helped Muriel in while I escorted Vivian, who'd left her scooter back at the residence and relied on a cane and my arm. We took it slowly but made it to the living room and a firm but comfortable armchair. Then we all sat around with drinks and talked about the morning's sting and how upset the Prime Minister was—justly so.

"Jocelyn Massé said not a word the entire time," I said. "She just stood there behind Coulombe with eyes like saucers, watching her boss's career circle the drain."

"I doubt her prospects are much better, given how long she's been with Coulombe," Muriel added.

"The boys took *Baddeck 1* out for a spin this afternoon," Lindsay said. "I can confirm that it is no quieter than the last time I heard it fly by."

"Is that the famous hydrofoil I read so much about last year?" Vivian asked.

"Hovercraft, an air-cushion vehicle," Angus said. "A hydrofoil is a different beast altogether, but the two are often confused."

"Well, you certainly made a big splash back then."

"The splash part is still relevant," I said. "We were both drenched from the spray before we were out of sight of the boathouse."

We moved to the table a few minutes later. Angus and I served the three women, while Lindsay sat next to Muriel and discreetly cut her meat for her. Parkinson's had not only left her with tremors and reduced control over her movements but robbed her of strength in her hands and fingers.

A man of many talents, Angus had conjured up a pot of fresh butternut squash soup while I'd been chauffeuring Muriel and Vivian. I have to say it was an amazing meal, right down to my gravy.

"What a glorious dinner," Muriel said. "We're grateful, Angus and Daniel, for your efforts in the kitchen. This sure beats the pot roast to which we'd have been subjected back at Riverfront."

"I'll drink to that," Vivian said. "Angus, the beef is perfection. My roasts turn out in multiple shades of grey and are tougher than drywall. How do you get it to turn out so well?"

"Vivian, roasting beef is more art than science," Angus said. "It's instinct and observation, and an appreciation for the variables that dictate the rate of cooking. How big is the roast? What temperature is the beef when it goes in? How hot is the oven? How much fat and marbling is there in the beast? And of course, what kind of cow donated the beef? It all comes together with a sixth sense, a feeling—call it intuition—and voila, perfection."

"Well, there is some science involved," I said.

Angus sighed. "Aye. All right, all right. The meat thermometer is helpful when everything else fails."

"Is it true that what we now know as Angus beef was actually named in honour of your worldwide contribution to advancing roasting techniques?" Lindsay asked.

"I'm a humble man," Angus said, with head bowed. "And modesty prevents me from responding." Then he stood and lifted his wine glass. "Whilst I have the floor, this gathering is to honour the three of you," he started. "These past few weeks have been an adventure for Daniel and me, and for all of you, too. It was concluded successfully, save for the unfortunate and expensive loss of the Champlain Centre—though I doubt many are shedding tears over that, while multitudes are hoisting glasses at the river's edge."

We all laughed.

"But most of all, there was no loss of life, and we all know there could well have been plenty. So tonight, we raise a toast to you, for we'd have been lost without you, start, finish, and all points betwixt. Muriel, for bringing Vivian into our midst, and for adding a touch of silver to disguise the stakeouts. Lindsay, for your automotive tracking and tailing skills and prowess with a cellphone video camera, all at a time when you should be occupied with closing out your master's degree. Oh, and for being there to help Daniel when he drove into the back of Eugene's car in an effort to avoid drawing attention to himself."

Lindsay smiled and nodded.

"Very kind of you, Angus," I said. "Thank you."

"'Twas nothing, lad," Angus replied. "And to Vivian, whose insight, experience, contacts, and deductive powers really led to the breakthrough. I, for one, will never forget her line 'The bomb is not in the building. The building *is* the bomb.' All roads led to that epiphany."

I started to raise my glass to drink to the three of them.

"Not so fast, Daniel," Angus said "And to young Daniel, whose brilliant investigative legwork took us from knowing only that there may be two Chechens living in or around Ottawa, to giving them faces, names, a home address, and places of work. Without that, nothing else would have mattered. So I raise my glass—"

"Not so fast, Angus," I said, rising to my feet and lifting my glass. "And here's to Angus, a man of action, whose bravery and split-second decision-making put our lives in peril and my sanity at risk, but ultimately, and literally, brought Eugene and Tatyana down."

"Hear! Hear!" said our three compatriots.

"Thank you, lad," Angus said humbly. "Right, then, since we've all been implicated in this all-inclusive toast, let us raise our glasses in mutual thanks and admiration."

"I just wish Pete1 and Pete2 could have been here tonight," Muriel said, smiling. "They would have loved this."

"Aye," agreed Angus. "That would have been grand."

The two Petes had been stalwart members of the Angus McLintock election team. Both engineering students and hard-core punk rockers, they pushed back the frontiers of sartorial splendor in their attire. Piercings, fluorescent mohawks, and multiple tattoos made door-to-door canvassing interesting, to say the least. They also worked part-time in Angus's constituency office. The two friends had recently left for a backpacking trip around Europe and weren't due back until August.

When we'd almost finished dessert, Lindsay kicked me under the table and nodded towards Angus.

I shook my head. She kicked me again. I sighed. I'd learned, three kicks and you're out.

"Um, Angus, great dinner, by the way. So good," I babbled. "Um, are you familiar with *The Nutcracker*?"

"Aye. I'm surprised its notoriety has reached your tender ears."

"I'm afraid to ask this, but what do you mean by that?"

"The Nutcracker was a particularly successful technique my rugby mates and I pioneered that proved effective in neutralizing opponents in scrums."

"Neutralizing or neutering?" Muriel asked with a laugh.

"I'll plead the fifth on that one, Muriel," Angus replied.

"Angus, I wasn't talking about rugby," I said. "I was referring to the popular seasonal ballet."

"Oh, that *Nutcracker!* The Tchaikovsky masterpiece. Brilliant and colourful," he said. "I believe it debuted in the early 1890s, yet it remains a Christmas staple more than a century later. I don't know about you, but I'd contend it's the most accessible ballet ever performed. For the uninitiated, I think of it as a gateway drug to the more complex and challenging ballets like, say, *Don Quixote*. Why do you ask?"

I was no longer surprised when the breadth of Angus's general knowledge was on full display. He never intended to seem all-knowing and pedantic. He was genuinely interested in a vast diversity of pursuits. Apparently, ballet was one of them, and I hadn't known until that instant.

"Well, have you ever seen a performance of *The Nutcracker?*"

"Of course, man. Many times. Have you not?"

"Um, no, I can't say I have."

"Well, you must. You'd love it." Angus turned to the three women. "Have you all seen it?"

Lindsay, Muriel, and Vivian all nodded. Turned out I was the philistine, again.

"Anyway, so you're familiar with the role of the two cannon dolls?"

"Ha, it's one of the highlights in the show. Just before the end of the first act, if my memory doesn't betray me," Angus said. "They're the comic relief. Very funny. And I understand they're sometimes portrayed by local celebrities who—" He stopped. He had always been a quick study. "No. No way," he said. "I don't mind crashing a car into a speeding plane, but I'm not donning that ridiculous costume with the pom-pom-festooned jester's cap. Not in my lifetime."

"Angus, don't write it off so quickly," I said. "You're always telling me not to make hasty decisions, but to let ideas sit in my brainpan and steep for a bit. That's all I'm asking. It's the National Ballet of Canada. They're touring *The Nutcracker* in December, and it's coming to the National Arts Centre. I think it would be a blast."

"I've had my fill lately of blasts," Angus said. "Being onstage amidst truly talented professional dancers as part of a classic ballet is not my idea of a pleasant afternoon, when I could otherwise be at the dentist, or cleaning my carpets."

"Angus, dear, you'd be wonderful in the role. Your particular hairstyle seems well suited to the part," Muriel said. "And getting to release your inhibitions and bounce around the stage like a lunatic would be so cathartic and so much fun! I really think you should do it."

"I second that," Vivian chimed in.

"Angus, the Prime Minister and Bradley are always telling caucus to accept these kinds of community opportunities," I said. "They help put a human face not just on Members of Parliament but on the government. I think this is a great chance to endear yourself to Canadians, without risking any lives."

"Angus, you'd be wonderful," Lindsay said. "And just think, you could forever say that you performed with the National Ballet of Canada. Not many can boast that."

Now that it was out in the open, we kept up our, shall we say, encouragement and exhortations, and broke out the Lagavulin to lubricate the decision. After about twenty minutes of our full-court press, Angus gave his final word on the matter.

"Out of respect for you all and the celebratory nature of this evening, I'll not rule it out tonight. My flat refusal can wait at least until tomorrow."

After dinner, Lindsay and I drove Muriel and Vivian, who were buzzing from their evening out, home. Just before I turned in for the night, Bradley emailed confirming receipt of Coulombe's resignation and said to expect a call from the PM the next morning. I couldn't even muster the energy to ask what it was about. It had been a long and very eventful weekend. I fell asleep minutes later, pressed up against Lindsay with her arm around my chest.

It did not feel like a Monday morning. I thought Angus and I needed a few days off to recover from the excitement, but alas, we had work to catch up on. On the drive in to Ottawa that morning, the CBC national news reported that the Prime Minister had announced the Honourable Emile Coulombe's resignation from Cabinet, citing personal reasons. For the time being, the PM would assume responsibility for Public Safety, signalling just how important the portfolio was in the wake of the weekend's assassination attempt. Finally, the news report said, neither the PM nor Emile Coulombe would be making any further public comment.

The PM called our office at nine thirty. I put him on speakerphone.

"Thanks for making some time this morning, gentlemen. I'll be brief," he said. "I remain very troubled by the role of MI6 in all of this, in London and here in Ottawa. That a trusted ally could violate the Five Eyes agreement and ignore the threat to human life, my life, just to see Pudovkin removed from office in the most extreme and irrevocable way, is breathtaking. I'm itching to call Downing Street and rage at the Prime Minister, but I want to be as prepared as I can be. That's where Paul Wilder comes in. I mentioned him to you earlier."

"Yes, we remember, Prime Minister," Angus replied. "An independent study makes sense."

"Paul is a retired Supreme Court Justice of British Columbia," the Prime Minister continued. "We go back to our university days together. There is no more thoughtful, balanced, and thorough legal mind I know of in the country. I've asked him to, in a very short time, examine this entire affair, tie together all the disparate threads, and draw the many links and connections into a coherent story. I need to be in full command of the details when I start going after Downing Street for—well, for their ignorance at best, and their complicity at worst."

"I think that's an excellent idea, Prime Minister," Angus said. "And we offer our full and immediate cooperation in the task."

"I knew you would say that, Angus. Paul is in town now and I've given him a week to turn this around, which I know is almost ludicrous. But I believe we know much of the story already, thanks to the stellar work you two have done in the last week or so. But I want it all presented in one place, simply, clearly, and powerfully. So your assistance in this is not just appreciated, it's crucial."

"Of course, Prime Minister. Daniel and I will speak with Mr. Wilder today."

"Oh, Angus, while I think of it, I understand the National Ballet fancies you as a cannon doll in December."

Angus turned to glare at me.

"Angus," I protested, "I've said nothing to anyone beyond our Cumberland circle about it, and I certainly did not discuss it with the Prime Minister."

"He's right, Angus. Daniel would never be so indiscreet. The artistic director wrote to ask if I would encourage you to accept their invitation. And I agreed. Particularly after what's just happened, your stock is high. By doing this, you'd certainly be helping an important arts organization and burnishing your own image, but more importantly, you'd be putting a positive sheen on the government. I hope you'll consider their offer."

We spent three hours with Paul Wilder later that morning and into the early afternoon, giving him every detail of the preceding few weeks. And because Fleming's cover had already been blown, though we still did not know her real name, Angus and I were completely open in telling our full story, from the very beginning in the Copper Cup pub. We left nothing out, all the way up to and including the whole Coulombe trap at Mamma Teresa's. With her blessing—I called her first—we even described Vivian's important role, and the support Lindsay and Muriel had provided.

Angus and I were both impressed with Paul Wilder. It was evident from the very beginning that he was a clear thinker who could separate the important from the merely interesting. We both figured his report would be fair and compelling.

Later that afternoon, Angus skipped Question Period, so we decided to take it easy for the rest of the day. We sat in our Centre Block office and just talked, which was nice. Then, around four thirty, we bailed and began the drive home. I was back at the wheel of the Buick.

"So, just to close the loop on *The Nutcracker*," I said. "I swear I never breathed a word of this to anyone in the PMO. I wouldn't do that." *At least not yet*, I thought.

"I know you didn't," he replied. "I just dinnae like that kind of thing. You're centre stage and everyone's looking at you."

"Well, being a cannon doll involves far fewer people staring at you than are already watching you on the news and YouTube. At this moment, you're front and centre on the world stage, so having a thousand ballet fans watching you should hardly seem daunting."

"I'm afraid I wasn't considering many, or any, of these implications when behind the wheel of that rusty Ford. I was only thinking a second or two ahead."

"But if you had carefully planned everything and accounted for all the outcomes, Eugene and Tatyana would probably be safely on a trawler somewhere off the East Coast, chugging for Europe."

"Maybe you're right, lad."

"So, what do you say? Can you spend two minutes onstage in the name of humanizing the government?" I asked. "Tough to say no to the Prime Minister."

"Blazes! All right, I'll do it if it means we can stop yammering about it. And I'm not doing it alone. The performance calls for two cannon dolls, so you'll be by my side, as you usually are."

"I had hoped it would not come to this, but I can tell by your tone that there's no other path to yes. Okay, it'll be the two of us in December."

"If we can survive an airport crack-up like we did a couple days ago, I reckon we can withstand the slings and arrows of the ballet."

CHAPTER 13

On the following Sunday evening, less than a week after we'd met with the retired Justice of the B.C. Supreme Court, Bradley Stanton emailed a password-protected copy of the Wilder report to Angus and me. He then texted the password to my personal cellphone. It was *Champlaingoboom*. Nice.

Angus and I had been playing chess, but we suspended the game to read the report. Angus was kicking my carcass all over the board anyway. I was happy for the reprieve.

We reviewed Wilder's findings on Angus's laptop. The Prime Minister had directed that the report be long enough to present compelling justification for its findings but short enough to be read, understood, and acted upon quickly and decisively. This was a delicate balance to strike, particularly in the space of a week. But as we read the forty-two-page document, it was clear to us both that Justice Wilder had done a masterful job at walking that fine line. It was very impressive. Angus shared my view though he was a little perturbed by how often his name—and mine—appeared in the report.

"Well, I don't know how he could complete a major examination of the whole affair and not talk about us," I said. "We were involved in almost every aspect of it, because we seemed to be the only ones who accepted it was actually real and happening."

"Aye, I know, I know. But if this report finds its way to the media, the circus will be back in town. I dinnae like the circus," Angus said. "But that aside, this gives the Prime Minister all the ammunition he needs to deal with Britain. It's a fine piece of work."

"Yes, and it's nice the PM invited us to the party," I said. "Let's not be late tomorrow. I don't want to miss the fireworks."

Speaking of fireworks, we eventually resumed our chess game so Angus could complete his rout.

The call was set for nine thirty. Angus and I arrived at the PMO in good time. The Prime Minister had been sequestered all day Sunday with Bradley and senior advisors from Global Affairs Canada and the Department of Justice. Now, the PM took a seat at the table and began to review his notes. Bradley, Angus, and I sat across from him.

"Prime Minister, it's time," Bradley said. "We'll be right here listening, so if you get into trouble, look to us and we'll help."

The PM donned his headset while we slipped on our headphones. Bradley dialled the private line and we were off.

"Hello, Prime Minister, good of you to call," the familiar plummy voice said.

"Thank you for taking the call, Prime Minister."

"Such a close shave you experienced a week or so back," the British leader said. "I was heartened in the end that only a building was lost."

"Yes, it could have been a lot worse. But it was in fact worse than it appears, for reasons that, if you'll bear with me, I'll proceed to make clear. And, not to bury the lede, it does involve your government."

We could almost hear the temperature drop on the call.

"I'm afraid you have me at a disadvantage, Prime Minister."

"That, sir, is an understatement. Let me start from the beginning, and I'd be very grateful if you could allow me the courtesy of completing my summary of the events before you pose any questions. I know we have limited time, so with your concurrence, I'll begin."

"By all means."

So far, so good. I could see steely resolve in the Prime Minister's eyes, perhaps for the first time since I'd known him.

"Prime Minister, I do not assume that you have been privy to, or responsible for, any of the grave transgressions your government has committed as part of the dramatic events that unfolded here in Ottawa just over a week ago."

"I beg your pardon, sir," the startled voice on the phone said.

"Please, allow me to proceed, and then you will have ample opportunity for explanations and questions. And believe me, I'm eager to hear your response."

The PM now stood up as he began to present the facts. He stuck to his talking points, but it did not for one instant sound like a recitation. He was angry, and that was evident in his tone of voice.

It took the Prime Minister about twenty minutes to hit all the key points. The Madrid cover-up. The sleeper cells in capital cities. The documented links to MI6. And all the rest. He skillfully combined telling the story with drawing conclusions and assigning blame. He was careful to fully support our claims that someone in the British High Commission, likely Thomas Maynard, had manufactured evidence knowing it would cause the arrest and detention of an innocent Canadian professor.

"Excuse me, Prime Minister, I must stop you to say in the clearest possible terms that I am utterly shocked by what you have told me, and can profess with complete honesty that I have no idea what you're talking about," said the British PM.

The PM glanced at us and rolled his eyes before continuing. I was proud of him. Angus looked at me and nodded in approval.

"Prime Minister, I pray you know nothing about this personally, but even if that's the case, your government had the intelligence to thwart this potential tragedy but remained silent. Instead, your government abrogated the UKUSA agreement, to which we have been mutual signatories for decades, and took active steps to help the Chechen sleeper cell succeed. For Christ's sake, man, we're a Commonwealth country!"

"Prime Minister, if I may . . ."

"Not yet! One more point and the floor will be yours. A former Justice of the Supreme Court of British Columbia has prepared a comprehensive and fair report on this sordid and unprecedented international incident. I will encrypt it and send it directly to you. I expect to hear back from you within forty-eight hours with your official response, including the steps you are taking to ensure this never happens again, and how you propose to compensate Canada for this completely avoidable calamity."

There was silence for a time.

"Prime Minister, am I free to speak now?"

"Yes, sir, you are," our PM replied. "Thank you for your patience."

"Sir, I reiterate that to the best of my knowledge, no one in Downing Street had even the slightest inkling of any connections between our government and the unfortunate events in Ottawa."

"So you were not aware that an MI6 employee had been relieved of her duties and placed under house arrest, and now faces multiple charges under the Official Secrets Act?"

"Well, um, yes, I was made aware of that, but the details were not revealed during the briefing, so I knew nothing of the Ottawa connection."

"Well, Prime Minister, Fleming—the code name used by this brave MI6 operative—has been atrociously treated, when she deserves to be honoured for taking the appropriate and noble course. I fervently hope you will terminate Mr. Acton's employ, drop the scurrilous charges against Fleming, and reinstate her immediately. Whatever her real name is, she deserves a medal, not house arrest and an ankle beeper."

Angus and I were looking at each other through much of the call with ever-widening eyes. We'd never seen the Prime Minister in a state of such pure, unadulterated leadership. He was confident and authoritative, quite a departure from his customary demeanour. It was a breathtaking transformation that certainly fit the occasion.

"Mr. Prime Minister, again, you have presented some allegations that are very extreme. You must understand that I can say nothing until I have carefully examined and corroborated the evidence you are providing and spoken to my colleagues at MI6 and the High Commission in Ottawa. I cannot yet accept on your word alone that this is a true representation of the facts. It falls too far outside the standard of conduct I expect from those who serve my government. I cannot believe it."

"Believe it, Prime Minister!" our PM snapped. "Read the report. Validate its findings. Talk to your people. Then tell me you don't believe it. If this fiasco were to become publicly known, it would serve neither of our nations' interests. But I will not hesitate to release all of this information if I do not receive full satisfaction from you and your government. Is there anything else you'd like to say, Prime Minister?"

"Not at this time," the U.K. PM replied.

He sounded defeated, almost as if he was beginning to accept that what he'd just heard might well be true.

"Very well, Prime Minister. I expect to hear from you within forty-eight hours, preferably sooner. Goodbye, Prime Minister."

He did not wait for a response but quickly pushed the button to end the call.

Wow. Even Bradley was at a loss for words. He looked dazed by what he'd just witnessed.

"Sir," Angus said, "I truly believe that call was your finest moment as Prime Minister thus far. I only wish Canadians could have heard your performance."

"Oh, gee, that's great. Thanks, Angus," the PM said. "So you thought I was okay? Really? I wasn't sure if I was coming on too strong, or not strong enough. I just couldn't tell. But I really appreciate your support. I'm glad you were all in the room. I must say I found the whole encounter exhilarating, but still distressing and quite unsettling."

The spirit of the Prime Minister we knew so well had re-entered his body.

Later that morning, I got a call from the Governor General's office. It was the staff person who supported the GG's advisory committee on Decorations of Bravery, and she had a few questions. She couldn't tell me why she needed answers, but despite the occasional lapse, I'm not a complete idiot. Her questions were not challenging, and I was able to answer them without the need to consult Angus. There was no way I was going to tell him about the plans that were almost certainly afoot to express the nation's thanks. Let it be a surprise. If he doesn't want public recognition, maybe he should stop running into the flames and throwing himself on grenades. I noticed that half her questions had been about me and, as I've recently noted, I'm not a complete idiot. I'd been on the field with Angus for the whole game, so I guess it should have been no surprise that I was to be included somehow. I felt a little guilty. Angus deserved the recognition. I was just tagging along, and not always voluntarily. Best to let it happen without making any noise about it. It would pass.

I called Bradley.

"Addison," he said. "I know it's still early, but any heroics today so far?"

"Well, I almost tipped over my glass of orange juice this morning, but at the last second, I saved it. It was very close, but thanks to my heroics, a crisis was averted."

"Wow. You're incredible. I'm honoured to know you. Now, what do you want?"

"I gather something's going on in the House tomorrow," I said. "Anything I should know?"

"Just that the PM has boarded the crazy train and is insisting on doing this in the House. The GG is coming and will preside. I think it's a bit over the top, but the opposition parties have agreed. The PM believes that without your digging and action-hero histrionics, he'd be waterlogged under rubble at the bottom of the river. So, he's feeling it right now."

"Okay. I mean, it's all very nice. But Angus is going to be very uncomfortable," I said.

"Ah, poor baby. This is not about how Angus feels, it's about what the PM wants. And he wants to thank Angus, and you, too, in a formal and fitting way. That means the House."

"Well, I'm touched, Bradley."

"You're more than touched, Danny boy," Bradley said. "You're a full-on nutbar, right up there with Angus."

As I'd surmised, there was a big deal in the House of Commons the next day, led by none other than the Prime Minister and the Governor General. It was all quite lovely and embarrassing. They'd chauffeured Vivian, Lindsay, and Muriel into Ottawa to watch the whole affair from the

Member's Gallery, and their roles were also acknowledged. Angus hated every minute of it, including when the Governor General pinned the Star of Courage on our chests, apparently for "acts of conspicuous bravery in circumstances of great peril." Modesty prevents me from providing any more details, but warm and fuzzy feelings abounded.

After Angus and I extricated ourselves from the House of Commons, we jumped in the Buick and bolted for home. Halfway to Cumberland, my cellphone rang. I recognized the number and put the call on hands-free.

"Hi, Bradley."

"Addison, I assume the minister is with you."

"Aye, I'm right here, Mr. Stanton."

"Stand by for the Prime Minister."

The pause was short.

"Congratulations again, Angus and Daniel. And thanks for indulging me in the House."

"Thank you, Prime Minister, it was very special," Angus said while scowling at me.

"More importantly, gentlemen, I just heard back from the British PM. He's been burning the midnight oil, and I must say I'm very pleased with his early response."

"That is good news, Prime Minister. What did he say?" asked Angus.

"I've yet to see the transcript from the call, but I did take some notes. Let's see here. Right. He was mortified and enraged by what he read in the Wilder report, yada, yada.

He quickly sought and received responses from the British High Commission in Ottawa and the head of MI6, and he spoke to Fleming and to, what's his name, oh yes, Kendal Acton, blah, blah, blah. To his horror, he was able to confirm every relevant revelation in the report. He apologized early, often, and at great length."

"Fantastic!" I said.

"Yes, it didn't take him long to confirm the details," the PM continued. "The junior MI6 officer in the British High Commission in Ottawa—Maynard, I believe—apparently sang like a canary, implicating Acton. Said he was just following orders. Maynard will be immediately repatriated, likely on a flight tonight. Acton was quietly and summarily relieved of his duties. Let's see here—yes, Acton was warned of his permanent obligations of confidentiality. We'll hear no more from him. Our friend Fleming has been fully reinstated and even offered a promotion. In fact, she was asked to assume Acton's position, but it seems she's decided to retire now that her name has been cleared. I was assured that her service will be recognized."

"Congratulations, Prime Minister, that is splendid," Angus said. "Was there any mention of financial compensation for the loss of the very attractive architectural wonder that was the Champlain Centre?"

"I'm glad you reminded me. Yes, the British government will make a sizable contribution, details to be worked out, et cetera, et cetera. He also strongly urged me to approach the

Russians, since it was their citizens who actually bombed the building. I agreed but doubt that will come to anything."

"How did he move so fast?" I asked. "Governments can't usually react so quickly."

"As the Prime Minister put it to me, embarrassment, humiliation, and shame are great motivators," the PM said.

DIARY

Tuesday, May 20

My love,

Today was an odd one, love. While it may be strange for a politician to admit, you've always known that lusting after the spotlight and the public's admiration will never be found in my DNA. I surely want a life with purpose, and work-ing for the common good, in service of Canadians, delivers me that. But personal satisfaction is the only reward I seek. I feel queasy all over when oth-ers start fussing and fawning. Of course, on those rare occasions when you saw fit to fuss and fawn over me, I was quite happy. But this is adulation I cannot countenance. But when the Prime Minister spearheads it, and enlists the Governor General as a willing accomplice, my hands are tied, even if my fists are clenched.

*You were there, I'm sure. You saw it. It's not that
I don't understand why they would feel compelled
to bury us in accolades. I've seen the blasted
airport video. I can hardly believe we did what we
did. But I have no use for a bleedin' medal and
all the flippin' foofaraw that came with it. I've
never been more disquieted in all my days. Aye,
it's a pretty little bauble and well-intended, I know.
And I confess that deep, deep down, it arouses a
flickering and faltering sense of pride. But I put
a stop to that quick enough. Let's get back to what
we're elected to do, and to hell and gone with
the ceremonial frills and frivolities. Damnation.
But as Daniel says, it's tough to say no to the
Prime Minister.*

*Sorry for the outburst, my love. But better it hap-
pen here than in the blasted House of Commons.*

*The British PM has fallen on his sword and bled
profusely for the sins of his intelligence agency.
We left him little choice, but good on him for
stepping up and owning it all. Could not have
been easy, and heads will be rolling in London
for some time to come!*

My love, I need the moderating effect you used to bring me. You'd know just what to do, just what to say. I miss that and so much else.

AM

CHAPTER 14

Three weeks after we'd been feted in the House of Commons, we were standing at the baggage carousel in Domodedovo International Airport, just over an hour's drive from downtown Moscow.

"I cannae believe we're here," Angus fumed. "I dinnae understand why this is more important than the mountain of work that awaits us in Ottawa."

Angus's question was rhetorical. He knew why.

Pudovkin had insisted in three different calls to our Prime Minister that he had to meet and thank personally the "two heroes of Mother Russia" and show us the glories of Moscow.

Our friend Mikhail Koskov, Russia's ambassador in Ottawa, had also been persistent in promoting the "goodwill" visit.

"Angus, you've never been to Moscow," I said now. "We're actually going to have an audience with the President. They're going to put on a big show, and very likely give us a medal. It's not exactly a hardship assignment."

A woman in military uniform approached us as we wrestled our bags off the carousel. "Drs. McLintock and Addison?" she said. "Thank you for what you did. Thank you. Thank you! This way, please."

She walked and we followed.

"Have our reputations, or at least our faces, preceded us?" Angus whispered.

"They have YouTube over here. Considering the number of views our recent little movie has earned, I figure most Russians would recognize us."

"That explains why everyone has been smiling, waving, and bowing since we disembarked," Angus said.

"And it also explains why that older woman over there wanted to give me a Mason jar of borscht."

We walked past long lines and were escorted to, and then through, what I could only conclude was a VIP passport-control booth.

As we passed through sliding glass doors into the vast arrivals area, I glanced up at a TV screen mounted on the wall. It was broadcasting Rossiya 1, the state-owned news and entertainment network. Now I understood why Angus and

I, but probably mostly Angus, had been recognized. Clips of our airport heroics were playing on the screen. I guess news of our visit was not restricted to the upper echelon of the Kremlin.

I recognized the Canadian ambassador stationed in Moscow from the headshots I'd seen of her. She was walking our way.

"Minister, and Dr. Addison, welcome to Moscow," she said, shaking our hands in turn. "I'm Ambassador Marie-Christine Boudreau."

"Please, I'm Angus and my sidekick is Daniel, and those names work just fine."

"All right, then please call me Marie-Christine."

A big black Lincoln was waiting for us just outside. The driver loaded our luggage into the trunk, and I slid into the front passenger seat, leaving the back seat for Angus and Marie-Christine. As the unelected Chief of Staff to the minister, I sit at the kids' table with the driver—and I don't say that with any ill will, let alone contempt. It is how it's always been and how it should be.

"The entire country is very excited that you are both here," Marie-Christine said as we started our drive into Moscow. "The assassination attempt and your role in uncovering it and then stopping it has been openly shared on all state-run and private networks. The YouTube video didn't hurt, either. On a per capita basis, Russia leads the world in how many citizens have viewed it. In short, you are rock stars here."

"Aye, I was afraid of that," Angus said. "I had hoped leaving Canada for a few days might represent a brief respite from the wall-to-wall coverage back home."

The Canadian Embassy was located on a high-traffic street a little west of the Kremlin. We settled in to our small but adequate rooms and got ourselves cleaned up from the flight. Luckily, the formally programmed visit didn't begin until the next morning. With no discernible jet lag, Angus wanted to see the chess museum before our afternoon briefing with Marie-Christine. She was a little nervous about Angus and me traipsing around Moscow on our own but relented when we agreed to restrict it to the short walk to the museum. Ambassadors tend to worry about things like losing visiting Cabinet ministers.

It only took seven minutes to get there using my cellphone's maps function. Walking in that part of Moscow didn't feel that different from walking in any other major city. There were buildings, streets, sidewalks, traffic lights, people, noise, and plenty of that commodity that cities can't do without . . . concrete. The chess museum was interesting, but I discovered that nothing triggers jet lag like viewing far too many obscure and ornate chess sets in glass showcases. Angus had a little more capacity for such things, but after forty minutes or so, even he was ready to start back.

We took an alternate return route to the embassy, just to see different streets. I took in as much as I could, frequently turning around to get the full 360-degree view. That's when I noticed something.

"I saw those two guys behind us before we got to the museum, and there they are again," I said quietly to Angus.

To his credit, Angus did not suddenly spin on the spot and stare. Rather, he casually shifted his position to make it appear from a distance that he was talking to me. Then he pointed to something in the distance as cover for sneaking a look behind us.

"I do believe those two lads were in a car down the street from the embassy," Angus said. "I remember noting the awful colour of the one guy's coat. I've never seen a shade of green quite like it and hope never to again."

"If they're following us, they're probably FSB," I said. "Why don't we stop in at that café up the block a ways? If they follow us inside, that moves it from the 'we're imagining things' column to 'they're definitely following us.'"

"A fine stratagem," Angus replied. "I could use a coffee before our briefing, anyway."

We turned in to the café and took a page out of Fleming's tradecraft handbook when we snagged a seat in the corner with a full view of the only entrance. Our waiter was at our table in an instant, serving us some dark bread and butter and speaking just enough English to take our order. Angus had coffee, while I decided on a hot chocolate. Just as the waiter left us, our two minders entered the café. They looked around until they spotted us, then they looked at each other, shrugged, and promptly walked over to our table. After what we'd been through in the last month, I didn't think we needed to worry, unless of course we discovered they were Chechen nationalists.

"Hello, I am Dimitry, and this is Sergei," said the one in the memorable green coat. His accent was thick, but we could easily understand him. "We know who you both are. Welcome to Moscow."

"Thank you very much," Angus said. "We're pleased to visit such a famous city."

"Would you mind if we take photo with you?" Sergei pulled out his cellphone. "It is great honour to meet the heroes who saved our leader."

I looked at Angus, who nodded with a *Why not?* expression.

"Of course," I said, chuckling. "You know, it's funny, but we thought you were FSB and were following us."

"We are FSB and we are following you," Dimitry said. "But is protection. The President wants you safe and so do we. We are like—how you say—bodyguards."

"That's very good of you lads," Angus said. "Why don't you join us?"

Sergei fetched our waiter, to take their order and to take about fourteen photos with us. Then the waiter wanted a photo with us. Word spread and the kitchen staff filed out for pictures, as did several of the customers. Our bodyguards were nice guys but didn't really fit my idea of FSB operatives. I guess I'd read too many thrillers and watched too many spy flicks. Eventually we had to leave to make it back for our briefing, so we said goodbye to Dimitry and Sergei, who hugged us. A minute after we left, they took up their position about fifty yards behind us for what was left of our walk back to the embassy.

"Gentlemen, you've been fully briefed in Ottawa about your itinerary tomorrow and have no doubt seen the full briefing book waiting for you in your rooms," said Marie-Christine when we had gathered in her embassy office. "Do you have any questions I can answer before jet lag inevitably catches up with you?"

Angus and I looked at one another and shook our heads. "Thank you, Ambassador," Angus replied. "Courtesy of your excellent briefing binders, I think we're fully informed about tomorrow's proceedings. But thank you."

"Very well. May I just leave you with a few final points, and then I'll let you rest up before a more casual dinner here at the embassy? First of all, it is quite common for Canadian delegations to be followed by the Russian intelligence service. If you notice suspicious vehicles or individuals following you for some or all of your stay, that is not unusual and poses no risks, unless you decide to take pictures of military installations while in the company of known dissidents and Pudovkin critics."

"Good to know," I said, leaving it at that.

"Secondly, while Pudovkin is clearly grateful for what you did in Ottawa, he remains a tough, ruthless, and power-hungry expansionist. This is not a formal and substantial bilateral meeting between Canada and Russia. This is more of a ceremonial goodwill encounter to help set the stage for more important economic and trade discussions in the coming months. So forgive my bluntness, but even if the President asks you pointed questions about Canadian policy or actions, your latitude when with him is limited to polite social interactions. This is not a time for policy discussions, so I encourage you not to be drawn into them."

"Your message is sound and has been received," Angus said. "Thank you for your candour and clarity. It saves time."

"And he may well push you for more insight on the intelligence that pointed you in the right direction. Obviously, we know you'll be circumspect in that regard," Marie-Christine said. "Finally, Pudovkin will have a translator with him when you are in his presence. Please know that the President's English is better than he lets on. Do not assume he cannot understand what you're saying, even as he focuses on his translator. And of course, if the translator is within earshot, he has been trained to listen to whatever you might be saying to one another, even when the President is not with you. So, caution and circumspection are your guides."

Angus and I nodded.

"And that's it for me," Marie-Christine said. "You may want to flip through your binders this evening or before your whirlwind tour tomorrow morning, but I'm not anticipating any issues."

As the ambassador had promised, the time change caught up with us by the early evening, and it took considerable effort not to dip my head into my soup bowl and nod off. But we both managed to make it through the dinner the embassy laid on. We declined the post-dinner vodka shots and retired for the night.

Marie-Christine was right. The next morning was a whirlwind. In just a few hours, we zipped around Red Square, toured the Bolshoi Theatre, hustled through the impressive Museum of Cosmonautics, and marvelled, ever so briefly, at the beauty of one of Moscow's most ornate Metro stations.

After lunch and a carefully controlled tour of the Kremlin, we were finally led into President Pudovkin's office. Both Angus and I were wearing dark suits, as were President Pudovkin and his translator. Pudovkin was all smiles when he came out from behind his massive wooden desk to greet us.

"Angus, my friend, and Daniel, thank you, thank you," he said in halting English as he embraced us in turn. "Thank you. Sit. Please." He gestured to a sitting area off to the side.

The four of us sat in comfortable chairs around a glass-topped coffee table. President Pudovkin glanced at his translator, then started speaking in Russian, looking mostly at Angus but throwing me the occasional glance.

"I am so delighted that you have made the long journey to Moscow, though I'm sure the weather here is not so different from Ottawa," he said through his translator. "I wish to thank you personally for risking your lives to save mine. I don't usually need help to protect me. My security staff and intelligence service are very good, but they did not see this coming."

"Thank you, Mr. President" was all Angus said. I added a great deal by nodding in agreement.

"How did you know this was happening? How did you figure it out when so many others missed it?"

"Well, Mr. President, it started when we realized that steel beams in the building that were supposed to be hollow, were not. After we determined what was in the beams, we started looking at who had access to them," Angus explained. "Daniel here discovered that a man from Chechnya worked at the steel plant and was very involved in fabricating and delivering the beams. Also, we learned he lived with another Chechen, who worked in our main Parliament building. This would give them access to the perfect spot to detonate the bombs. And that's the whole story."

"I'm sure you are being modest and that there is more to it than that," Pudovkin said. "Please, more details, please."

"I'm sorry, Mr. President, there's nothing else to tell. If you've seen the infernal video of the finale at the small airport in Ottawa, you know everything."

Angus did very well not to be drawn in. We'd prepared for this, but still, he parried the President's queries with care and skill.

"It was like a movie," Pudovkin said through his translator. "And she had a gun, too. But still you went close with the car to make sure they could not escape. It was very brave of you."

Angus and I said nothing, because I wasn't sure the translator would be familiar with the phrase *Aw shucks, it was nothing*.

When President Pudovkin stood up, we followed suit. The meeting was over.

As we'd been warned, the ceremony and reception later that afternoon were lavish and over the top. No need to dwell on the formal part of the affair. President Pudovkin sang our praises and pinned more medals on our chests. People clapped. Caviar and vodka shots were consumed.

When the President was about to leave the reception, he made his way over to us with a serious look on his face and his translator in tow.

"Mr. President, thank you for a very moving ceremony," Angus said as he shook Pudovkin's hand.

The President leaned in and said, "Mr. Angus, I want two Chechens back here. Not Canada. Moscow."

We'd been expecting this. We knew Pudovkin wanted them back.

"I cannot speak for my government on this issue, but I know we do not have an extradition treaty between our two countries. The crime was committed in Canada, so I don't believe extradition is even appropriate to consider."

The translator did his thing, which did not help the President's mood. Pudovkin then switched to Russian, which the translator eventually conveyed. "Mikhail Koskov will be making a formal extradition request for the two assassins, and he hopes you will support it with your Prime Minister."

"Mr. President, I will certainly ensure that our Prime Minister is informed of your wish to repatriate Anzor Dudiyn and Elina Shishani. But I cannot in good conscience support your request."

"I am glad we have already given you the medals," the President said through the translator. "Thank you again for what you did to protect me in Ottawa. You saved my life. But we want Anzor and Elina in Moscow to stand trial. And do not worry. We are not like the United States. We abolished the death penalty in Russia in 1996. They will be treated fairly."

"I will ensure my Prime Minister understands your position," Angus replied, with steady eye contact.

The President spoke his final words directly to us in English. "I think is time you go back to embassy now."

"Excellent suggestion. Thank you, Mr. President," Angus replied with a nod.

Angus told me later that he'd been tempted to inform Pudovkin that Canada would be seeking compensation for the loss of a new, expensive, and very ugly building, but held off, figuring we'd already worn out our welcome. Wise decision. We had.

Our early-morning four-hour flight landed at Heathrow around noon the next day. It was the second and final stop on our international victory tour. We were back in the same hotel where the adventure had started. It seemed like a very long time ago but was only a matter of weeks. We both had naps—a highly underrated restorative—and donned our best finery. That means we both put on the dark suits we'd worn in Moscow.

A chauffeur-driven Jaguar picked us up in front of our hotel for the short drive to Buckingham Palace. Neither Angus nor I had ever been inside the palace, though we'd both watched the Changing of the Guard from beyond the wrought iron gates.

"Do we even know what's to happen when we get there?" Angus asked.

"It's all rather vague," I replied. "We know Fleming is being honoured for her service by at least one member of the royal family. And that it's a very small, private, and secret ceremony."

"'Tis the lot of the spy that the public knows little of their exploits on the nation's behalf. But it's grand that they invited us."

It was really something to drive right through the gates and onto the grounds of the palace. We went through the central arch into the inner courtyard and stopped in front of the main doors, where a red carpet swept down the stairs and ended underneath our Jaguar. When we got out of the car, a woman in military uniform escorted us up the steps and inside, leading us up a beautiful staircase and eventually to our final destination, the Blue Drawing Room. Whoever came up with that room's banal name deserves some kind of royal recognition in the category of understatement. I briefly laid my hand on Angus's shoulder to steady myself. It's hard to describe the Blue Drawing Room's splendour and opulence. There was a high-arched, ornate gold ceiling, four beautiful crystal chandeliers, several marble pillars, enormous royal portraits, and a stunning red carpet with swirls of blue and green and gold and countless other colours. I realized I'd stopped breathing when I entered the room—I'd just never seen anything like it. Angus was similarly affected. The last time I'd witnessed him wrestling with his emotions based purely on visual impact was when I'd first walked him into the Library of Parliament in Centre Block.

After taking all of this in, I noticed four chairs placed in a row in the centre of the royal carpet. Seated at one end, her cane beside her, was Vivian Kent. And she was smiling at us. I blinked twice and yet she still was there. What a shock. Angus spied her at the same time and was clearly caught off guard, too.

"Um, Angus, your mouth is open," I whispered.

He closed it and moved towards Vivian.

"My dear, whatever are you doing here?" Angus asked, as he leaned down to kiss her cheek.

"I wanted to surprise you," she said.

"Well, you've succeeded, madam."

I gave her a hug, too. "But what brings you to this royal sanctum?"

"All will be revealed in time, but it appears our guest of honour has arrived."

An older woman had just entered the room. No, it was not the Queen. It was Fleming, looking much more relaxed than when we'd originally met. She was dressed in a beautiful, flowy red dress that perfectly matched the carpet. I wondered if that had been intentional. She strode right past us and embraced Vivian in a way that suggested a long and close friendship. Angus looked at me with eyes wide. Then it all made sense.

Eventually, their clinch ended, and Fleming warmly greeted us. Then we all sat down. The door opened again and a well-dressed man entered, followed two beats later by Her Majesty the Queen. She wore a classic yellow dress, with shoes and purse that perfectly matched. To my untrained eye, the dress looked like almost every other I'd ever seen her wear. My mind raced back to the protocol briefing note that I'd read earlier on the off chance that the Queen would be presiding over the ceremony. Well, she was. We all stood as she approached. The man, who I gathered was her Private Secretary, followed at her shoulder. The Queen extended her hand when she reached Fleming, who was beside me.

"Ms. Marion May Potts, London," intoned the Private Secretary.

"Good afternoon," the Queen said. "The guest of honour, I'm told."

"Your Majesty," Fleming said, bowing slightly.

"Dr. Daniel Addison, Ottawa, Canada."

"How do you do," she said.

I felt my hand and voice trembling, I hoped only slightly.

"Your Majesty," I said, mimicking Fleming—or Marion, I guess I should say.

"The Honourable Angus McLintock, Ottawa, Canada, by way of Scotland."

"I'm very pleased to meet you, Minister," she said.

"And I, you, Your Majesty."

"Ms. Vivian Kent, Cumberland, Ontario, Canada."

"I'll not squeeze tightly," the Queen said, extending her hand. "A dear friend has arthritis and I know how it pains. I do hope you're feeling well."

"Thank you, Your Majesty. Today, I feel wonderful."

A discreet lectern with a chair next to it had materialized in front of us. The Queen turned and sat down, while her Private Secretary stood at the lectern. He waited until the Queen had settled in her chair before turning to us.

"Good afternoon. I am the Queen's Private Secretary, and I'm pleased to assist in this ceremony. As you will see, there is no one else in the room beyond the six of us. That is as it must be, given the particular nature of this recognition. I remind you, with regret, that there is no medal or certificate or citation to commemorate this proceeding. There is no formal record of it occurring at all. What happens in this room this afternoon remains among us only. It is not to be spoken of to others. It seems cruel to impose such a stipulation, but it is for the greater good of Great Britain and the Commonwealth and is common practice when recognizing outstanding contributions by members of our intelligence service."

He stepped back and turned to the Queen.

"Ma'am."

The Queen rose and approached the lectern, where her notes lay.

"I am pleased to be here this afternoon to recognize the extraordinary service to Britain of Ms. Marion May Potts. While this is for a long and successful thirty-five-year career in the intelligence service, it also reflects a recent and particularly noble episode in which she put the interests of her country and those of another Commonwealth nation ahead of the ill-conceived and wrong-headed directives of a superior. The chain of command is almost always to be honoured, except when it means violating the trust, and agreements, we have with Commonwealth allies. On behalf of my government, I apologize unreservedly to Marion May Potts for the ordeal and the injustice she was forced to endure until sanity eventually prevailed."

The Queen then walked over to Marion, who rose to her feet. The Queen took both Marion's hands in hers. "I speak for all of Great Britain and the Commonwealth when I offer my deepest gratitude, not only for your creditable and exemplary career, but for your unwavering commitment to do what is right when it is far from what is easy."

At this point, Marion's eyes were glistening.

The Queen returned to the podium and turned to a new set of notes.

"Before we conclude the formal part of this ceremony that never was, I wish to pay tribute to the Honourable Angus McLintock, Dr. Daniel Addison, and Ms. Vivian Kent, all three of whom, with additional support from Ms. Muriel Parkinson and Ms. Lindsay Dewar, exemplified intelligence, dedication, and bravery in preventing what could have been a tragic international event that, in the end, would not have reflected well on my government or nation. I speak for both when I express my profound thanks."

And that was it. We had not expected to have some of Marion's glory splashed over us. It was thrill enough just to meet the Queen. She stayed after the ceremony, and we chatted as informally as one can ever chat to a bona fide living sovereign. After about fifteen minutes, her Private Secretary subtly leaned in and whispered to her. She talked for a few minutes longer before thanking us all again and leaving the room for parts unknown. It *is* a big palace. The four of us waited a few minutes longer while Vivian's scooter was retrieved, then made our way back out to the inner courtyard, where two Jaguars waited.

"I propose a celebratory drink at a little place I know called the Copper Cup," Marion said with a smile. "Who's with me?"

"I've heard a lot about that particular pub," Vivian said. "And I've got nowhere to be. Count me in."

"A few fingers of Lagavulin would not be unwelcome," Angus said.

"I'm with Angus, so I'm in, too," I said.

Marion and Vivian left in one Jaguar, with Angus and me a minute or two behind in the other. The Copper Cup wasn't the best choice for Vivian as she would have to navigate the stairs, but she insisted on seeing the site of our first clandestine encounter. Angus and I helped her down the stairs while Marion, whom I will always think of as Fleming, went ahead to grab a table. With the scooter stowed in the cloakroom, we found Marion seated at the very table where we'd first met. We settled Vivian beside her, and Angus and I sat across from them. We ordered drinks and nachos—you know, that classic traditional English pub food.

"Now, just before we cloud our senses with illicit liquids and Mexican finger food," Angus said, "pray explain the history and nature of the obvious bond the two of you share."

"After you," Marion said, looking at Vivian.

"Well, it's hardly a mystery," Vivian started. "When you work in the intelligence game—yet another bastion of male dominance—you gravitate to others of your own kind. Marion and I met soon after I came to London as the CSIS lead at the embassy."

"She was like a breath of fresh, testosterone-free air," Marion said. "We sat on a joint task force on intelligence-sharing with three backward blokes from Australia, New Zealand, and the U.S. In that kind of setting, we would have hit it off even if we didn't really like each other."

Vivian laughed. "As it turned out, we became very close friends. Despite a bit of an age gap."

"I'm not sure either of us could have skated through some rough patches in our careers without each other's support," Marion said, briefly resting her head on Vivian's shoulder.

"So you were in on this from the beginning," I said to Vivian.

"Well, Marion was on the horns of a dilemma, so we talked it all through endlessly and finally mapped out a strategy for resolving it. Muriel had been singing your praises up and down and non-stop since I moved into Riverfront, and when I learned you were both going to London, the plan pretty well wrote itself."

"It all becomes clear," Angus said.

"And were the two of you talking throughout the affair?" I asked.

"I called Vivian almost every day," Marion said. "It was helpful to get a confirming perspective, particularly after speaking with you two."

"Let me guess," I said to Vivian. "You sent me the burner phone."

"Well, I might have had something to do with that." She grinned.

"And now I understand how you were always primed and ready when we needed help," I said. "You already had Newton's phone number on a piece of paper, ready to hand to me. I don't know why I didn't pick up on that."

"Because she's good at what she does," Marion said.

"Good at what I *did*," Vivian said. "I'm sadly out of the game now."

"You certainly didn't seem out of the game to me. We'd have been stranded and struggling without you," Angus said. "But why not welcome us into the tent right from the start?"

"It's just how we spies work," Marion said. "You keep the circle as small as possible, minimize the risk, and protect you gents in the process."

"You boys were very good on the ground, solving problems, cracking codes, making solid progress," added Vivian. "There was just no real advantage to telling you. Had you been well-meaning, humbling idiots, we might have played it differently."

"So, tell us, if you can, what happened over here to move you from house arrest to Buckingham Palace?" I asked Marion.

"The short answer is, you three happened," she said. "Vivian sent me the documentary evidence that her friend Newton gathered on both the emails and the listening devices, proving the link with MI6 in Ottawa. Combined with your brilliant work identifying Eugene and Tatyana and figuring out the beam bombs, and the earlier Madrid work, I finally had enough real evidence to go over Acton's head."

"And you blew your whistle long and loud," Angus said.

"I surely did. And they had to listen, because of what you gave me. But it really happened when your Prime Minister sent over the report that judge prepared, which I've only recently read. That was the final nail in Kendal Acton's coffin. After that, I was safe."

"So he's gone for good?" I asked.

"Kendal Acton will be lucky if he escapes prison time. But he will never darken MI6's doorway again. Several of his acolytes were also either dismissed or demoted. They even offered me Acton's job. It was unquestionably gratifying, but I was very happy to say no and retire on a high, with the Queen's blessing."

"Aye. That's what I call making a grand exit," Angus said.

"Well," Vivian said, raising her glass, "I believe I can now duly declare that Operation Angus is officially closed."

CHAPTER 15

We'd only been gone for a few days, but all I could think about was seeing Lindsay again. Angus knew about love, so when Lindsay picked us up from the airport, he immediately ensconced himself in the back seat so she and I could hold hands in the front. We dropped Angus at his front door and drove further down the driveway to the boathouse. There's nothing like having your life put in peril to make you hold on to those you love a little tighter. The experience seemed to crystallize the shared belief that we belonged with each other. I'm glad we both felt the same way. It would have been very awkward if watching me crash into the side of a speeding airplane had prompted her to pack up her things and move back in with her mother.

"So, I made a decision while you were away," she said as were lying in bed in the dark.

"You'd like to give up your studies and chase after your dream of becoming a mime," I suggested.

"Close, but not quite."

"Professional wrestler?"

"That could be my side hustle, but not just yet."

"Okay, I've got it now, by the process of elimination," I said. "You want to translate the Prime Minister's public statements, live, in real time, through interpretive dance."

"You are good. But no."

"Those were my best shots. I've run dry. Tapped out."

"I've accepted the Ph.D. offer from Carleton."

"Oh, you meant a serious decision," I said, turning to face her. "Were you accepted at Harvard and Oxford?"

She just nodded.

"Linds, why turn them down? If I thought for one instant that you were declining Oxford or Harvard because we'd be apart, I couldn't live with that. Don't stick in Ottawa on my account."

"Don't flatter yourself," she said, straight-faced—for just two seconds. Then her bottom lip started vibrating, and finally she dissolved into giggles and hugged me.

"Remind me to play poker with you sometime," I said with some relief.

"Daniel, leaving you would be very difficult, but I know we could make a long-distance relationship work. Millions have before us."

"Long-distance? I'd follow you to London or Boston or just about anywhere without poisonous snakes," I said. "I could maybe get back to teaching."

"I know I've said it before, but I picked Carleton for two major reasons. Firstly, the program is much more focused on the Canadian Parliamentary system, which is what I'm studying. It seems silly to move to Oxford or Harvard to study the Parliament of Canada when Carleton is respected internationally and is just down the street. If I were at Oxford or Boston, I'd be coming back to Ottawa often, because my subject matter is here. It makes no sense. Secondly, my grandmother is in decline. No one is saying it out loud, but she is. You've seen it yourself. Parkinson's may be slow at the beginning, but when you hit the latter stages, it progresses faster. I think we're close to that now. I do not want to be out of town when the phone call comes. I want to spend as much time with her as I can, while she still can. I think she still has a few stakeouts left in her, so I want to be close."

"And . . ." I said.

"Well, I'd miss the Ottawa Senators, too. And I hate the Boston Bruins."

I just elevated my left eyebrow.

"Daniel, having you here, as well as the Sens, is a huge bonus. But it's not why I picked Carleton. Being with you was a given regardless of which school I chose. I knew we'd make it work wherever I ended up."

"Plus, I do think the professional wrestling scene in Ottawa is heading for a renaissance," I said.

I lay awake for a while as she slept beside me. Part of me was relieved she was staying in Ottawa, but another part was already regretting we wouldn't have a new adventure together in a completely different place, where neither of us knew anyone. I would have followed her. In a heartbeat. Provided she respected my no-poisonous-snakes caveat.

Cabinet met the next day to answer a question that had arisen when the Champlain Centre fell. What do we do with the blast site? For Canadians, the wreckage of the Alexandra Bridge, just a twisted steel girder away from what was left of the Champlain Centre—and there wasn't much left—was a stark double-whammy reminder that the government had infrastructure problems. So the Prime Minister and the rest of Cabinet were eager to be seen taking action. A quick start to redeveloping the Champlain site could turn bad optics into good optics—that is, if you're one of those loose adherents to proper English usage who actually accepts the word "optics." Neither Angus nor I can stomach the term.

Because I'm a veteran on the Hill who used to work in the Leader's office, and because I'm Chief of Staff to a rookie Cabinet minister, I'm one of the few staffers—along with

Bradley, of course—who can attend Cabinet, though naturally I sit against the wall, well away from the table.

As soon as we entered the room, the assembled ministers broke out in applause. It was our first Cabinet meeting since the Rockcliffe airport showdown. I just nodded once and took my seat. Angus sat down at the table.

"All right, all right, enough of that, please," he said, waving his hand.

The ovation collapsed quickly, as you might expect from a room full of ministers who were probably unhappy that a colleague was getting so much more press and profile than they were.

"All right, ladies and gentlemen, we all have work to do, so let's try to get through this as effectively and efficiently as we can," said the Prime Minister, who was seated at the head of the table. "Our major priority today is to chart a course for developing the site of the former Champlain Centre. We want shovels in the ground as quickly as possible, to erase the voters' memories not just of the explosion a few weeks ago, but also of the whole spider redesign fiasco. I'm going to ask Michael Zaleski to brief us on the state of public opinion on the issue. Michael."

I'd nodded to him when I'd entered. We'd been through the wars together. Michael "the Z-man" Zaleski was an outstanding market researcher and devout Liberal. He and his firm had been the pollsters for the Liberal Party for a decade, and the market research firm of record for the Privy Council and several other major federal departments since we'd become the government. He was smart, understood his audience, and knew how to tread the very thin line that always ran between politics and policy.

"Thank you, Prime Minister," Michael said as he stood. "We have undertaken a three-pronged research approach on this question. First, focus groups across the country, to help frame our quantitative questionnaire. Second, the full quant piece, a national survey with a large enough sample to give us solid regional numbers, and third, a digital public engagement, which I think of as a blend of quantitative and qualitative research. You have seen the topline results from all three in your Cabinet binders, so I won't go through it all, chapter and verse. Rather, let me summarize the highlights to, I hope, frame your discussion this morning."

Michael had gotten better over the years at giving the party and now the government just what they needed to know to make decisions in the public interest, and, it must be said, the party's interest, too. You can always tell the respect and esteem in which Cabinet presenters are held by the level of background noise in the room. That morning, there was only silence.

"While the government's hands were tied, Canadians did not support the redesign of the Champlain Centre. They initially understood the fiscal realities of starting over, but these were completely overshadowed when the final redesign was approved and the support braces were installed. When they watched as the beautiful, sleek, glass-fronted maple leaf transformed, like something out of a Kafka story, into a big black spider, the public no longer cared about financial prudence and fiscal responsibility. We found this across all three research vehicles."

The Z-man let that sink in for a moment. We all waited.

"Rightly or wrongly, fairly or unfairly, the research also shows a clear link in Canadians' minds between the collapse of the Alexandra Bridge and the destruction of the Champlain Centre, even though they are completely different disasters with completely different causes. The common thread is the government's performance on infrastructure.

"Finally, among residents of the National Capital Region, there remain strong negatives for the government for the loss of the Astrolabe Theatre, which was razed to make way for the Champlain Centre.

"The bottom line, ladies and gentlemen, is that on the question of what should be built on the site of the Champlain Centre, if anything, there was a modest consensus nationally, and a strong consensus here in the National Capital Region, that it should be a successor to the Astrolabe. That it should be a new and state-of-the-art outdoor theatre for a broad range of cultural events. And I think I've taken up enough of your time already. Thank you for your attention."

He then returned to his seat against the wall opposite me and sat down.

"Thank you, Michael, for your compelling findings," said the PM. "The floor is open."

Given the strength of Michael's presentation, there was still more debate than I'd expected. Several ministers argued against the numbers and advocated for considering the runners-up in the design competition that had selected the cantilevered maple leaf. Some of the designs were just as striking but could be built in spite of the geology of the cliff face. For a time, there was some momentum building for this position. I watched as Angus raised his hand and the PM recognized him.

"I support the position the majority of Canadians seem to hold, as Mr. Zaleski so clearly outlined in his address," Angus said. "I accept that it is possible to build a conference facility similar to the erstwhile Champlain Centre that does not at all resemble a spider, beetle, centipede, silverfish, or any other invertebrate. However, I would simply suggest that we already have ample conference facilities in Ottawa to handle future and growing demand for such space. What we surely and sorely lack since the demise of the Astrolabe is any kind of open-air amphitheatre for concerts, plays, literary readings, and other cultural events, open to all Canadians. And might I add, Prime Minister, that from an engineering perspective, which is never far from my thinking, the unfortunate blast has rather conveniently carved out of the cliff face what appears to be a nearly perfect space for the in-ground seating bowl. That should save us some money. My vote is for just such an outdoor theatre."

As Angus sat back down, I counted several ministers nodding in agreement.

"Thank you, Angus," said the Prime Minister. "I should also remind ministers that the British government will be subsidizing this development project, and it's possible, though far from confirmed, that Russia may also contribute. This aspect of the issue is not yet to be made public and will not be as long as it threatens to compromise the work of our national intelligence organizations."

Several more ministers offered their occasionally informed and often ill-informed views on the question, but as the meeting progressed, few spoke in favour of another conference centre.

A short time later, the Prime Minister called for a vote. The strong majority sided with the open-air theatre option, a nicer and better-equipped successor to the lamented and long-gone Astrolabe. They agreed to call it the Champlain Amphitheatre for the Arts.

"Thank you. Decision made, and I think it was the right one," said the PM. "Now, may I invite the Minister of Finance to give us a brief fiscal update. And while he does, I'd like a private word with Angus, if I may."

Bradley and I looked at one another. His facial expression and shrugged shoulders conveyed that he had no idea what it was about. While we both wanted to accompany our bosses to be part of the conversation, we stayed where we were as the PM and Angus left the room. When the Prime Minister asks another minister for a "private word," it does not include staff.

I barely registered the fiscal update from the Finance Minister, and I don't think Bradley did, either. We both kept looking at the door like dogs awaiting their masters outside the grocery store.

Ten long minutes later, Angus and the PM returned. Angus gave me a quick look as he passed. I couldn't tell if he was troubled or elated, or somewhere in between. I feared Bradley and I would have to wait until after the meeting to learn what the private chat had been about. But I was wrong.

Before the PM started to speak following the fiscal update, I figured it out. It shouldn't have taken me so long. But there'd been a lot going on in the last few weeks.

"Ladies and gentlemen, if I may depart from our agenda briefly, I have an announcement. I'm pleased to tell you that I have just appointed the Honourable Angus McLintock as the new Minister of Public Safety. I don't need to tell you, or Canadians for that matter, how easy a decision this was. Congratulations, Angus."

I looked over at Bradley. He was still rocking his *I had no idea* countenance.

"Thank you, Prime Minister," Angus replied. "As ever, I'll do whatever is in my power to justify your faith in me. May it not be misplaced."

The next day, the PM appointed Deborah Dawson, MP for Yukon and a member of the Kwanlin Dün First Nation, as Minister of State for International Relations, taking over from Angus.

The next morning, the Russian ambassador, Mikhail Koskov, arrived on Parliament Hill for his appointment. It took the Prime Minister just ten minutes to decisively reject President Pudovkin's demand that Canada immediately extradite Anzor Dudiyn and Elina Shishani to stand trial in Moscow. It was not a pleasant meeting for Ambassador Koskov, but at least it was short.

As expected, two days later, President Pudovkin revoked Marie-Christine Boudreau's diplomatic papers and expelled her from Russia, though he did not rescind our medals. In a perfectly proportionate response, the Prime Minister expelled Mikhail Koskov. This may well have been redundant, as I figured that in light of Koskov's failure to secure extradition of the Chechens, Pudovkin would recall him anyway. My theory was strengthened when, a few months later, Koskov was appointed ambassador to Benin and sent to Cotonou, its administrative capital. Not exactly a plum post, though the weather is warmer than in Ottawa. Around the same time, the Prime Minister appointed Marie-Christine Boudreau our ambassador to the United States in Washington.

It was late fall before we set the date and actually got it organized. By rights, it was no longer our responsibility since Angus had been appointed to the Public Safety portfolio, but we'd committed to it earlier and he wanted to close the circle and make it happen.

About five hundred men and women crowded into the ballroom at the Château Laurier on a Thursday evening in early December. I recognized a few of them, including the security guards who'd so often waved us onto the building site, and some of the landscapers. But many of those attending had never even been to the site. They had supported the construction at their own premises, sewing curtains, supplying drywall, custom designing and manufacturing light fixtures and wall units and windows and signage. One major contractor was not in attendance, by mutual agreement. Red Pine Steel remained under investigation, not for complicity in the plot, but for negligence in quality control. After all, the Government of Canada never asked for C-4 to be stuffed into every second hollow steel beam. So we had agreed with Red Pine Steel's president that their attendance might not be appropriate.

Angus worked the room as effectively as an introverted mechanical engineering professor turned Cabinet minister could. Infrastructure Canada had been generous enough to lay on wonderful canapés and hors d'oeuvres, and they were very popular with the invitees. We had debated having the beautiful original scale model of the Champlain Centre, in its pre-arachnoid state, set up in the ballroom, but ultimately decided against it, worried it might bring everyone down and simply serve as a reminder that the building now rested on the bottom of the Ottawa River—and we didn't have a scale model of the Centre's twisted wreckage poking above the water's surface. So we nixed the whole scale model idea.

Despite the odd circumstances, everyone seemed in good spirits, delighted to be invited to a thank-you celebration. The open bar likely helped, too. At the appointed time, when folks had eaten their fill, had a few drinks, and were starting to grow restless, Angus mounted the riser at the front of the ballroom and tapped the mic.

"Good evening, ladies and gentlemen. I'm Angus McLintock, the Member of Parliament for Cumberland–Prescott. I also have the honour to serve in the Cabinet as Minister of Public Safety. I'm glad so many of you could come, so we can express the government's thanks and admiration for the hard work and heavy lifting you all did to complete the Champlain Centre under unreasonably tight timelines. And you delivered. The building, additional black spider-leg braces and all, was completed in time to welcome President Pudovkin last May. As you all know, the President never quite made it to the Centre, nor did our Prime Minister, for which we all ought to be grateful."

Angus paused and scanned the room. All were attentive, and most were smiling.

"I'll not dwell on the unfortunate story we, and much of the world, know all too well by now. But I will say that none of you in this room ought to be jaded or discouraged because the building you set out to create had to be altered halfway through construction. That has no bearing on your efforts. Also, that the building, unique as it was, is now resting at the bottom of the Ottawa River is no reflection on your service. Rather, it is simply a manifestation of a malevolent and bitter dispute rooted in a troubled nation far from here."

Angus stopped again to take stock of the room. It was still with him. And so was I.

"Ladies and gentlemen, on behalf of the Prime Minister and the Government of Canada, we thank you for the dedication, perseverance, and blessed sweat that finished the Champlain Centre in record time, even if it was then finished in a different sense a short time thereafter. Your efforts are not diminished by this unusual and unexpected outcome. Rather, we honour your contributions, I thank you, and the people of Canada thank you."

Muriel, Lindsay, and Vivian were very excited. Angus and I, not so much. We had to be there early, so Lindsay agreed to drive her grandmother and Vivian. We would see them at intermission, when our responsibilities would be over.

It was kind of cool to be entering through the stage door at the back of the National Arts Centre. If you've ever witnessed my acting, singing, or dancing, you know that stage doors of any kind were never part of my life plan. Yet there I was. And for someone who had to be coaxed, then cajoled, and finally coerced, Angus seemed to have a spring in his step that evening.

We were greeted by the choreographer, who walked us to a rehearsal room complete with mirrored wall and, running its length, a barre—you know, the one you hold when you plié, not the one you hold up when you drink. She put us through our paces. The cannon doll scene takes place shortly before intermission; our little comic sketch would consume all of about two minutes on stage and mark the start of the big battle scene. Angus was to play the aggressive, militaristic, war-mongering cannon doll, eager for the cannon to fire to start the hostilities, while I was to play his antithesis as the timid, terrified, whimpering one pleading for the Cannon Master to keep his powder dry and not light the fuse.

It was perfect. My part didn't require much acting, as I naturally tend towards timidity where cannons and battles are concerned. And Angus, too, was quite comfortable in his take-charge, damn-the-torpedoes—or in this case, cannonballs—approach.

To heighten the comic relief of the scene, at one point I was to leap into Angus's arms, cowering and snivelling. Then I'd faint dead away and Angus would drag my limp body to one side of the stage, where he would proceed to perform CPR in a bid to save me. Failing in his efforts, he would then mime the successful use of a defibrillator to revive me. Finally, we'd follow the Cannon Master and trot offstage to thunderous and rapturous applause that would threaten to delay the very battle itself. Everyone would be happy, and

I'd have great photos for our next Cumberland–Prescott constituency newsletter.

In the rehearsal hall, the real dancers, including the principal ballerina, were warming up and doing things with their
limbs that I'd not thought possible for people with bones.
I had expected Angus to be a reluctant participant, but he
seemed engaged, almost as if he was enjoying himself. He
made some suggestions to the choreographer about what he
might do to convey his gung-ho, full-steam-ahead attitude. It
involved a lot of windmilling arms, crazed facial expressions,
and some might say lewd hip action that appeared more con-
vulsive than controlled. But the choreographer loved it.

We were then ushered into a small dressing room just for
the cannon dolls. It kind of made one feel like a big shot.
The costumes were multicoloured, and baggy to accommodate dolls of different sizes. Complete with matching boots,
wild wigs, and jester's caps festooned with pompoms, we
looked utterly ridiculous, and that was before vibrant rouge
makeup was applied to our cheeks to complete the doll look.

In a move that was apparently unprecedented, the choreographer asked Angus not to wear the wig provided. It seemed
the ridiculous otherworldliness of the wig fell well short of
the statement his natural head of hair made all on its own.
Nutcracker history was made that evening.

We were backstage when the Cannon Master materialized
between us and it was time. My heart pounding, I looked over
at Angus, who was grinning maniacally. And then we strode

onstage into the spotlight and gave the performance of our lives. When we finished and retreated behind the curtain, the audience erupted in applause. Lindsay told me afterwards that they had announced Angus and me as the cannon dolls before the performance started, so the crowd was ready.

"Lad, you put on a first-rate show," Angus said as soon as we were offstage. "You really felt limp as I dragged you around out there."

"Thanks, Angus. I've been working on my going-limp technique. And you were, um, very animated yourself under the lights."

"I wanted my leg kicks to be a little higher, and I think I may have damaged my rotator cuff when swinging my arms so violently. But it was better than sitting around the House of Commons watching the Table Clerk's hair grow."

During the intermission that followed shortly after our big scene, we quickly doffed our costumes, did our best to remove our makeup, with limited results, pulled on our street clothes, and met Lindsay in the lobby, where drinks were being served.

As soon as we entered the lobby, where a good chunk of the audience was milling about, spontaneous pockets of applause broke out. Angus's hair was a dead giveaway, not to mention the still-visible red cheeks.

"Oh my gosh, you two were hysterical," Lindsay gushed after she'd kissed me. "Angus, that was a side of you I'd never seen, and I hope we see more of it."

"I dinnae think I'll be recruited for the ballet company, but playing the fool is right up our alley," he said, looking at me.

We helped Lindsay take lemonade back to Muriel and Vivian, who had remained in their seats.

"I thought there was going to be wine," Muriel said.

"Grandma, they only serve the wine out in the lobby," Lindsay said. "Sorry about that."

"No matter, dear. I can drink when we get back home." She spotted Angus and me behind Lindsay. "There you two are," Muriel said. "I think you were probably the very best celebrity cannon dolls they've had in this performance for at least the last several days."

We laughed.

"I'm just joshing, gents. You were both spectacular. The audience was obviously overwhelmed."

"I saw two older women pass out a few rows ahead," Vivian chimed in. "Seriously, you were both wonderful."

"Who knew there was a secret longing for the stage lurking in them both?" Lindsay said.

After the performance, Lindsay and I drove Muriel and Vivian back to Riverfront, then headed home. As soon as we made it back to the boathouse, I put on my pajamas and a sweatshirt and flopped on the couch. I didn't turn on the TV but just looked out the window into the darkness, where the moon illuminated a swath of the frozen river and the swirling snow. With the whole ballet thing behind me, there were only the daily pressures of my job to stress me out. But all was well on that front. So I just lay on the couch and closed my eyes, content, happy. Then Lindsay, pajama-clad, too, squeezed in beside me and laid her head on my chest. "Content" and "happy" don't quite capture it.

DIARY

Sunday, December 14

My love,

I put up a fight, I did, but not only did I agree in the end, I wanted to. Not because I like being onstage and the centre of attention. You know I abhor that. And not because the Prime Minister wanted me to do it for the sake of humanizing our damned government. And certainly not because it would give Daniel a grand photo to put in our next bleedin' constituency newsletter for the good voters of Cumberland–Prescott, although all of that is undeniably true.

No. I wanted to do it because I knew it would please you. It would appeal to your sense of adventure and mischief. You were always encour-aging me to live a little larger and sip more often from the cup of new experiences. I tried to follow your advice when you were beside me, and I try still, even now when you're not. And you would

*have laughed — as I'm sure you did — when I acted
my antics in the spotlight, my face powdered
and rouged, my aging body sheathed in vibrant
colours, my head topped by a jester's pompoms.
I was surely a sight.*

*I did it for you, love. And there's not much I
wouldn't do if I thought you'd favour it. It keeps
you close. The unexpected bonus? It was much
more interesting, even exciting, than I could ever
have predicted. Daniel and I had a time, we did.
He's a good and loyal lad. But you know that, too.*

*Love, I'm ready for sleep and, if good fortune
reigns, the melancholy joy of seeing you in
my dreams.*

AM

THE END

ACKNOWLEDGEMENTS

I wasn't sure I'd ever come back to Angus, Daniel, Muriel, Lindsay, and the rest, but when I did, it felt like getting together with old friends. We got caught up, had a few laughs, engaged in some hijinks, endured some excitement, and generally had a good time. It was nice to be back where it all started. Who says you can't go home again?

This novel was written in 2020, during the Covid-19 pandemic. A year like no other. I offer my great respect and deep gratitude for the frontline health workers who got up every morning and did their jobs with bravery and dedication, under harrowing circumstances, to keep us safe.

I want to thank Phil Gurski, a thirty-year CSIS analyst, for his insights on the intelligence world. While few would mistake my novels for reality, I do want the stories to feel like they could possibly happen, even if it's a stretch. Phil helped with that and even had a hand in the novel's title.

I also offer thanks to the National Ballet of Canada for allowing me, alongside my son Ben, to make our debuts in *The Nutcracker* in December 2019. Based on my performance, I doubt I'll get the chance to do it again, but it did equip me to write a particular scene in this novel from first-hand experience.

As always, I owe a debt of gratitude to my McClelland & Stewart family. My editor, Bhavna Chauhan, has done it again. She's made the novel better while always being clear and kind in the process. My publisher, Jared Bland, has been such a strong supporter, and for that I am grateful. Daniel French, my outstanding publicist, helps keep my calendar full and my novels in the right hands. And once again, my copy editor, Erin Kern, brought her astonishingly sharp and focused insights to the manuscript. Finally, a big shout out to Matthew Flute who created such a creative and arresting cover for this novel. Thank you!

I will always be fortunate and thankful that my literary agent, Beverley Slopen, took a chance on me in early 2008. Eight novels now and counting.

I'm blessed that celebrated publisher, editor, and writer, Douglas Gibson, my *editor emeritus*, continues to support my writing life through his wise counsel and friendship.

My twin brother, Tim, played his customary and important role in this novel. He was among my first readers and provided valuable feedback that improved the story.

My wife, Nancy Naylor, and our two, now grown-up sons, Calder and Ben, end up shouldering a heavier load when I'm toiling on a new novel, particularly when the pandemic has the entire family isolating together. But, as always, their support has been unwavering. I know I'm a very lucky guy.

Terry Fallis, Toronto, February 2021